Even Vampires Get the Blues

"A wild zany private-investigative romantic fantasy . . . a frenzied, fun frolic." —The Best Reviews

"Another hit for Katie MacAlister. I absolutely love it! It is full of the humor that you expect from her books, and on top of that you get mystery and great chemistry from the characters. . . . This book is wonderful and must be read by everyone." —Romance Junkies

"Cheerful mayhem and offbeat characters enliven another MacAlister gem. Witty banter that sparkles with humor and a plot that zips along make even the most outlandish situation seem perfectly reasonable. MacAlister is a rare talent." —*Romantic Times* (4½ stars)

"A laugh riot . . . invigorating and steamy. . . . If you are in the mood for a comedy with chills, thrills, and heat, then look no further." —A Romance Review

"A delightful heroine . . . wickedly hot and unusual . . . The story is fast-paced, with something exciting happening with every turn of the page. . . . MacAlister has written another titillating romantic tale that readers of paranormal romance are sure to enjoy. With electrifying characters, an entertaining storyline, and spicy sex, *Even Vampires Get the Blues* is a stimulating read." —Romance Reviews Today

"Like all of Ms. MacAlister's books, this is a delightful charmer. Her vivid imagination is revealed throughout, as she reinvents the vampire myth and concocts killer butterflies. You won't be disappointed with one of her books, ever." —The Eternal Night

"Demons, poltergeists, ghosts, and alastors populate this romp on the dark side, lightened with MacAlister's offbeat humor that includes a cloud of killer butterflies, sword-wielding ghosts, and a faery in denial." —Monsters and Critics

continued . . .

Other books by Katie MacAlister

THE LAST OF THE RED-HOT VAMPIRES

Katie MacAlister

A SIGNET BOOK

SIGNET
Published by New American Library, a division of
Penguin Group (USA) Inc., 375 Hudson Street,
New York, New York 10014, USA
Penguin Group (Canada), 90 Eglinton Avenue East, Suite 700, Toronto,
Ontario M4P 2Y3, Canada (a division of Pearson Penguin Canada Inc.)
Penguin Books Ltd., 80 Strand, London WC2R 0RL, England
Penguin Ireland, 25 St. Stephen's Green, Dublin 2,
Ireland (a division of Penguin Books Ltd.)
Penguin Group (Australia), 250 Camberwell Road, Camberwell, Victoria 3124,
Australia (a division of Pearson Australia Group Pty. Ltd.)
Penguin Books India Pvt. Ltd., 11 Community Centre, Panchsheel Park,
New Delhi - 110 017, India
Penguin Group (NZ), 67 Apollo Drive, Mairangi Bay,
Auckland 1311, New Zealand (a division of Pearson New Zealand Ltd.)
Penguin Books (South Africa) (Pty.) Ltd., 24 Sturdee Avenue,
Rosebank, Johannesburg 2196, South Africa

Penguin Books Ltd., Registered Offices:
80 Strand, London WC2R 0RL, England

First published by Signet, an imprint of New American Library,
a division of Penguin Group (USA) Inc.

First Printing, April 2007
10 9 8 7 6 5 4 3 2 1

Copyright © Marthe Arends, 2007
All rights reserved.

 REGISTERED TRADEMARK—MARCA REGISTRADA

Acknowledgments

The usual group of suspects are in line for my fervent appreciation for their support and many lattes provided during the writing of this book: my darling agent, Michelle Grajkowski (who, every book, tries to get me to include a character named Honey Grajkowski); my editor, Laura Cifelli (who makes me laugh with her praise over my ability to put the correct end quotes after an em dash); and my husband, Michael (the one responsible for bringing me all the lattes).

In addition to the Gang of Three, I owe much gratitude and thanks to all the readers who enjoy my books, even the ones who demand that I write faster. And for those readers who are concerned about the title of this book—no, it won't be the last of my vampire romances.

Chapter 1

"Oh, look, a crop circle. Let's stop and see if we will be abducted by aliens."

"Why on earth would you want to be abducted by aliens? From what I hear, they're all about strange implants and anal probes. Neither is my idea of fun."

Sarah glared at me as we whipped past a sign noting that tours of a local farm famous for its crop circle were available for a modest fee. "You have the soul of a nihilist."

"On the contrary; I don't believe in either assassination or terrorism. Is this the turn we need?"

A map rustled next to me as my friend consulted the driving directions we'd received from a local travel company. "I don't think so. The directions say the town is called Newton Poppleford. There should be a bridge we go across. And you know full well that's not the sort of nihilism I meant."

"Ah. Newton Poppleford is another kilometer," I answered, nodding to a small sign partially hidden by a dense shrub. "So you're saying I have the soul of a disbeliever?"

"Yes, I am. It's all that science stuff you do."

I couldn't help but smile at Sarah's comment. "You make it sound like being a physicist is tantamount to being a crack addict."

"It's not quite that bad, but it's definitely rotting your mind."

"Oh, come on, that's being a bit extreme." I avoided a startled rabbit in the narrow country road, and spotted a humpbacked stone bridge in the distance. No doubt that was the exit we needed to get to the tiny little village that was Sarah's destination.

"Not in the least. Just look at how your precious skepticism has ruined the trip so far. First, there was the ghost walk in London."

"At which, I feel obligated to point out, no actual ghosts were present."

A look filled with suspicion was leveled at me. "We had you and your doubting Thomas attitude to thank for that, no doubt."

"Hey, all I ask is that people who insist someplace is haunted show me a ghost. Just one, just one little, itty-bitty ghost. That tour guide couldn't produce so much as a spectral hand, let alone a whole ghost. I don't think it's expecting too much for people to back up their claims with empirical proof."

"Ghosts aren't like you and me! They don't like to materialize around non-believers. All that negative energy is bad for them. So if they don't show up around you, you have no one but yourself to blame."

I would have rolled my eyes at that ridiculous

statement, but I was negotiating the crossing of an old, narrow stone bridge, and decided safety was more important than expressing my opinion. "Is that the inn?"

Sarah peered out the window at a rustic pub. "No, ours is the Tattered Stote. That's the Indignant Widow. Top of the hill, the instructions say."

"OK. Cute village. I didn't know people here still had thatched roofs."

"Then there was the mystery tour in Edinburgh. I was never so mortified as when you told the tour guide that the spirit facilitators were lame."

"I didn't say lame: I said ineffective and inadvertently comical rather than frightening. Their idea of ghostly attire looked pretty off-the-rack to me. At best it was from a theater company. And besides, the man said he wanted feedback on the quality of the tour. I simply gave him my opinion."

"Everyone else thought it was very scary when one of the body snatchers' victims leaped up off the table! I came damn close to wetting my pants at that, and all you did was laugh!"

"Of course I laughed. Only the very gullible would have been frightened in that situation. For one thing, we were on a mystery tour that promised thrills and chills. For another, it wasn't in the least bit realistic. Dead bodies do not spontaneously resurrect themselves, let along shriek with abandon as they lurch after tourists."

"Do not speak the word 'spontaneous' to me again," Sarah warned with a potent look. "I doubt I will ever recover from the memory of you lecturing the curator of the Museum of the Odd about why spontaneous combustion of individuals was due wholly to people smoking cigarettes."

"Documented cases have proven that people who supposedly combusted by some mysterious force were all smokers and prone to falling asleep in chairs and beds—"

"Speak not to me of your rationalities, O ye skeptic," Sarah said, holding up a hand.

"But that's why you brought me along on this trip—to keep your feet on the ground," I pointed out as we drove slowly through the small village, avoiding dogs, geese, and the village inhabitants who had a disconcerting habit of stopping and staring as we drove past.

"I brought you on my research trip because Anthony refused to leave his bird-watching group for what he called 'yet another excuse to spend money in foreign countries,' and also because I thought exposure to real psychic phenomenon would do you good. You're too hidebound, Portia."

"Uh-huh."

"You are so set on demanding proof of anything before you believe in it, you're positively rigid."

"Right. So understanding the building blocks of our universe is hidebound, not just healthy curiosity."

"But most of all, you're going to be forty soon. You need a man."

I couldn't help but laugh at that. "You're a romance writer, Sarah. You want everyone to be madly in love with someone else, but it's just not practical for me. I was married to Thomas for three years and gave it the best shot I could, but things didn't work out. I think I'm just one of those women who is comfortable going through life without a permanent partner. At least of the human, male kind. I would like a cat . . ."

Her blue eyes considered me carefully as I drove slowly up a long hill. "Well, I agree with you about the Thomas Affair. I didn't think anyone could be more analytical than you, but he was positively androidlike."

"Honestly, I'm perfectly happy as I am now. I have male friends. There's a researcher at a local software company with whom I get together occasionally."

"Geek boy."

"And I've gone out a couple of times with the vet who lives next door to me."

"In the brown house? I thought those were Wiccans?"

"No, other side, the yellow one."

Sarah wrinkled her nose. "Ah, him. Nice enough personality, but ugly as sin."

"Looks aren't everything, O ye of the blond hair and blue eyes. Some of us have to make do with more mundane appearances. But just to point out I appreciate eye candy as much as the next girl, there's Derek."

"Who's that?"

"Fireman. We bumped carts at the grocery store. There was a line of women following him around the store."

"That good-looking?"

I flashed her a grin. "Oh, yes. We had coffee. He is a bit intense, but so easy on the eyes."

"Hmm." She looked thoughtful as we crested the hill. "But none of them really knock your socks off! What you need is a handsome, dashing foreign man to sweep you off your feet."

"Who says I want to be swept up?"

"Oh, come now, every woman wants to be swept up in love! Every man, too! I mean, who doesn't want to be loved? Not even you want to spend the rest of your life in loneliness."

"Of course I don't, and I want to be loved just as much as the next person, but I don't intend to be swept up on the sorts of grand passions you write about. Love is simply body chemistry, in the end. People are compatible because their particular physical makeup jibes with someone else's. Pheromones trigger sexual excitement, endorphins generate pleasure from the contact, and voila! You've got love."

Sarah's mouth hung open a little as she gawked at me. "I cannot believe I'm hearing this! You think love is just a . . . a chemical reaction?"

"Of course. That explains why people fall out of love. The initial chemical reactions fail, leaving the relationship cold. Why else do you think the divorce rate is so high?"

"You're insane, you know that?"

I smiled as I turned to the left. "Why, because I popped your romantic bubble about being swept off my feet? Ah, here it is—the Tattered Stoat. One authentic English pub with rooms to let above the bar, milady. Watch out for the ducks when you get out. They seem to be interested in us."

"You've gone too far this time," Sarah said slowly, getting out of the car carefully so as to avoid the small herd of ducks that descended upon us from a nearby soggy field.

I stopped in the process of pulling our luggage out of the trunk. Sarah sounded offended, and although I spent just as much time trying to point out rational explanations for things she insisted were unexplainable, I wouldn't for the world want to hurt her feelings. Sarah might insist on believing in the unbelievable, but she was still my oldest friend, and I valued her company. "I'm sorry if I stepped on your toes, Sarah. I know you truly do believe all those romances you write—"

"No, it's not your unwillingness to fall in love that I'm talking about." She waved an expressive hand, her face serious as I set her bags down next to her. "No, I take it back, that's part of it."

"It's part of what?"

"Your lack of faith."

The muscles in my back stiffened. I grabbed my two bags from the trunk, locked it, and tucked the keys away before looking at her. "You know what my family was like. I can't believe anyone who knows what I went through would chastise me for rejecting religion."

"No one would blame you in the least, certainly not me," she said gently, a genuine look of contrition filling her eyes as she put her hand on my arm and gave it a little squeeze. "I'm not talking about religious faith, Portia. I'm talking about faith in general, in the ability to believe in something that has no tangible form or substance, something that is, but which you can't hold in your hands."

I took a deep breath, willing my muscles to relax. "Sarah, sweetie, I know you mean well, but I'm a physicist. My whole career is focused around understanding the elements that make up our world. To expect me to believe in something that has no proof of its existence is . . . well, it's impossible."

"What about those little tiny things?" she asked, grabbing her bags and following me to the pub's entrance.

"Little tiny things?"

"You know, those little atom things that no one can see, but which you all know are there? The ones with the *Star Trek* name."

I frowned down at the top of her head (Sarah, in addition to being petite despite the birth of three children, was also a good six inches shorter than me) as I opened the door to the pub. "You mean quarks?"

"That's it. You said that scientists believed in quarks a long time before they ever saw them."

"Yes, but they saw proof of them in particle accelerators. The detectors inside the accelerators recorded tracks of the products generated by the particle collisions."

Her eyes narrowed as she marched past me into the inn. "Now you're doing that physics-speak thing that makes my brain hurt."

I smiled and followed her in. "OK, then, here's a layman's explanation: We knew quarks existed because they left us proof by way of particle footprints. That tangible proof of their existence was enough to convince even the most skeptical of scientists that they were real."

"But before those fancy particle accelerators, no one had proof, right?"

"Yes, but calculations showed that they had to exist to make sense—"

Sarah stopped in the doorway to a wood-paneled room. A woman at the bar who was serving a customer called that she'd be right with us. Sarah nodded and turned back to me. "That's not the point. They believed in something of which they had no proof. They had faith, Portia. They had faith that something they couldn't see or touch or weigh existed. And that's the sort of faith that is lacking in you. You're so caught up in explaining away everything, you don't allow any magic into your life."

"There is no real magic, Sarah, only illusion," I said, shaking my head at her.

"Oh, my dear, you are so wrong. There is magic everywhere around you, only you're too blind to see it." A little twinkle softened the look in her eye. "You know, I've half a mind to . . . hmm."

I raised my eyebrows and forbore to bite at the "half a mind" bait she had dangled so temptingly in front of me. Instead, I reminded myself that I was her guest on this three-week trip to England, Scotland, and Wales (classified, for tax purposes, as a research assistant), and as such, I could keep at least a few of my opinions to myself.

It wasn't until a half hour later, after we'd taken

possession of the two rooms the pub boasted for visitors, that Sarah continued the thought she'd started earlier.

"Your room is nicer than mine," she announced after admiring the view of grassy pastureland outside my windows. Sheep and cows dotted the landscape, the few trees set as windbreaks waving gently in the early summer breeze.

"I told you to take it, but you liked the other room better."

"It has much calmer feng shui," she said, turning back to me. "And speaking of that, I have decided we're going to have a bet."

"We are? Is there a casino around here? You know I suck at card games."

"Not that kind of a bet. We're going to have one between us. A wager."

"Oh?" I leaned back against the headboard as Sarah plumped herself down in the room's only chair. "About what?"

"I am going to bet you that, before the end of this trip, you will see something that you can't explain."

"Something like . . . quarks?" I asked, thinking back to our earlier conversation.

"No, you believe in those. I mean something you don't believe in, like spirits and UFOs and faeries. I will bet you that before the end of our trip, you will encounter something that can't be explained away as a hot air balloon, or settling house, or any of those other unimaginative excuses people like you come up with to explain the inexplicable."

I sat up a little straighter on the bed. There's nothing I loved like an intellectual challenge. "Well now, that's an interesting thought. But it's hardly fair for you to throw something like that at me without allowing the inverse."

"Inverse?" She frowned for a moment. "What do you mean?"

"You can't take me to a haunted house, and when I point out that the plumbing is archaic and responsible for making the suggested poltergeist knockings, refuse to allow that as a valid explanation. You have to be open to rational deductions as to the source of your *mystical events*."

She bristled slightly. "I am the most open person I know!"

"Yes, you are; too open. You're much more willing to believe in something paranormal than normal."

"Oh," she said, glaring at me. "That's it! Put your money where your mouth is!"

"A bet, you mean? I'm perfectly willing, not that I have much money, but what I have I will happily use to back myself."

She got to her feet. I stood up in front of her.

"Then we're agreed. We will have a bet as to who can prove"—I raised my eyebrows—"or disprove a paranormal being or event." She thought for a moment. "Beyond a shadow of a doubt."

"Beyond reasonable doubt," I agreed, and we shook hands. "You know, I'm skeptical even without a bet."

"Yes, I know you're perfectly happy trying to rain on my mystical parade. But this adds just a smidgen of spice to it, don't you think? A little friendly competition?"

"Mmhmm. How much is the bet for?"

"Oh, we're not betting for money," she said, waving away such a mundane thought. "This is our honor we're betting, here. Honor, and the right to say 'I told you so' to the other person."

I laughed at that. "Sounds good to me. For every haunted house we visit, for every psychic you take me to see, for every crackpot who claims he has crop circles, I'll show you the truth behind the paranormal facade."

Her smile lit up her eyes as she opened the door to the tiny hallway. "We can start this afternoon. This area is a hotbed of paranormal activity, but most well known is the faery ring just outside of town. Get your faery-hunting clothes on, Portia. The game is afoot!"

Chapter 2

"Na then, t'get ta the faery circle, gwain ye doon the road past Arvright's farm—ye know where that be, then?"

By focusing very, very hard, I managed to pick out words in the sentence that I understood. "Yes."

"Aye. Gwain ye doon the hill past Arvright's, then when ye see the sheep, ye turn north." The old man pointed to the south.

"Is that north?" Sarah asked in an undertone, looking doubtfully in the direction the man pointed.

"Shh. I'm having enough trouble trying to get through his West Country accent." I turned a cheerful smile on the man. "So, I turn left at the sheep?"

"Aye, 'tis what I am sayin'. Na then, once ye've skurved past they sheep, ye'll come to a zat combe."

"Zat combe?" Sarah's face was fierce with concentration. "I'm not sure I . . . a *zat* combe?"

I wrote down the old man's directions, praying we wouldn't end up wandering into someone's yard.

"Aye, 'tis right zat. Full o' varments."

Sarah looked at me. I shrugged and said to the man, "Lots of them, eh?"

Behind my back, Sarah pinched my arm.

"Chikky, too. They needs a good thraipin', but none here'll be doin' it."

"Thraipin'," Sarah said, nodding just as if she understood.

"Well, thraipin' chikky varments is an acquired skill, I've always found," I said, continuing to take notes that made no sense. "So we go through the zat combe with the varments? Then . . . ?"

"Ye be up nap o' thikky hill."

"Ah."

Sarah leaned close. "I recognized a word in that sentence. I think I'm getting the hang of this language. It's good to know that all those years of watching BBC America are paying off."

"And that's where the faery circle is?" I asked the man, trying not to giggle. "Up nap o' thikky hill?"

"Aye." The old man narrowed his eyes and spat neatly to the side. Sarah looked appalled. "Dawn't ye go kickin' up t'pellum on thikky hill."

"We wouldn't dream of it," I promised solemnly.

"Ye maids be master Fanty Sheeny t'gwain ye ta the faery circle. 'Tis naught good ye find up nap o' thikky hill."

"Well, now, that's just lost me," Sarah said helplessly, turning to me for translation.

I winked at the old man. "Really? Bad, is it?"

"Aye. 'Tis evil." He winked back at me, and spat again.

"That's a common fallacy, you know," I said,

tucking away the notebook. Beside me, Sarah groaned. "Although faery rings have been considered places of enchantment for many centuries, they aren't really made by faeries. They are the result of a fungal growth pattern. Mushrooms, you know?"

The man blinked at me. Sarah tugged on my shirt and tried to pull me to the car she'd rented for the duration of our trip.

"I know this area is rich in folklore, and faery rings certainly have their share of believers, but I'm afraid the truth is much more mundane. It turns out that there are three distinct types of rings, and that the effects on the grass depend on the type of fungus growing there, although not all rings are visible . . ."

"Ignore her, she's a heathen," Sarah said, yanking me toward the car. "Thank you for your help! Have a good day!"

The old man waved a gnarled hand, spat again, and hobbled past us toward the pub.

"You are so incorrigible! Honestly, spouting off all that stuff about fungus to that very colorful old man."

I got into the car, taking a moment to readjust myself to the English-style cars. "Hey, you started this bet, not me. I'm just doing my part to win serious 'I told you so' rights. Ready?"

"Just a sec . . . oh, whew. Thought I'd forgotten this." Sarah folded a wad of photocopied pages and stuck them in her coat pocket. "I can't wait to see what effect these spells have on the faery ring!"

"I am obliged by reason to point out that some weird quasi-Latin words found in a Victorian book on magic are not very likely to have any result other than making your friend and companion don a long-suffering look of martyrdom."

Sarah lifted her chin and looked placidly out the window as we crept through town. "You can scoff all you want—these spells were written by a very famous medieval mage, and passed down through one family over the centuries. The book I found it in was very rare: only fifty copies printed, and most of them destroyed. And I have it on the best authority that the spells are authentic, so I have every confidence that you'll be eating that long-suffering martyred look before the sun sets."

"Uh-huh."

By dint of Sarah consulting the hiking map she'd picked up in London, we tooled along the lazy river that wound around the town, headed over the stone bridge, and turned the car in the direction of farmland and the famed Harpford Woods.

"Left side," Sarah pointed out as I strayed to the right.

"Yup, yup, got it. Just a momentary aberration. Let's see . . . down past the big farm, then take the road south to a bunch of trees. Beware of the varments. What do you think a zat combe is?"

"I have no idea, but it sounds fabulously English. Here, do you think?"

We pulled off the road and got out of the car to eye the field stretched out before us. It was the perfect day for a walk in the country, what with pale blue, sunny skies, the bright green of the newly dressed trees, hundreds of daisies scattered across the field bobbing their heads in the breeze, birds chattering like crazy as they swooped and swirled around overhead, no doubt busily gathering nesting materials. Even the sheep that dotted the hillsides were picturesque and charming . . . at least when viewed from the distance.

We gave them a wide berth as we followed what the hiking map showed as a right-of-way through a huge open pasture and up a hill to where a sparse crowning of trees waved gently in the June breeze.

"This is so awesome. It's absolutely idyllic! And the emanations—my god, they're everywhere. We have to be close, Portia," Sarah said emphatically, looking around us with happiness. "I feel a very strong sense of place here."

"Yeah, me, too," I answered, stopping by a fallen tree to scrape sheep poop off my shoe.

"I knew you'd feel it, too. I can't wait to try the mage's spells—they simply can't fail. Interesting arrangement of the trees, don't you think? They appear to make a circle around something. Shall we investigate?"

"Lead on, MacDuff." I followed obediently as Sarah, glowing with excitement, broached a sparse ring of trees. In the center, a space of about eighteen feet was open to the sky, covered in lush, emerald grass.

"There it is!" Sarah grabbed my arm and pointed. Her voice dropped to an awe-filled whisper. "The famed West County faery ring! It's perfect! Just what I imagined it would be! It's like a holy place, don't you think?"

I left her hugging herself with delight, marching

over to squat next to the bare earth that marked the boundaries of the faery ring. The ring was about four feet wide, a perfect circle of bare earth surrounded by lush grass growing on the inside and outside of it. There was nothing to indicate the cause, no mushrooms visible, but I knew they weren't always seen. I touched the sun-warmed dirt, and mused, "I wonder if there's a lab around here where I could send a soil sample so we can find out just which fungus caused this ring?"

"Infidel," she said without heat, slapping her coat pockets, pulling out the spell pages, and turning around in the way women who have forgotten their purses have. "Do you have the camera?"

I cocked an eyebrow at her. "You took it away from me at Denhelm, if you recall."

"Oh, that's right—you insisted on taking pictures of the farmer's son rather than the bog man mummy. I must have left the camera in my bag."

"You have to admit, the son was much better looking than that moth-eaten old bog man."

She straightened up to her full five-foot nothing. "That bog mummy is said to have been used in a druid sacrifice, and thus could well contain the spirit . . . oh, never mind. I can see by the mulish expression on your face that you are closing yourself up to any and all things unexplainable. Let me have the car keys so I can run back to town and get the camera."

"I'll do it—"

A little sparkle lit her eyes. "No, you stay and meditate in the faery ring. Maybe if you open yourself up to the magic contained within, you'll see how blind you've been all these years. Here, you can read the spells over while I'm gone, but don't try them out until I get back. I want to see everything the ring has to offer!"

I took the pages she handed me, plopping down to sit with crossed legs in the middle of the circle. "All right, if you're sure you're OK with driving on the wrong side of everything." I plucked a piece of grass and chewed the end of it as I shucked off my light jacket. "I'll soak up a bit of sun while you're gone."

"Portia!" Sarah's eyes grew huge. "You can't do that!"

"Do what, sunbathe? I'm not going to take off my clothes, just roll up my sleeves," I said, suiting action to word.

"You can't eat anything that grows in the faery ring. It's . . . it's sacrilegious! In fact, I don't think you should be in the ring at all. I'm sure that's going to anger the faeries."

I rolled my eyes, chewing on the blade of grass. "I'll take my chances against the fungus. Remember to stay on the left."

She hurried off after delivering herself of a few more dire warnings as to my fate if I continued. I sat enjoying the sun for a few minutes, but that quickly lost its charms. I made a search of the area surrounding the ring, but there was nothing there but trees, grass, daisies and buttercups, and the wind whispering through the leaves.

"Right. A little scientific investigation is in order," I said aloud to break the silence. I seated myself again in the faery ring, plucking another blade of grass to chew while I consulted the photocopies Sarah had thrust upon me. The text explaining the purpose of the spells was couched in dramatically obscure language, no doubt fooling the more gullible reader into believing its authenticity. "It's going to take a lot more than some lame attempts at mysticism to fool me," I muttered as I ran my finger down the spells. "*Magicus circulus contra malus, evoco aureolus pulvis, commutatus idem dominatio aqua* . . . oh, for heaven's sake, how hokey can you get? I bet this isn't even real Latin—"

A glimmer of something caught the corner of my eye. I turned my head to look at it, thinking someone had dropped a penny or bit of glass on the ground that had caught the sunlight, but there was nothing.

The hairs on the back of my neck stood on end, as if something that posed a threat was approaching.

"Honestly, Portia, how pathetic is it that you're letting Sarah's chat about magic get to you?" I rubbed my arms against a sudden prickling of goose bumps, and gave myself a mental lecture about allowing someone's enthusiasm to sway my common sense.

A little flash of light in midair had me whipping around to look at it.

There was nothing.

"Oh, this is ridiculous. I'm spooking myself, and over what? Figments of an overactive imagination . . ."

Directly in front of me, something twinkled in the air again, just as if tiny motes of metal had reflected the sunlight.

To my astonishment, the twinkling continued,

growing thicker until the air around me seemed to collect, flashing like a thousand tiny, nearly imperceptible, lights.

"I'm hallucinating," I said, closing my eyes. "It's the sun. I'm sun blind, or having heatstroke, or the fungus in the faery ring is a hallucinogenic."

I opened my eyes, sure I would see only the top of a sunny hill, but instead gawked as the twinkling lights gathered themselves into an opaque form.

"It's got to be the fungus," I said quickly, getting to my feet and backing up out of the ring. "It's from the peyote family or something—"

As I backed away, I stumbled over a lump in the grass, falling onto my butt. My mind came to an abrupt stop as the form turned into a person. I shook my head, blinking rapidly to clear my vision. "All right. Time to get some medical aid. This silliness has gone on long enough."

"Oh, there you are!" the hallucination said as it turned to me. "Thank heaven you called me. Quickly, we don't have much time. I must pass on the Gift and be on my way before they find me."

The hallucination—in the form of a woman, slightly shorter than me, with long black hair and brilliant blue eyes—stood over me with her hands on her hips, an exasperated look on her attractive face. "Merciful sovereign, are you faery struck?"

"Don't be ridiculous," I answered, my voice coming out as a croak. I cleared my throat. "There are no such things as faeries. Oh, man, what am I doing? I'm talking to a hallucination?"

The woman—I couldn't help but think of her as

such when she looked so real—rolled her eyes for a moment, then startled me by grabbing my arm and hefting me to my feet. "Don't tell me they didn't conduct the preliminaries with you? You passed the trials, yes?"

"That must be some serious fungus," I answered, brushing the bits of grass off my butt as I looked at the faery ring. "I could swear I felt someone touch me."

"Hello! Can't you hear me? I'm talking here!"

"It's amazing, absolutely amazing. I'm going to have to get a sample for the nearest lab to analyze. This could be dangerous if children came across it— who knows what sort of thing they would hallucinate." I dug through my pockets, hoping for a plastic bag or something I could use to hold a sample of the earth. Unfortunately, I had nothing on me other than a package of gum. "Damn. I'll just have to wait for Sarah, then pop back to town to get something—"

"Are you deaf?" the woman in front of me shouted, waving her arms in the air. I watched her, amused at the lengths my imagination would go to under the influence of a delusionary drug. She looked quite normal, dressed in a tight pair of green pants and a chunky tan and green sweater. She was frowning, clearly unhappy about something.

"I suppose I could humor my brain," I said, eyeing her. "At least until Sarah gets here. Hello."

"What is wrong with you?" the woman asked, slapping her hands against her legs. "Didn't you hear me? We don't have time for you to stand here and be strange!"

"You'll have to forgive me. I've evidently been

poisoned by hallucinogenic fungus spores. What did you want to know? And . . . this is silly of me, I know, but could you tell me your name, if you have one?"

"Oh, for the love of . . . they were supposed to meet with you and fill you in when they gave you the summoning spells! Honestly, the incompetence these days, it's frightful. You'd think they could do something right after having a few millennia to work it out. My name is Hope. Who are you, please?"

I smiled at the illusion, giving my brain and the fungus full marks for creativity. "I'm Portia Harding, of Sacramento, California, and I'm currently employed by a biomedical firm as a researcher in Atomic Scale Technology. Is there anything else about me you'd like to know? Favorite color? Perfume? Shoe size?"

The look from her intense blue eyes had me forgetting for a moment that she wasn't real. "Your shoe size is irrelevant. We don't have much time at all, and even less now that I have to do everyone else's jobs and fill you in. I swear, if I ever get back to the Court, I will file a grievance about their slack ways . . . Where was I? Oh, yes, we don't have much time. Listen carefully, Portia Harding. What I am about to say to you is going to change your life."

"Oh dear—the fungus isn't doing some sort of permanent brain damage?" I said, backing away from the circle a bit more. I took a few deep breaths of sweet summer air and tried to calm the worry in my mind. This circle had been here a long time—I couldn't be the only person to suck the fungus off a blade of grass, could I? If it was truly dangerous, surely the authorities would have done something about it.

"I am a virtue. I am in danger, grave danger, and I cannot stay or all will be destroyed. Do you under-stand? Everything! Life, existence as we know it, light and dark—it will all be destroyed. Your request came at the perfect time."

"Indeed." The results of inhaling the fungus spores paced around me in an agitated way. I won-dered how long the delusions would last. "I hate to sound stupid, but what request—"

"There is no time for lengthy explanations," she said, snatching up my hand and pressing it between her own. I stared down at them, amazed again at how real the whole fantasy seemed. Her fingers tightened around mine in a grip that I was almost ready to swear was real . . . *almost*. "I must leave now. As you summoned me, so I answer: unto you I bequeath the Gift. Use it wisely. The penalty for abuse is too horrible to speak of."

The wind whipped past us as my hand grew hot in hers.

"This is absolutely amazing," I said, wishing I had my laptop to take notes on the experience. Heat from her hand seemed to creep up my arm, gaining speed and intensity. "I'm sorry, but I have to try this . . ."

I tried to yank my hand from hers, but her grip was too strong.

Her eyes lit with a soft glow as she looked deep into me, all the way down into my soul. It was such a piercing, intense gaze, that for a moment my body froze, leaving me unable to move. As she spoke, she released my hand and touched me on the center of my forehead. "My virtue passes to you, Portia Harding. May the sovereign protect you from those who would destroy you."

The heat that had started in my hand now swept through me, a fever of such intensity that I wanted to shred my clothes and find the nearest body of water. My skin burned, my blood boiled, my mind cried out for relief.

"Oh, great. Now this stupid fungus is making me feverish. I just know I'm going to end up in the . . . the . . . whatchamacallit. Hospital."

The need for something to quench the raging inferno inside me left my brain confused and unable to focus, driving out all other thoughts but relief. I struggled to maintain control, to breath slowly and deeply until the worst of it passed, but the fever that burned me from the inside out didn't abate. It consumed me, sweeping me along in its inferno, pushing me deeper into its burning depths until I threw back my arms and screamed to the heavens for deliverance.

A cold, wet drop hit my forehead. Another struck my cheek.

"What . . . I . . . rain?" I panted, watching with wonder as, out of nowhere, clouds formed overhead, at first soft, hazy white wisps, quickly merging into clumps that darkened until they were heavy and foreboding. Soft little pats of noise indicated the rain that gently touched my heated skin wasn't just my imagination . . . all around me in the secluded copse, raindrops fell, caressing me, soothing me, blessedly taking away the fever and leaving behind a calm tranquility that gently eased the fire within. I closed my eyes and tipped my head back to welcome the blissful wetness. "Sweet mother of reason, I've never felt anything so good in my life. This is sheer heaven."

"No, this is the Gift. I thank you for your help. And now, I must be gone before they find me."

So wonderful did the rain feel that I had forgotten for a moment about my hallucination. I cracked an eye open to see if she was still there. The faery ring, and everything around it, was empty of all life but me.

"Good. Maybe the hallucinogen is losing its power," I said as I swung around to make sure I was alone. Something odd struck me. I turned in a circle again, slower this time, my frown deepening as I looked upward to the cloud that still gently rained down on me.

There were no other clouds visible in the sky— just a small one over my head.

"You're part of the whole mushroom thing," I told the cloud. "I'm only imagining you're there, and imaging that I'm wet, and imagining that strange women are appearing and disappearing without cause. Oh, hurrah, Sarah is back. Sanity returneth."

Through the trees that ringed the hilltop, a flash of red heralded my friend's return. I was relieved to see her, and struggled with the idea of not mentioning to her that I'd been inadvertently poisoned by potent fungus, but concern that I might suffer some sort of permanent damage convinced me that it would be best to admit all, and seek medical assistance.

"Sorry I took so long. I had a little difficulty with

a right turn . . . dear god in heaven, what are you doing?" Sarah stopped about ten feet away from me, her eyes huge.

"Hallucinating, if you must know, and all because you wanted to see a silly fungus ring. Would you mind taking me to the nearest hospital? My mind is under the influence of some pretty psychedelic mushrooms, and I think I need to detox somewhere quiet."

"You're . . . you're raining!"

"No, that's just part of the hallucination." I stopped, a little chill rippling down my back. "Wait a sec . . . are you saying you can *see* the cloud above me?"

"Of course I can see it," Sarah answered, walking around me in a big circle. "I'd have to be blind to miss it. It's right above you, one cloud, raining on you. Nowhere else, just you. How on earth are you doing that?"

"No," I said shaking my head, refusing to believe the impossible. "It's not really here; it's just an illusion brought on by hallucinogenic fungus. You must have been close enough to the ring to have breathed it in as well. We should get to the nearest hospital if this fungus is so potent."

"Don't be ridiculous, Portia," Sarah said, coming to a stop in front of me, her face beaming awe and delight. "It's the faery ring! This is part of the magic, although I have to admit I've never heard of rain faeries. Still, even you can't dispute that this is something well out of the realm of normal!"

"Oh, I admit it's not normal to get high off of fungus found lying around on the top of a hill, but it's certainly nothing that can't be explained by an understanding of chemistry, medicine, and biology." I thought for a few seconds, my eyes narrowing as I mulled over a possible explanation. "It could have been Hope."

"It could have been what?"

"Who, not what. A woman by the name of Hope. Perhaps she was real after all. It's entirely feasible that this whole thing was a setup, you know. She may well have known that there was a fungus here with properties that left someone susceptible to hypnotic suggestion."

Sarah fixed me with a confused gaze. "Someone named Hope hypnotized you while I was gone?"

"It would explain the delusion about the rain cloud. And the lights could have been the hallucinogenic starting to work on my synapses. Yes. I like that hypothesis. I am willing to bet that if Hope hadn't heard you coming up the hill, she would have tried to rob me. It's probably some sort of a scheme to fleece innocent tourists. We should definitely report this to the police, after we go to the hospital to get checked out, naturally."

"Portia, you're not making a lick of sense," Sarah said, shaking her head and pointing to where the fantasy cloud hovered over me, still gently raining. "I have not been hypnotized, nor am I under the influence of any drugs, hallucinogenic or otherwise. You have a cloud over your head, raining only on you. You are standing in the middle of a very famous faery ring, and you ate something that grew out of that ring."

"You're right," I said, stepping outside the ring.

The rain cloud followed me. I ignored it as best I could.

Sarah looked remarkably cheerful. "Really? You admit I won the bet? You concede that this is a bona fide paranormal event?"

"Of course not! I meant that you were right about me ingesting the blades of grass I was chewing on. Not that I ate them per se, but if the fungal spores had been brushed onto them, and I put them into my mouth, it could well mean that Hope had no part in it, and it's all just an unfortunate coincidence."

"I think you'd better tell me exactly what happened while I was gone," Sarah said, pulling out a small voice recorder. "Start with the moment I left. Er . . . I don't suppose you can make that go away?" She pointed to the cloud.

"It's not really here. You just think it's here. No, I mean I just think it's here . . . wait, that doesn't fit the hypothesis . . ."

"Start at the beginning and tell me everything," she said in a businesslike, brisk fashion.

I spent the time it took to fill her in puzzling out how she could be witness to my delusion. "It must be mass hypnosis after all," I concluded, eyeing the dirt ring. "There's just no other explanation for it."

"There's one all right, only you are too stubborn to admit it. Oh, Portia, this is the most exciting thing! I never thought to have met someone who's seen a real faery, but you've done it!" She gripped my arm, excitement bubbling off her. "And you said the faery gave you some sort of gift? What is it?"

I lifted my eyes skyward for a moment, hoping for

patience, but all I got for my effort was an eyeful of rain. "We need to leave. Now. This fungus is clearly muddling both our thinking."

Without waiting for Sarah to answer, I spun around and marched toward the ring of trees, hoping by the time I reached the road that I might be free from the effects of the fungus.

"I'll be along in a couple. I want to get some pictures of this ring," Sarah called after me.

"If you start to see sparkly little lights and a strange, paranoid woman, don't say I didn't warn you."

The wind picked up as I approached the trees, the circular arrangement of them giving the wind that whipped past an oddly hollow sound, like a mournful sigh. For some reason, the sound of it made me feel jumpy.

"It's the drugs," I told myself as I pushed aside a branch, the hair on the back of my neck prickling. "I'm just a little susceptible to imagination right no—grk!"

For a fraction of a second I thought a tree branch had slapped backward, striking my neck, but as a dark face hove into view, I realized that it was a man who had me in a stranglehold.

"What have you done with Hope?"

I was so surprised at being assaulted that my brain, rather than coming up with an escape plan, took a few minutes to notice that his voice was low and mean, with a faint Irish tone to it, while the eyes that burned into mine had a slightly exotic tilt to them. That wasn't what held my attention, though . . .

his eyes were black, solid black, with no difference in color between iris and pupil.

With both hands I grabbed the man's arm where he clutched my throat, subsequently cutting off my air supply, but his grip on me was steely and unmovable.

"Let go of me," I wheezed, letting go of his arm to search my pocket for car keys or a pen or something I could use to defend myself against the attacker.

He hauled me closer until little black dots swam before my eyes. "Tell me what you've done with her, or by god, I will snap your neck."

Chapter 3

I twisted in the man's grip, attempting to knee him in the groin, but he anticipated my move, releasing my neck and jerking me around suddenly. I had time to suck in one large lungful of air before he grabbed my throat again, his other hand immobilizing my arm nearest him. "Where is she?" he demanded.

"She left," I managed to squeak despite the spots that were once again dancing before my eyes. I tried to get some air into my lungs, but his grip was on this side of fatal, leaving me just barely alive. Desperately, I tried to remember everything I knew about self-defense, but my brain seemed sluggish and slow to cooperate.

"Left for where?"

"I . . ." I threw myself backward, hoping to knock him off balance, but it was no use. "Don't know."

The world swam around me in a nauseating way, and just when I thought I was going to pass out—or die—a bolt of blue from the sky startled my would-be murderer into releasing me.

I collapsed on the ground into a fetal ball, my lungs heaving as I sucked in air. Even as I rubbed my neck and welcomed oxygen to my body again, I was aware of the man standing over me, his body silhouetted against the sun. He was tall, taller than me, solidly built, with skin the color of a latte, and thick black hair that came to a widow's peak in the front. He peered upward for a moment.

"Stop that!"

"Stop what, breathing? You almost did it for me, thank you."

He glared at me as I continued to massage my neck. "Stop the rain."

If he saw the rain cloud, he couldn't be real. Then again, Sarah said she saw it too. He must have breathed in the fungus as well, triggering the same response Sarah and I had. "I would be delighted to stop that particular hallucination if I could."

"Will it away," he demanded, taking a step toward me.

I scrambled backward like a crab, braced and ready to run if he looked like he was going to attack me again. "I don't think you can will away hallucinations by just saying, 'Rain, rain, go away!' "

The small cloud over my head dissipated until nothing was left of it.

The man looked at me, one eyebrow cocked.

"This just proves it's not real," I grumbled, still watching him carefully, looking for an opportunity to run like hell.

"You are mortal?"

I frowned up at him, rubbing my neck as I got to

my knees. "What do I look like, a baked potato? Of course I'm mortal."

My voice was a croak that sounded almost as bad as my throat felt.

He swore.

"If you lay so much as one finger on me again, I will scream bloody murder. My friend is just beyond the trees, and she went to great trouble to illegally smuggle pepper spray into the country."

He was about to say something, but the wind brushed past us, the hollow note more pronounced. Inexplicably, the skin on my back crawled at the sound of it.

"Portia?" Sarah's voice sounded distant, and very worried.

"Over here," I yelled, slowly getting to my feet, my eyes on the man in front of me. If he even looked like he was going to grab me again, I'd bolt.

"Portia? Did you hear that voice? Oh my god, it was awful! I don't like to hurry you, but I really think we need to get out of here." She burst through the trees, a frightened look on her face that turned to confusion when she saw the man in front of me. "Oh. I didn't realize someone else was here."

"The Hashmallim has come. Move quickly, or die," the man said, grabbing my arm and giving me a none-too-gentle shove toward the sheep pasture.

"Stop that!" I yelled, twisting out of his grip. "If you touch me once again—"

"What's going on here?" Sarah asked, stumbling as she ran down to where I'd stopped to face my attacker.

"That man tried to strangle me," I answered, pointing at him.

"He what?" She turned to glare at him. "You hurt my friend?"

"It was a misunderstanding. I did not realize she was mortal."

"What the hell else should I be?" I demanded to know.

The wind swirled around us, eerily sounding as if voices were whispering dire warnings. I shivered, despite the fact that I knew it was just the effect of the wind through the circle of trees.

"We do not have time for this," he said, stalking toward me. "If you wish to die, stay here and continue talking. If you wish to live, run!"

"Run?" Sarah asked, looking around.

Wordless voices swept past us, setting off my flight instinct. I didn't stop to analyze the situation, I just acted.

"Run!" I screamed, grabbing Sarah's arm and hauling her with me as I hurtled down the hill.

I felt the man's presence behind us as we raced down the hill, stumbling over occasional clumps of earth and rocks, but a long-buried, primal sense told me I had less to fear from him than whatever it was the wind heralded.

Sarah would have stopped by her rental car, but the man grabbed the back of my shirt and her dress, and pushed us on, toward a small shed that sat near a curve in the road. "Do not stop! Your car is within sight of the hill."

He half dragged us over a low stone wall, shoving

us without any ceremony around the edge of the shed. I ran straight into the front bumper of a car, slamming onto the hood with a breath-stealing, "Ooof!"

"Get in," he ordered, opening both doors on the driver's side.

"Are you insane?" I snapped, limping over to where Sarah stood. "We are not going anywhere with you—"

I like to think of myself as reasonably able to take care of myself in dangerous situations, but the man in front of me was several inches taller than me, probably a good fifty pounds heavier, and evidently spent his spare time working out with weights, or throwing unwilling women into the backs of vehicles, because he had no difficulty in doing the latter. He tossed small, delicate Sarah into the car as if she weighed no more than a bag of grapefruit, flinging larger and more substantial me in on top of her before slamming the door behind us.

"Hey!" I yelled into Sarah's left hip.

"Oh my god, get off me. I think you're breaking my rib."

The car lurched forward as the potential murderer, now kidnapper, started the engine and slammed his foot on the accelerator.

"I'm sorry, it wasn't my choice to be here," I grumbled, scrambling off Sarah and onto the car floor. I flailed around for a moment, but only ended up wedged in between the back and front seats. "Ow! That's my head you just kicked!"

"Sorry. Hey, you! This is kidnapping! International kidnapping! If you pull over right now and let us out, I won't get my husband, a renowned criminal lawyer, to sue your ass into a life sentence at the nearest penitentiary where you will spend the rest of your days as some burly axe murderer's girlfriend."

"Stay down or the Hashmallim will see you," was all that the kidnapper said.

"Hit him," I whispered furiously to Sarah where she crouched above me on the seat. I tried to pull myself out of my predicament, but there was nothing I could grab to give me leverage.

"What?"

"Hit him," I said again in a voice pitched low enough that just she could hear. "On the back of the head. Knock him out so we can escape."

Sarah looked wildly around the backseat of the car. "Knock him out with what? My camera bag? It has my digital camera in it!"

"Oh, for Pete's sake, do I have to do everything . . . move aside so I can get out of this horrible deathtrap."

Sarah managed to move aside just enough for me to grasp the fabric of the car seat with both hands and heave myself out of the trench. The car swerved slightly as the kidnapper glared in the rearview mirror at us.

"I told you to keep down. The Hashmallim could still see you."

"You are kidnapping us," I told him, untangling my purse strap from my person. I didn't have much in it but my travel wallet and miscellaneous tourist items, but I had to do something to stop our abduction. Spending time trapped in a psycho's lair while he did who-knew-what to us was not on my vacation to-do list. "Stop the damned car and let us out!"

"What you're doing is illegal!" Sarah added, scooting over ever further as I hefted my bag.

"I answer to higher laws than yours," he muttered as he swung the car around a corner. Ahead of us, the town of Newton Poppleford hove into view.

"It's now or never," I whispered to Sarah. "We have to get out before he goes through the town. I'm going to bash him on the head with my bag while you open the door and throw yourself out. I'll jump out my side at the same time."

Sarah bit her lip as she watched the water rush past while we drove over the humpbacked bridge, no doubt worried about the folly of jumping out of a moving car, but she didn't let a little thing like possible death or dismemberment stop her. She nodded that she understood.

"On three," I told her, taking a deep breath and a firm grasp on my purse.

"One . . . two . . ." I swung my arm back, prepared to wallop the kidnapper on the head as he slowed down to maneuver through the town.

As I was about to bring it forward, his head whipped around, his black eyes flashing a warning. For a moment his gaze held mine, and I was aware of a strange fission of warmth that seemed to come to life inside me. "I am trying to save you, you foolish woman!"

"Save us from what?" I asked.

"Death," he snapped.

"Three!" I yelled, and brought my purse down as hard as I could on his face. The car jerked to the left, brakes squealing as he tried to stop.

Sarah jerked open the car door and threw herself

out of the vehicle without waiting to see if I was following. The man yelled something as I wrenched at the door handle, pausing for a second at the sickening sight of the pavement passing so quickly outside the door. I didn't wait around to see what he had to say, however. I flung myself forward, wrapping both arms around my head to protect it from injury. I hit the ground with my right shoulder, skidding and rolling at the same time, pain blossoming from a dozen different spots as I tumbled along the road, finally coming to an abrupt stop courtesy of a parked car.

I lay dazed for a few minutes, too stunned by the fall to rally much awareness, but at last my senses started returning to me. I was aware that the exposed skin of my arms and hands burned, my shoulder ached, and my back and legs felt as if someone had beaten me with a baseball bat, but I was very much alive. Several horrified voices calling out questions and exclamations indicated the townsfolk had seen our unorthodox arrival. I got to my knees, flinching at the sting as my abraded palms touched the ground. Several pairs of hands reached out to help me to my feet while voices asked question after question.

"I'm OK," I said, weaving dizzily for a moment when I made it to my feet. "Thank you for your help, but I'm just fine. A few cuts and bruises, nothing more. Has anyone seen my friend—oh there she is."

"Why on earth did you go that way?" Sarah asked, standing on the verge of a grassy square. She brushed a few last strands of grass from her dress and straightened up. "It was much nicer falling on soft lawn. Oh! Someone stop that man!"

The benevolent bystanders turned as one to watch our abductor's car drive off down the street with a squeal of tires. I memorized the license plate number, swearing revenge, or at least justice for the assault and kidnapping.

I had expected that, as foreign visitors to the country, we would be caught up in endless red tape in both getting medical care and reporting the abduction, but to my surprise, a short two hours after we had made our dashing escape we tottered up the stairs of the Tattered Stoat to our respective rooms, bruised, battered, exhausted, and in my case, utterly confused.

The hospital had done three blood tests (two at my insistence since I was positive the prior results were incorrect), all of which showed I had not ingested any form of fungus, hallucinogenic or otherwise.

"Are you going to be OK with the séance we are supposed to go to tonight?" Sarah asked wearily as we slowly made our way up the dark back stairs to the upper floor. The pub was a popular one with the younger crowd, as evidenced by the large flat-screen TV blaring music videos. The building, however, was thankfully thick-walled, so the noise was muted on the second floor.

"You heard the doctor—I'm fine. Just a few bumps and bruises; nothing a couple of aspirin can't fix."

She paused at her door and gave me a concerned once-over. "I know, but I still feel like you should be in bed, not attending séances with me."

"Don't worry about it," I said with a careless wave that I felt far from feeling. "I wouldn't miss the opportunity for exposing some hokey medium."

"Portia!"

"I know, I know. I promised I'd go into this with an open mind. But I'm going to enjoy proving you wrong."

"There's that little matter of the cloud that followed you that you have yet to explain," she said with obnoxious cheerfulness.

"I explained it perfectly well. It was either the result of hallucination by a yet-as-undetermined source, hypnosis, or visual trickery."

"Smoke and mirrors, you mean?" she asked archly.

"Smugness ill becomes you," I said sternly, pulling my room key from my pocket. "I will offer scientific proof as to the non-existence of the cloud just as soon as I have soil from that faery ring analyzed. It could well be that there are elements at work other than possibly hallucinogenic fungi."

"Uh-huh. I'm willing to let you get away with this one because I've never heard of a cloud associated with a faery ring, but I'm not going to go so easy on you next time." Sarah smiled as she spoke, digging her key out of her camera bag. I rolled my eyes. "Dibs the bathtub first."

"You're mean," I answered, fitting my own key into the lock.

"You're not supposed to get your owies wet."

"I am not Tyler," I said with infinite dignity, despite the various bandages swathing my arms, hands, and one eyebrow. "He is six and an extremely precocious child whom you spoil shamelessly. I am just a friend who is subjected to your abuse under the guise of concern." I opened the door on the last of my words, flipped on the light, and stared with stunned disbelief at my room.

"Uh . . . Sarah?"

"Hmm?" She paused in her doorway, looking back at me.

"The kidnapper is here."

She stared at me for a moment, then hurried after me as I entered my room. "Oh! The nerve! I'll get the police—"

I snatched up the nearest item at hand to use as a weapon—which turned out to be a paperback Agatha Christie novel—and threw myself in front of Sarah, fully intending to protect my friend despite my injuries, as the deranged kidnapper moved toward her.

The man moved faster than I thought, however. He seemed to blur as he moved, one minute standing next to the chair on the opposite side of the room, the next in front of Sarah, his hand on the door to keep it from opening any further, his head tipped down so he could look her in the eyes.

"There is no need for you to call the authorities," he said in his deep, slightly Irish voice that contrasted so oddly with his dark skin and exotic eyes.

"There most certainly is!" Sarah protested.

I added my two cents, stalking forward with my book held in a threatening manner. "I'd say assault and kidnapping is grounds for arrest. The police were very interested in having a word with you. I'm sure they will be delighted to discuss the issue."

Sarah, to my surprise, did not knee the attacker, or even scream for help. Instead, she stood in front of him, her mouth slightly opened, an odd look of absorption on her face.

"Sarah," I said loudly, waving my book around.

Neither she nor the man gave me so much as a glance.

I moved next to them, peering first at him, then her. Their eyes were locked, their posture that of two lovers about to kiss.

It bothered me intensely that she would stand and gawk at an (admittedly handsome) insane criminal.

"Sarah? Hello?"

"You have nothing to fear from me," the man told her gently, and to my complete amazement, she nodded her head and closed the door.

"Oh my god, you're some sort of hypnotist, aren't you?" I told him, watching Sarah. Her eyes had a slightly dazed look to them, her breath coming with soft little panting sounds. She was blushing, as well, her cheeks pink with some strong emotion. "I insist that you stop this right now. I will not have you victimizing my friend."

"I . . . I'm glad," she said, ignoring me. She licked her lips nervously, her eyelashes fluttering as she sent him coy little glances.

"Sarah, stop it! Snap out of it!" I grabbed her shoulders and forcibly turned her toward me. Her head swiveled so she could continue to gaze at the man. I grabbed her chin and turned her face so she was looking at me. "Sarah!"

"Hello, Portia. It's all right. We don't have anything to fear from him." Her eyes were slightly dilated, but other than her strangely flustered state, she seemed to be all right.

Her words, however, made it clear she was far from in her right mind. "I'm going to take you back to the hospital," I said slowly, so she would understand. I looked over her shoulder to where the man stood. "And if you try to stop me, I will scream bloody murder and bring up everyone in the pub."

"I have saved your life," the man said, his brows pulling together in a frown.

Sarah smiled at him and nodded, a devoted look on her face. "He did. He saved us."

"There was nothing threatening us except you," I said firmly, trying to steer Sarah toward the door. "I will call the police from the pub downstairs. And if you try to kidnap us again—"

"Blast it, woman, I am not a kidnapper!" he exploded.

I took a few precautionary steps backward, glared at Sarah's head for a moment as she stood simmering at him, finally yanking her back to stand with me. "Look, you can yammer on about saving our lives all you want, but I know what I know."

"You know *nothing*," he said, scorn dripping from his voice. He stalked toward me, his black eyes fairly shooting sparks. I looked around quickly for a sturdier weapon than a book, but other than the bedside lamp, my room was horribly weapon-free. "I *did* save your life, and by the laws governing the Court of Divine Blood, I demand recompense in the form of exculpation."

Chapter 4

I felt behind me for the table lamp, grasping it firmly and shifting slightly to the side to hide the fact I was holding it. It wasn't much of a weapon, but it was better than a paperback.

The man stopped in front of me, so close I could smell his woodsy aftershave.

"I want you to leave this room now," I said in a calm, but firm, voice. Beside me, Sarah made a slight noise of unhappiness. "I don't know anything about a court, but I do know that you have violated several laws, and the police are even now searching for you. If you leave right now, I will not harm you, but I am fully prepared to defend my friend and myself from you if you insist on attacking."

An annoyed look flitted across his face. "Stop saying that! I have not attacked you!"

"You strangled me!" I answered, part of my mind pointing out that reason never worked with deranged madmen, but too irritated to listen. "I almost died! If that's not an attack, I'd like to know what is!"

"I told you—that was before I knew you were mortal," he snapped, irritation replacing the annoyance.

I waved the book around in a vaguely threatening manner. "I'd just like to know what you think I could be if not mortal!"

"You're a virtue," he answered quickly, reaching behind me and wrenching both lamp and book out of my hands, tossing them onto the bed. "Thus, you must be a member of the Court of Divine Blood, and as such, bound to uphold the laws therein. You wish for an accounting? I will give you one. The Hashmallim do not enter the mortal world unless it is to capture someone intended for destruction. Since I saved the lives of you and your friend by spiriting you away from under the nose of the Hashmallim, you are in my debt. I am calling in that debt, and the price shall be exculpation."

"I forgive you," Sarah said with breathy adoration, her eyes glowing as she gazed at him.

"The first thing I do after this guy is locked up is get you to a good head shrink," I told her.

"Woman!" the man roared, and grabbed me by the neck, hauling me up until my face was close to his. His eyes burned into mine, his breath skittering along my mouth.

"My *name* is Portia," I said without thinking. "I hate being referred to as if I was nothing but an object!"

"You push me too far, Portia!"

Sarah made faint mewing noises of distress as she pushed in close to us, her hands on his arms.

"You're assaulting me again." I waved my arms frantically for the lamp or book.

"Eee!" Sarah said, half demanding, half plaintive as she brushed her lips on his cheek.

The man turned his head slightly, and gave her another soul-piercing look. "You are not for me, sweet."

"Oh," she said, pulling away, an oddly content look on her face as she stood watching us.

"Stop hypnotizing—"

The man took a deep breath, closed his eyes for a moment, and twisted his body as I tried to knee him. Without dislodging his hold on my throat—nowhere near as debilitating as the first time he strangled me, but still inhibiting—he spun me around so I was pressed up against the wall, his body pinning me into submission. "I do not have time to play ridiculous games with you. You will exculpate me now, before I lose my temper."

"Fine," I said, exhausted, sore, and heartily tired of the handsome man whose mouth was close enough to kiss . . . and bothered by the fact that I could even *think* such a thought. "I forgive you for kidnapping us, assaulting me, and attempting to strangle me. Happy now?"

"Stop playing with me!" he snarled, his fingers tightening. "You have the Gift! I saw it! I demand my reward! I demand exculpation!"

"I forgive you!" I bellowed back at him, praying he would go away and be deranged with someone else.

He really was an incredibly handsome man . . . I firmly squelched that line of thought. Physical attractiveness had nothing to do with anything.

The man sighed, releasing me as he stepped back.

I hadn't been aware that he had lifted me off the floor, but I slid down a few inches until my feet touched the floor, and kept on going when my legs gave out on me. I slumped against the wall, divided between the desire to cry and the urge to whack the man across the kneecaps with a blunt instrument.

"At last," he said, opening his arms. He stood that way for a moment, as if he was waiting for something, his ebony eyebrows pulling together as he looked down at himself. "It didn't work."

"What didn't work?" Sarah asked, watching him closely. I shot an unhappy glance at her as I got to my knees, hauling myself up onto the edge of the bed, where I clutched both the book and the lamp.

He looked at me, his eyes narrowing slightly. "When did you say you received the Gift?"

"What gift? No one has given me a gift."

"How long have you known her?" he asked Sarah. She plopped down onto the bed next to me. I was delighted to see that the smitten look was gone from her face, although her calm acceptance of the kidnapper was at odds with her very vocal threats to the local police about the actions her husband would take if the man was not caught promptly.

"Since seventh grade," she answered.

"Has she always been like this?"

"Obstinate, you mean?" Sarah smiled. "Stubborn? Unyielding?"

"Hey!" I objected, poking her in the hip with the book.

"Rigid and unimaginative and one-track-minded? Oh yes, she's always been that way."

The kidnapper looked at me, his lips pursing slightly. "Pity."

"I object to being talked about as if I'm not sitting right here!"

Sarah patted my hand. "She's also smart, very curious, has a soft spot for underdogs, and is unswervingly loyal to anyone she calls friend."

"I may have one less before the day is out," I grumbled, mollified by her praise.

"I see," the man said, frowning down at me. My fingers tightened around the base of the lamp.

Sarah laughed and put her arm around me. "She's also my best friend, and someone I trust with my life. If you need her help with something, she'll do everything she can to make it happen."

"Will you stop putting words in my mouth! I do not countenance criminals!"

"I am not a criminal," the man said with a thoughtful look at us both. He snagged the chair from the end of the bed and set it before the door, sitting on it with a belligerent look at me.

"I could scream for help, you know," I told him.

"No one would hear you over the noise," he answered. "I'm going to get at the truth if it takes me all night. When did you last see Hope?"

"Oh! The faery?" Sarah asked, clasping her hands together. "I can't believe I forgot about her! Portia said she saw her while I had run to town to get my camera. That would be about two—"

"Sarah." I cocked an eyebrow at her.

"I was just trying to be helpful."

I ignored that and leveled a long, hard look at the

man sitting across from us. My first impressions of strength had not diminished at all by exposure to him. His face was all hard angles, high cheekbones and a blunt, square jaw doing as much as his obsidian eyes in imparting a sense of ruthless purpose. His skin was darker than that of an Anglo-Saxon, a warm, rich color that hinted at an exotic heritage. Gleaming black hair swept back from a widow's peak that no doubt had women swooning to run their fingers through the silky black curls. For a moment my fingers itched to do just that, but the thought died just as quickly as it had been born.

"If I answer your questions, will you leave?" I asked with a resigned sigh.

"Portia! You don't have to be rude!"

I gave her a look that should have made it clear what I thought of such a ridiculous statement, but years of close acquaintance have made Sarah immune to such things.

"I begin to think that there might be more here than I anticipated," the man answered. "But I will swear to you that I mean you no harm."

I hesitated a moment, weighing my options. It was true that the noise from the busy pub below would drown out any screams for help that we might make, but we weren't completely helpless. There was the fact that we were two against his one. If push came to shove, I could fling myself at the man while Sarah made her escape to bring help . . . except I wasn't so sure that in her present hypnotized state of mind she would run for help.

Clearly, the solution lay in a peaceful resolution

of the situation. After we got the man out of my room, I'd call the police and they could deal with him. I'd give him a few minutes of twenty questions to lull him into a sense of control, then persuade him to exit the room.

"All right, I'll answer your questions . . . er . . . what is your name?"

"Theo North. When did you last see Hope?" he repeated.

"What a nice name," Sarah said with perky cheerfulness. "Theo. Warm and friendly. Short. A little different. I like it."

I did too, as a matter of fact, but I wasn't going to let him know that. "I saw Hope for the first and only time about two this afternoon, for approximately five minutes. At the time, I was under the impression— yet to be disproved to my satisfaction, given that lab tests can be mixed up, altered, or deliberately changed—that Hope was part of my hallucinations."

"Hallucinations?" He subjected me to a searching look. "Are you prone to them?"

"She thought the magic at the faery ring was due to mushrooms," Sarah said quickly. "She is an unbeliever, you see. You believe in the power behind faery rings, don't you?"

"Of course," he answered, making me want to scream.

The look of triumph on Sarah's face was directed solely at me. "There, you see? Even Theo believes in faery ring magic! And he's a . . . a . . . er . . ." She looked back at him. "What exactly do you do, if you don't mind me asking?"

He cast her a quick glance, but for the most part kept his attention on me. "I'm a nephilim. What did you do at the ring to summon Hope?"

This was torture, sheer and utter torture, so I figured I'd get it over with as quickly as possible. Although Sarah had heard most of it, I described how I had sat in the faery ring and muttered aloud some of the spells on her photocopy.

"Hmm," Theo said when I was done. He stroked his chin, a perfectly normal gesture, but one which held some bizarre fascination for me. It drew my attention to the lines of his jaw, and the sweet curve of his lower lip . . . good gravy, what was I thinking? Just because he was a handsome devil didn't mean I had to think about his lips and his jaw and that hint of manly stubble that seemed to hold an unholy fascination for me.

I realized that both of them were looking expectantly at me.

"Sorry, I was thinking about . . . er . . . did you ask something?"

"I asked you why Hope said she responded when you summoned her."

"I didn't summon her." I frowned for a moment, remembering something the hallucination woman—not a hallucination if the man in front of me was to be believed—said when she popped through those funny lights in the air. The lights themselves gave me no trouble: they were clearly pollen in the air, which I in my half-sun-blinded state interpreted as sparkling. Hope was a bit less easily explained, but no doubt she had been hiding behind a tree, and took advantage of an inattentive moment to make her appearance. "She said something about being glad I summoned her when I did, and that she was in danger and couldn't stay or she'd be killed."

"She is a virtue," Theo said as he rubbed his chin. The sweep of his thumb across his square chin distracted me for a moment, but I was firm with myself and looked at the grain of the wood in the door behind him, instead. "She cannot die unless she is removed from the Court. If she was in danger from someone, that would explain why I had such a difficult time tracking her down . . . Very well, continue. Who did she say she was in danger from?"

"From whom," Sarah corrected with a smile.

Theo looked at her. "Sorry. I'm a writer. It's second nature."

"She didn't say. She just told me she was in danger, and that if she stayed, all would be destroyed. She was very drama queen about the whole thing, frankly, which is why I had no trouble believing she wasn't real. What exactly is a virtue, other than the normal definition of the word?"

Theo's black-eyed gaze swept over me. I wouldn't be a woman if I didn't notice that it lingered for a shade too long on my breasts. "You really don't know, do you?"

"If I knew, I wouldn't ask. How can someone not be killed just because they're a member of a court?"

He got out of the chair and paced to the end of the room, turning to face us. "This complicates the situation greatly. If you unintentionally summoned Hope, and she was desperate enough to use the escape you offered . . . but I'm getting ahead of myself. A virtue, my dear mortal, is a member of the Court of Divine Blood."

I sighed and leaned back on the headboard, adjusting a pillow so it supported my aching shoulder. "You're going to say things I don't want to hear, aren't you? You're going to spout all sorts of make-believe stuff in such a way that Sarah will buy it hook, line, and sinker, and I'll spend the entire rest of the trip trying to explain to her why immortal people don't suddenly pop into faery rings."

"I've heard of the Court of Divine Blood," Sarah said slowly, her eyes scrunched up as she hunted through her memory. "It's another name for heaven, isn't it?"

"No," Theo said, much to my relief. Religion was a bit of a touchy subject with me, one I certainly had no intention of discussing with a strange man who quite possibly had mental issues. "The concept of heaven is loosely based on the Court, but the Court of Divine Blood is not dogma for any specific religion. It just is."

"Good gravy, you're not going to tell me that the woman who snuck up behind me and popped out when I wasn't looking is an angel!" I sent Theo a look of utter disbelief.

He looked annoyed in return. "I just told you that the Court is not heaven. There are similarities, but that is all. The members of the Court are not angels, although their jobs are classified in a hierarchy that Christians took for their own. A virtue is a member of the second household, and controls weather."

"The cloud!" Sarah said triumphantly. "I knew it! Proof! Oh my god, that means you . . ." Her mouth hung open for a second as she looked at me with huge eyes. ". . . you spoke to an angel! She gave you her job! Good heavens! *My best friend is an angel!*"

I rolled my eyes. "Theo just said that there are no such things as angels. Use your common sense, Sarah. Some woman pops out of the woods at me, and you're convinced that everything Theo says is gospel . . . no pun intended. Who's to say the two of them aren't working together? He kidnapped us, after all. This is no doubt some elaborate scheme to get money from us." I thinned my lips at Theo. "And it's not going to work. Get out."

"Portia!"

"Pardon?" Theo asked, frowning.

I stood up slowly, holding my lamp. "I said your little scheme isn't going to work, and I want you out of here. Right now. I've listened to this crap long enough."

"Portia!" Sarah gasped again, looking appalled at my bad manners.

I didn't care. I was sore, tired, and sick of being made a fool. I wasn't going to stand for any more bull from this man and his accomplice.

Theo straightened up and looked as intimidating as he could, but I'd had enough. I didn't care what he did, so long as he did it away from me. I stomped over to the door, and jerked it open. "Leave. *Now!*"

"And just how do you expect to bend me to your will? Scream? I told you, no one below would hear you over the music."

Anger, frustration, and the suspicion that I had been made to look a fool grew within me, until I thought I would explode with it. I sucked in a deep breath, prepared to rip him up one side and down the other, but before I could, a storm broke directly overhead. Brilliant blue light exploded around the pub, followed immediately by thunder so loud it shook not only the glass in the windows, but could be felt in the walls and floor of the pub. Before the rumble of thunder disappeared, the lights went out, the music of the pub suddenly silenced. The silence was almost smothering in its thickness.

I tipped my head back and screamed for all I was worth. Sarah threw herself sideways and covered her ears as I released every bit of pent-up emotion. It was a scream the likes of which I'd never made before, and one I doubted I'd be able to duplicate.

Sudden voices from below indicated they had heard me.

Theo snarled something in the darkness. I stumbled to the bed, finding and clutching Sarah as she made odd little squeaking noises. Lights flashed in the hallway outside my room, visible through the open door. A shadow a hair darker than the surrounding blackness paused in the doorway for a moment.

"You foolish woman," the Theo-shaped shadow said. "Do you not realize you will need a champion for the trials? To try it alone is folly. You will end up destroying yourself . . . and me as well."

The pub owner called up the stairs to ask if we were all right, the light from his flashlight flickering and dancing in an erratic pattern on the wall opposite us. I slumped against Sarah, relieved when Theo's shadow merged into that of the hallway, his last words echoing in my mind.

"I will not let you escape me as Hope did."

Chapter 5

"Could you have possibly been any ruder to poor Theo?"

"Shhh. Madame What's-her-face is gesturing for you. No doubt she wants to anoint you or something."

"It's Mystic, not Madame. Mystic Bettina, as you know well. Oooh! She must have picked me to be one of her assistants! Fabulous! I'll be in a perfect position for unbiased observation." Sarah jumped out of her seat and hurried over to where the local medium was standing with two women.

"Very unbiased," I said to myself, then smiled reassuringly at the man on my left as he glanced at me.

He leaned over and whispered, "Is this your first séance?"

I nodded.

"Mine too," he said in a confiding tone, and hazarded a shy smile. "My wife—that's her there with the others—is a member of the local ghost hunter's group, so she's been wanting to come to a séance for a long time. I'm not sure I believe in all this." He chuckled a little, watching me carefully to see if I was going to mock him for his skepticism.

"I'm a scientist by trade, and a natural-born skeptic," I assured him. I dropped my voice a little so the other four people in the room couldn't overhear us. "To be honest, I'm just here to explain to my friend how all the tricks are done. She's one of those people who is ready to give anyone the benefit of the doubt, no matter how unlikely the situation."

"Ah, a true believer," my new friend said, nodding. "There are a lot of those in the ghost hunter's group. I'm Milo, by the way."

"Portia," I said, shaking his hand. "Shall we join forces to bring reason to our loved ones?"

He glanced nervously at his wife, who was approaching the table with the small woman who claimed she was a "world-renowned medium." "Indeed we could, although I hesitate to disappoint my wife. She wants so much to contact her father, you see. He passed on when she was quite young. Still, I've told her that to have so much faith in such things is sheer folly."

"I've found that faith is vastly overrated," I said softly, then turned to Sarah as she slid into the seat next to me. "So are you to hold the ghostly tambourine, or rap on the table at the appropriate time?"

She whapped me on the arm and whispered at me to behave myself.

"Considering all that we've been through today, I think I'm behaving with complete circumspection," I said just as quietly, gingerly moving my shoulder.

The muscles, which had been strained but not torn, protested the movement.

Sarah noticed my grimace of pain, and leaned even closer. "Are you sure you're all right? Maybe I shouldn't have brought you tonight. What with the virtue and Theo and that horrible storm you conjured up—"

"Will you stop? I didn't conjure up anything. The pub owner himself said it was perfectly normal for storms to whip up like that."

"Yes, but he couldn't explain the way it completely disappeared a minute later. Nor why just the lights at the pub went out, and none of the other buildings nearby."

"The fuses were blown, nothing more. It's quite common in buildings close to a ground lightning strike."

"Hrmph."

Mystic Bettina (the name had me snickering softly to myself when we were introduced) returned to the round glass table with the others. Milo, Sarah, and I were already seated; Mystic Bettina took an elaborately carved chair I mentally dubbed "the throne," flashing a smile around the table. There were only five of us attending the séance—Milo and his wife, an elegant black woman who clutched a tattered bible, Sarah, and me. "Are we all settled, then? Very good. I'd like to welcome all of you to my mystic circle. I am sure that we will have a very good experience tonight with the spirits. They always know when people sympathetic to their beings are present."

I was going to say something, but Sarah was still

miffed at me for the way I had driven off Theo the kidnapper.

"I'm afraid one of us here is a skeptic," she said, shooting me an accusatory look.

"Oh, but everyone is welcome at my table," Bettina said quickly, turning her overbright smile on me. "Even non-believers. Especially non-believers! It is perfectly healthy to be skeptical of something so beyond our grasp as the spirit world."

"See?" I said softly to Sarah, nudging her with my elbow. "Skepticism is good!"

She made a sour face.

"It is one reason why I have a glass table," Bettina continued, nodding toward the table upon which were spread a number of tiles painted with the letters of the alphabet, like oversized Scrabble tiles. In the center, a normal-looking drinking glass sat upside down on a small square of crimson silk. "I do not want anyone to be able to claim the events they witness have a mundane explanation. There is no trickery performed here!"

Sarah elbowed me back. I ignored it and carefully examined the table. Despite the dim lighting of the small séance room, everyone's legs were clearly visible beneath the table.

"Now, if we're ready, perhaps we can begin with a prayer."

I bit my lip and said nothing as Bettina clasped her hands together and bowed her head before offering up a prayer of understanding and protection. Everyone followed suit except me—I took the opportunity to look around the room, trying to find anywhere an accomplice could hide, locations of possible hidden projectors, and anything out of the ordinary.

"Atheist?" a soft voice to my left asked.

"More a skeptical agnostic," I answered Milo in a whisper. "I grew up in a strictly religious household, but it didn't stick with me after I left home."

"Me, too," he said with a conspiratorial smile.

"If everyone would take a few moments to write down a couple of questions you would like asked of any spirits who may visit us, that would be very helpful." Bettina passed out small squares of paper and tiny pencils. "Please don't sign your name to the questions. The spirits will know who asked what."

I toyed with my pencil for a moment, debating whether I should pose questions that physicists have yet to answer, but decided it was hardly fair to expect anyone, even supposed spirits, to solve all the mysteries of the universe. I contented myself with asking a few simple questions instead, passing my paper along with everyone else's.

Sarah leaned closer and whispered, "I hope you didn't embarrass me by asking something impossible to answer, like what the meaning of life is, or what Einstein's favorite color was, or what that gnu thing is."

"Gnu?" I whispered back, confused. I'd never had any questions about cattle of any form, let alone exotic ones.

"That theory thing you're always talking about."

I stifled a giggle. "That would be GUT, the grand unification theory, but I've long since moved on to string theory—"

"Excellent," Bettina said, shooting me a glance that indicated she'd love it if I shut up. "For our new friends who haven't been here before, I'll explain what will happen during this séance. First, everyone will place their fingertips upon the edge of the glass. We will clear our minds of the trivialities of everyday life, and focus on creating a welcoming environment for any spirit who wishes to join us."

"Short of baking cookies and laying out a 'Welcome, Spirits' doormat, how are we supposed to do that?" I asked Sarah in a nearly inaudible voice.

"Shh!"

"Once a spirit has indicated that he or she is present, I will begin reading your questions. I ask that you be silent until the spirit has answered the question, at which point you may ask for clarification if needed, or if you have a follow-up. In order to keep the séance to a reasonable length, there will be only one additional question per person."

Well, at least this was going to be fairly short, I thought to myself as I prepared to clear my mind of whatever trivialities were lurking there. "Begone, value of pi to ten decimal points," I murmured softly. "Shoo, velocity of the pion. Take a hike, plum pudding model of the atom."

"Portia!"

I composed my face into one of absolute innocence, and placed two fingertips on the circular walls of the glass. Bettina did a few moments of communing with who knew what, swaying slightly, her eyelids fluttering in a suitably dramatic fashion.

"Spirits, entities, and loved ones who have passed

on before us," she intoned, still doing the swaying and fluttering thing. "Heed our plea, and grace us now with your presence."

Milo's arm brushed mine. I glanced at him out of the corner of my eye. His lips were twitching. I fought hard to keep from grinning at him, and was mostly successful, but Sarah glared at me nonetheless.

"We beseech you who have gone beyond the beyond—"

I bit my lip hard, using the pain to distract me from the need to burst into unseemly laughter.

"—share with us your knowledge and advice." Bettina took a couple of deep breaths, swayed forward, swayed backward, swayed forward again, then sat upright and opened her eyes. "Is there a spirit with us now?"

Beneath my fingers, the glass moved slowly to a tile upon which had been printed the word YES in bright red letters. I wasn't surprised the glass moved, being tolerably familiar with the concepts of auto-suggestion and self-delusion, although I had been content to simply rest my fingers on the glass and do no more. No doubt an overeager participant had nudged the glass across the table, possibly quite unaware that he or she was doing so.

"Very good. Let us see what the spirits have to share with us tonight." Mystic Bettina pulled a piece of paper from the stack, and opened it. "Does the velocity of an object in space determine the force of the vacuum through which it travels?"

Everyone looked at me. I cleared my throat and

smiled. "It was the only thing I could think of off-hand."

Behind my arm, Sarah pinched me.

Bettina gave me a stern look, and pulled another piece of paper from the pile. "I believe we will try a question a little less confusing. Here is one: is my brother James happy—"

"Sorry we're late," a voice interrupted as the door to the séance room was opened. Sarah gave a startled yelp, and jumped in her chair.

Silhouetted in the doorway were two shapes, the voice female. "Bloody badgers, it's dark in here. Tansy, find the switch, will you?"

We all blinked as an overhead light suddenly flooded the room with light. Two middle-aged women, both with close-cropped, greying hair, stood smiling at us. One was very short and rather round; the other was tall and had a brusque manner about her that reminded me of the late British actress Dame Margaret Rutherford. The Dame Margaret woman peered nearsightedly around the room, her frown clearing when she spotted me. "There you are! Knew we'd run you to earth somewhere around town. All ready, are you? That your champion?"

She looked at Milo, who appeared just as startled as the rest of us.

"Um . . . no, this a gentleman named Milo."

"Ah, it's the lady then? Excellent! Equality of the sexes and all that."

I scooted my chair back and got to my feet, feeling it necessary to clear up a misunderstanding that evidently involved me. "I'm sorry, but I think you have the wrong person. I'm not expecting to meet anyone this evening."

"Bloody badgers," Dame Margaret swore, turning to her companion. "Did we bollocks it up again?"

"Excuse me, but this is a private session," Bettina said with a determined smile, rising from her seat. "If you wish to book one of your own, you can do so tomorrow between the hours of nine and—"

"Where's the bloody card . . . I know I had it." Dame Margaret patted her navy jacket. "Had it when we left Court. Tansy, you pick it up?"

"Oh, let me check." The smaller woman rustled around in a voluminous purse, extracting a small gold card. She had a grandmotherly look about her, with twinkling brown eyes, a little pink nose that twitched ever so slightly, and soft grey curls that bobbed as she fussed in her purse. "Yes, I do. Here it is. The name is Portia Harding. Such a pretty name, Portia. I had a cat named Portia, once. Do you remember it, Letty? She was orange and white, and had a nasty habit of piddling in my shoes, but otherwise was a very smart cat. I was devastated when she was trampled by a contingent of Cromwell's men."

You could have cut the silence in the room with a mackerel.

"Honest to Pete, I know the English are supposed to be eccentric, but this is just ludicrous," I whispered to Sarah.

"They certainly are . . . *different* here," Sarah agreed, watching with interested eyes as the two women continued.

"That wasn't Cromwell's men. You have your history mixed up again. It was James II's party that fired the town and killed everyone, your piddling cat included."

"Ladies, I'm sorry, you're going to have to leave. We're in the middle of an important séance here, and we've just made contact."

"James II?" The short woman named Tansy wrinkled her brow, ignoring Bettina's plea. "Are you sure? I distinctly remember cursing Cromwell."

Dame Margaret shook her head. "Of course you cursed him; we all did. Don't you remember the group cursing parties we used to have with the powers and virtues? All that thunder and lightning and those absolutely glorious bonfires that lit up the countryside for miles."

"Ladies!" Bettina strode forward with a smile that was a bit tattered around the edges. "I must insist that you leave now."

"I liked the wine back then," Tansy said with a sad little sigh. "You just don't find wine like that anymore."

"You don't find plague anymore either, but you won't catch me bemoaning the loss of those days. Yes, yes, we hear you, whatever your name is." Dame Margaret turned to Bettina, who was standing at the opened door. "This won't take long at all."

"We're quite experienced at conducting trials," Tansy said as she bustled over to the door, patting Bettina's arm. "Why don't you take a seat, dear. It will all be over before you know it."

"She said trial," Sarah whispered, gripping my forearm. "Didn't Theo say something about a trial before you scared him off?"

"And a champion," I answered, nibbling my bottom lip. It was a bad habit from youth, but one I couldn't help in times of stress . . . and whether I wanted to admit it or not, I was suddenly a bit worried about the two women who were even now escorting an overwhelmed-looking Bettina back to her seat.

"What do you think it means?" Sarah asked.

"Ladies and gentlemen!" Dame Margaret clapped her hands and, without warning, the room was filled with an intense bluish light, seemingly coming from nowhere and everywhere at once. It must have dazzled me more than I realized, because without being aware of moving, I suddenly found myself standing in the center of the room, facing the two women, Sarah at my side. "We commence with the first trial of the virtue known as Portia Harding."

"I have a feeling this evening is going to end up being just as strange as the afternoon," I told my friend.

She nodded.

"Is your champion ready?" Dame Margaret asked me.

Sarah and I looked at each other. "I'm a champion? Isn't that like a knight-errant or something?"

"So I gather." I turned back to face the two women. Beyond them, Bettina, Milo and his wife, and the elegant lady watched us with startled eyes. They were oddly silent given the unexpected interruption. "I'm really sorry, but this has to stop."

Dame Margaret frowned. "You're not Portia Harding?"

"Yes, I am, but—"

"And this is your champion?"

"No, she's my friend, not a champion, but—"

"It is your right to waive the presence of a champion, although I can't imagine why you would do so," Dame Margaret said with a shrug.

"Look, this has gone far enough," I said, getting angry. "As I explained to Theo, we are not the gullible, helpless tourists we may look to be, and frankly, we've had a hell of a day and I'm really not going to put up with any more fun and games a la Theo. Feel free to trot back to him and tell him that your little scheme didn't work, and the police will be contacting him about this continued harassment."

Tansy pursed her lips. Dame Margaret frowned. Sarah clutched my arm even tighter.

"We are already late, Portia Harding. I don't understand the purpose of your little joke, but we have a job to do. Tansy, if you please?"

"This is absolutely insaaaaaaaaa—"

Before I knew what was happening, little round butterball Tansy threw herself at me, slamming into me with a force that knocked me backward several feet onto my butt. I stared in stunned disbelief at her as she did the flying dive toward me, knocking the breath out of me as her not-insubstantial form squashed me like a ripe bug. My head hit the ground, making me see stars for a few seconds, my already injured shoulder screaming with reawakened pain.

"Sweet mother of reason, what do you think you're doing?" I shrieked as Tansy grabbed my hair and started slamming my head against the floor. "Sarah, call the cops!"

"I can't move," Sarah yelled back, her voice strained. "Something seems to be holding me back."

"You are not the champion," Dame Margaret said with irritating calm. "Only a champion can assist a subject."

"Stop it, you crazy old lady!" I screamed as Tansy sat on me and continued to pound my head against the floor. I struggled against her, trying to push her off me, but for an old woman, she was remarkably strong. It didn't help that one of my arms was just about incapacitated due to my sore shoulder, or that my head was becoming more and more befuddled with each wallop on the floor. "Someone help me!"

Tansy's face was twisted with concentration, her teeth bared in a grotesque parody of a smile.

"Fifteen seconds," Dame Margaret said in a bored voice. "I suggest that you make your move soon, Portia Harding."

"Arrrrrrrgh!" I bellowed, trying to twist my way out of Tansy's vicious grip. Part of my mind, the part that annoys me the most, pointed out with abstracted amusement the irony of being beaten up by an overweight, elderly lady after having earlier survived attacks by an extremely fit man.

"Ten seconds."

"Are you all right, Portia?" Sarah called.

"No . . . I . . . am . . . not . . ." I answered in between head bangings. "Gaaaarr!"

"Can't you just push her off you?" she asked. "It's just one old lady."

"This isn't an old lady; it's a big-time wrestler in

disguise," I snarled, trying to pry Tansy's hands from my head.

"Five seconds."

"Well then . . . you're just going to have to persuade her to stop," Sarah said, quite unreasonably in my opinion. "Without striking her, of course. I do not condone physical abuse of the elderly."

"Granng!"

"And . . . cease."

In a twinkling, Tansy released me and hopped up, immediately straightening her shapeless wool skirt and blouse, the former of which had been somewhat rumpled during her attack on me. "What happened?" she asked, peering down at me.

"That's what I'd like to know," I answered a bit woozily. With slow, careful movements, I sat up, feeling the back of my head. There was a horribly tender spot, from which tendrils of pain snaked out and wrapped themselves around my brain. "I'm going to have a hell of a goose egg back there. What have I ever done to you that you'd attack me like that?"

"Why didn't you defend yourself?" Tansy asked, looking confused.

Sarah rushed over and helped me to my feet, her face red with anger. "You people are insane—insane! How dare you assault us! You may be elderly, but that does not give you the right to beat up whomsoever you feel like!"

The ground dipped beneath my feet for a moment. I clutched Sarah and tried to blink away the dizziness.

"Subject failed to manifest any sort of defense whatsoever," Dame Margaret said as she wrote in a small notebook. She tucked the pencil into the book and put both away in her pocket, cocking an eyebrow at me. "Let's hope you do better on the second trial. That will commence tomorrow."

"Could someone call the police?" Sarah asked, gently pushing me toward my chair. Bettina and the others still sat around the table, as still as statues. "And an aid unit. Portia looks very pale."

"I don't understand why she didn't protect herself," Tansy said, back to looking like a fluffy-haired, jolly grandmother. I knew just how deceptive that appearance was. "Why didn't she do something, Letty?"

"No idea," Dame Margaret answered, pursing her lips again. "But it's no concern of ours. Who's next on the list?"

Tansy pulled a piece of paper from her purse. "A throne applicant."

"Oh, good. Always like testing them. They have such polite manners. Good evening!"

"Someone stop them," Sarah said, heading for the door, but it did no good. The bright bluish light that had filled the room suddenly went off, plunging us into relative darkness. We were light blind for a moment or two, moments which the two women used to hurry out the door before anyone could stop them.

"What is wrong with everyone here?" I asked, rubbing my head and glaring at the people around the table. "Couldn't someone have pulled that old lady off me?"

Bettina gave me an odd look. "Pardon? What old lady are you speaking about?"

"What old lady? The one who just tried to bash my brains into mush on the floor!"

Four sets of eyes watched me warily, as if I was the one who was behaving oddly.

"Perhaps you would like to lie down for a few minutes while we continue with the séance," Bettina said kindly. "There is a sofa in the reception room which you are welcome to use."

I looked from person to person, then to Sarah.

"Didn't you just see the two women who came in here?" she asked them all.

All four of them shook their heads.

"No one? You're telling us you didn't see anyone else come into the room?" Sarah asked, her hands on her hips.

"No," Milo said. "No one but the six of us."

"Unauthorized visitors are not allowed at client séances," Bettina added. "Shall we continue?"

"What's going on?" Sarah asked, confusion written all over her face. It probably mirrored mine.

I shook my head very, very carefully. "I have no idea, but I think it's time to leave."

"Definitely," she said, helping me to my feet and opening the door for me. I felt like I had been run down by a steam roller. My head and shoulder were hurting so much it was making me sick to my stomach. Sarah paused at the doorway and looked back at the four people at the séance table. "You English are just downright mean sometimes!"

Chapter 6

"Well?" Sarah asked the next morning as I staggered into the small room on the first floor that the pub owner said would serve as our private dining room.

"I'm still alive, my head is still attached to my body, and no other evil elderly people tried to beat the crap out of me after I went to bed," I said, slumping gratefully into a chair.

"Did you talk to the police yet?"

"Just got off the phone with them. Good morning, Darla. Yes, thank you, coffee and toast. And perhaps an egg, and that delicious-looking marmalade. Is there any bacon? Oh, good. I'll have some bacon, too. And a grapefruit, if you have one."

The barmaid/waitress who fed us breakfast and dinner gave me a curious look, but toddled off to bring me the requested foodstuffs.

"And?" Sarah asked around a mouthful of eggs and grilled tomato, a combination that made me shudder just looking at it.

"It's not polite to talk with your mouth full."

She made a face that would be more appropriate on her youngest child.

"I talked to the same sergeant who interviewed us yesterday, and he said they haven't found Theo, nor the two deranged women who attacked me at the séance. They have an address for Theo, but it's somewhere up north, and whoever is checking on it hasn't reported in yet. They want us to go in later and look at mug shots, in case he has an arrest history."

"So basically there are no leads," Sarah said, blowing on her cup of tea.

"Exactly. Thanks, Darla." I sipped the coffee set before me with pleasure that approached bliss, and wondered if I couldn't just have it administered intravenously.

"I've been thinking," Sarah said as she set down her cup.

"Good gravy, not that! Shall I alert the newspapers?"

"Oh, ha ha. You should be a comedian." She dabbed at her lips and gave me a stern look that had me giggling into my coffee. "About those two women last night."

"If you're going to pick on me because I was beat up by an elderly woman—"

"No, I'm not. But that makes up a good part of my point. It's not normal for little old ladies to go around attacking people."

I rubbed the bump on the back of my head, wincing slightly when my fingers found a particularly tender spot. "Granted, but that doesn't change the fact that one did. While everyone stood around and let her, I might add."

Sarah's blue eyes were uncommonly grave. "I told you that I couldn't move. Judging by what happened with the others at the séance, I assume the same thing applied to them, only they had a mind wipe afterward."

"Mind wipe?" A horrible suspicion occurred to me. "Oh no, you're not going to tell me that what happened last night was something paranormal, are you?"

"Let's look at the facts," Sarah said, ticking items off her fingers. "First, two women show up at a séance knowing your name and that you are a virtue."

"I am not a virtue," I said, waiting for Darla to serve my breakfast and leave the room before continuing. "A virtue is not a person, it's a concept."

"Yes, but how did they know you would be at that exact spot at that exact time?" Sarah asked, triumph evident in her voice.

"Easy." I smeared a little homemade berry jam on my toast and took a bite. "They asked the pub owner. Or Darla. Or the shopkeeper down the road whom you told just about our entire schedule to. Any one of those three people knew we were going off to that séance."

"Yes, but how would someone know who to ask, eh?"

I rolled my eyes and chewed my toast.

"Second, the women were there to administer the first in who-knows-how-many trials. I'm not sure what that's all about, but I know we'll figure it out sooner or later."

I licked a smidgen of jam off my upper lip.

"Right, and since Theo mentioned something about trials earlier, it's obvious they are working with him. Honestly, Sarah, it's as clear as the noses on both our faces—you're a famous author. You have gazillions of readers all over the world. Somehow, Theo got hold of the news that you were going to be in the area, no doubt from your English publisher, and since you make no bones about believing in every out-there theory floating around, he decided to set up an elaborate hoax to sucker you in."

"Sucker me in for what?" she asked, looking mulish.

I waved the jam spoon around. "I don't know, but it has to be something to do with money. Why else would he go to all the time and expense of hiring people to playact the parts of Hope, Tansy, and the big, horsey Dame Margaret woman."

"You can't tell me you seriously believe that nothing paranormal happened last night!" Sarah's face mirrored her disbelief. "How on earth do you explain that bright blue light? Or Mystic Bettina and the others having their memories wiped clean? Or the fact that I was held immobile while you were being beaten up?"

"Flat-panel lights in the ceiling, they were lying, and hypnosis," I said, wiping the crumbs off my mouth and pushing my plate aside. "You ready to go? We can swing by the police station first, before we head out to look for the Hound of the Baskervilles."

"It's not the Hound of the Baskervilles, as you very well know. The Black Shuck is a ghostly black dog according to local legend, and evidently it's become quite active the last few years . . . oh, never mind. The Shuck can wait. It's not supposed to appear before dark anyway. You're being entirely unreasonable about this, Portia. The bet aside, I don't understand why you are so unwilling to admit that you have become involved with something highly paranormal."

"You have yet to prove to me that anything paranormal has happened," I said with complacency that I knew would drive her wild. I was right. She lectured me for the next few hours while we drove out to view a circle of stones known as the Angry Stones. We didn't see or hear either the singing reputed to be audible or the medieval fair that supposedly haunts the area, although we did have a pleasantly relaxing drive through the country.

"This has been a lovely day," I said five hours later as we drove past the area containing the faery circle and headed for the humpbacked bridge leading into our town. "Beautiful countryside, shopping, lunch at a five-hundred-year-old pub . . . it's everything I imagined this trip would be."

"It is pretty country, isn't it?"

"Yes." I sighed, reality pressing down on me again. "I suppose we should visit the police before dinner and do the mug-shot thing with them. Ugh. What a way to end such an idyllically normal day. Not one single event had your paranormal meter shrieking."

"I never shriek," Sarah said as she rounded the corner before the bridge. At the sight of a figure standing smack-dab in the center of the bridge, she slammed her foot down on the brakes, and shrieked, "Dear god in heaven, where did he come from?"

The car skidded to a stop a few feet away from the man on the bridge. I narrowed my eyes as the man walked around to my side of the car. "I'm beginning to think the local loony bin. Don't just sit there—drive!"

"What? Are you blind? That's Theo!"

"My point exactly. Drive!"

"But he obviously wants to say somethiiiii—Portia!"

"Whatever he wants to say, he can say it to a policeman," I said grimly, leaning backward at an odd angle so I could keep my foot on the accelerator.

"You could have killed him!" Sarah yelled. "Get your foot out of the way! I can't drive with your foot like that!"

We whipped past Theo at a faster-than-normal pace. Despite Sarah's exaggeration, he wasn't in any danger of being run over; he'd been in the process of walking around to my side of the car, and wasn't anywhere near the front. I ignored Sarah's continued demands that I put my foot back, waiting until we were through most of the town before assuming a more traditional passenger position.

"If you ever do that again—I swear to god, Portia, sometimes I just want to strangle you! What will Theo think?" We came to an abrupt halt in front of a small cluster of stone buildings.

I unhooked the seat belt and got out of the car, grabbing the replacement purse I'd purchased earlier. "Sarah, he's a con man, nothing more. We don't care what he thinks."

"I care." She had a familiar mulish look on her face again, one that warned she was going to do something unreasonable. "You can go look at your precious mug shots if you want." She put the car in gear and reversed smoothly away from the police station. "I'm going to go back and apologize to Theo for your rudeness."

"Sarah! It's not safe for you to see him alone—oh, crapbeans!" I watched with frustration as my friend drove off through the town, worried that she would put herself into Theo's power and end up regretting her naive belief that he was not a bad man.

I thought about washing my hands of her, but Sarah was my oldest friend, and I couldn't leave her to the mercy of such a possibly dangerous man as Theo. I marched into the police station, intent on saving Sarah despite herself.

A short, balding man was at the reception counter, the only other person in the entryway. Beyond him, walls that were half glass gave the room light, and allowed the occupants to see what was going on in other sections of the station. Two policemen, and one policewoman, sat at desks typing industriously on their keyboards.

"Hello. You must be Portia Harding," the policeman at the reception desk said, coming around to shake my hand. He had a pleasant smile, and warm, friendly brown eyes that had me smiling back despite my distress. "I'm Terrin."

"It's a pleasure to meet you. Is Sergeant Reading here? She's the one we spoke with yesterday."

Terrin glanced behind him at the people in the other office. "Looks like she's stepped out for a bit. Shall we get started? This shouldn't take too much of your time."

"I'd be happy to, but I've just seen the man who assaulted me outside of town, and my friend has gone off to talk with him. If you hurry, I'm sure you can nab him before he escapes again."

A slight frown wrinkled his forehead. "Who would that be?"

"Theo North. You know, the man who assaulted me and kidnapped us?" I slapped my hands on my thighs, annoyed that he wasn't springing to life to capture Theo. "Are you at all familiar with the situation involving myself and my friend?"

"Of course I am," he laughed, taking my arm and guiding me to the far end of the room. "It's what I get paid to do. So to speak. Theo North. Hmm. The name is ringing a bell, but I can't put a face to it. While I'm thinking on it, why don't we get started?"

I stared at the policeman in disbelief, marching over to where he stood. "I am not going to stay here and do nothing while my friend is in danger!"

"The sooner you're finished, the sooner you can help her," he said soothingly, gently escorting me back to the corner.

"Oh, this is ridiculous. I'm going to go get my friend, and then you can bet I'll be back to complain to your superior about your callous disregard of human life!" I took one step forward and stopped, my skin crawling with horror as the black and white checkered tile floor that filled the reception area melted away to nothing. Everything but the two tiles I was standing on, and the two where Terrin stood across the room, was gone, a black pit of emptiness in its place.

"Sweet mother of reason," I swore, closing my eyes for a moment in hopes that whatever optical illusion I was seeing would disappear.

It didn't.

"All you need do to complete this trial is walk over to me," Terrin said with a happy little smile that I badly wanted to smack right off his face.

"This is not happening," I told him, shaking my finger at him. "Floors do not just disappear. And since I haven't been around any faery rings to breathe in hallucinogenic spores that don't show up on hospital tests, I doubt if this is a hallucination. Thus, I must be dreaming. An extremely lucid dream, one I want to stop right this very minute."

I closed my eyes tightly and willed myself to wake up.

"I'm afraid I don't have a lot of time to give to your trial," Terrin said.

My eyes popped open at the word *trial*. He looked at his watch. "This isn't a timed event, but I do have other appointments I must attend to, so I would appreciate it if you could please focus on the matter at hand."

"Good gravy, you're another henchman?"

Terrin's eyebrows rose. "Pardon?"

"You're another one of Theo's henchmen, aren't

you? Just like those two ladies? How many of you are there? It must be hugely expensive hiring so many people to play these silly roles. Regardless, I'm not going to do whatever it is he is paying you to get me to do, so feel free to go on to your other appointments." I crossed my arms and tried to look decisive and absolute without appearing bitchy.

"I assure you, Portia Harding, I am not in the pay of Theo North." Terrin's gaze on me was steady. "Now if we could dispense with the drama, could you please walk over to me?"

"You have not begun to see drama," I warned, giving him a look that should have singed off his eyebrows. "I consider this harassment of the purest form, and I will have no qualms whatsoever about lodging a complaint with the police about you if you do not cease with this ridiculous persecution!"

Terrin laughed, genuine amusement in his face. "The police? They have no jurisdiction over me, at least not the mortal sort. Please, time is passing quickly. If you could just walk over to me, we will both be free to go about our respective ways."

"You are insane if you think I'm going to walk anywhere near you," I told him, glancing at the floor. "Not that I believe your little optical tricks."

The amusement in his eyes deepened. "I see. You don't believe that I have made the floor disappear?"

"Absolutely not. This is nothing more than an illusion. It's done with lights and mirrors, or holograms, or some other sort of sophisticated projection."

"An interesting supposition. Would you care to prove it?" he asked, holding out a hand for me.

I glanced nervously from his hand to the floor. I knew, I *knew* that the floor hadn't disappeared into nothing despite the apparently yawning chasm in front of me. It was physically impossible. Thus, what I was seeing had to be an illusion. And if it was an illusion, then it was perfectly safe for me to walk across the floor.

At least, that's what I told myself. My legs refused to move, however.

A little bell jangled over the door to the street, heralding the arrival of someone . . . someone tall, dark, and incredibly handsome, someone whose mere presence had me grinding my teeth.

"What have you done with Sarah?" I asked before Theo was fully into the reception area. He stopped as soon as he stepped over the threshold, two tiles suddenly appearing beneath his feet. He glanced down at the apparently missing floor, then over to me. "I see the trial has begun."

"Ahhh," Terrin said, giving Theo a shuttered look. "Now I remember. You are the one who has been petitioning the Court for the last two hundred years."

Theo made a small bow. "Two hundred and twelve, to be precise."

"Indeed. And you are also now a champion?" Terrin looked thoughtful.

"Yes." Theo shot me a quick look.

"That might just do it, you know," Terrin told him. "Hasn't been done in a few centuries, but there is precedent."

I mustered up as much of a glare as I could, given the odd circumstances. "Where is Sarah? What have you done with her? And don't tell me you haven't seen her; she drove off to find you, and she's very single-minded when she wants to be."

"She went back to her room. She wished to see the trial, but I told her that you would no doubt prefer to conduct the trial without an audience." Theo's gaze swept around the room. "Unusual spot you chose to have it."

"I didn't choose anything! You people keep hounding me wherever I go, and I'm getting sick and tired of it." I carefully turned and waved my hands in the air to catch the attention of the police behind the glass walls. "And I'm going to put a stop to it right here and now. Hey! Hello! Need help out here! Dangerous criminal and his buddy right here in your station!"

The police people paid no attention whatsoever to either my frantic arm-waving or shouts, not so much as a single person looking up to see what was going on in their reception area.

"Portia, they can't see or hear you. They can't see or hear any of us until the trial is over," Theo said, holding out a hand for me. "Walk over here and it will be over, and then I can explain to you what's going on."

"Dream on," I snapped, wondering if they'd drugged everyone in the police station. Maybe some sort of drug in the water cooler that made everyone unaware of what was going on around them?

"I'm afraid I'm going to have to put this down as a refusal," Terrin said, pulling a small notebook out of his pocket. "This will be the second trial you've failed, I believe. You know, of course, that if you fail a third you will be disqualified and your application denied?"

"What is it you want?" I asked Theo. "Money? You won't get it, you know. I don't have any, and Sarah's husband is a lawyer who would grind you under his heel if you so much as thought about holding her for ransom."

Theo dropped his hand. "Is the floor here?"

"Yes, of course it's here," I answered, avoiding looking directly at the abyss in front of me. I'm not afraid of heights per se, but they did make me a bit nervous. Even though I knew what I was seeing was an optical illusion, it was good enough to make my palms sweat.

"Then walk over here and prove that you believe what you are seeing is not real."

I licked my lips, looking from him, to Terrin, to the floor. It's not real, I told myself. It's just an illusion, a very high-tech illusion, but an illusion nonetheless. Things like floors do not just disappear into nothing. If I march over there now, I will be able to prove to both of them that whatever their nefarious plan is, it won't work on me. I will laugh in their faces.

Despite my brave pep talk, my feet remained rooted to the two tiles.

"I'm sorry, I have no choice," Terrin told both Theo and me. He made a few notes and gave me a sad look. "I must mark this as a failure. I do hope you do better in your remaining trials, the third of which will commence tomorrow. Good afternoon to you both."

He turned and walked out the door, each step he made causing the tiles to appear in front of him, slowly rippling out until the entire floor was once again visible. I nudged the newly reappeared tile in front of me with the toe of my shoe. It seemed perfectly normal, perfectly solid.

"Hello, can I be of help?" a policeman asked as he walked in from the back rooms. He set down a cup of coffee and peered inquiringly over the desk at us.

"I am Portia Harding. I filed a complaint for assault and kidnapping against this man," I said, pointing at Theo. To my horror, my hand was shaking. "If you could arrest him now, I'd would be eternally grateful."

"Portia Harding?" The policeman frowned, seating himself in front of a computer. His fingers danced over the keys for a few seconds. "I'm sorry, but I don't have a record of a complaint by you, Miss Harding. What is your assailant's name?"

"Theo North. Er . . . Theodore, I assume."

"It's Theondre, actually," Theo said, walking over to the counter. "You will have to forgive Miss Harding. She has had a trying last few days, and is a bit confused at the moment."

"I'm sorry," the policeman said again, tapping away at the keyboard. "I see no entry for a Theo or Theondre North."

"Sweet mother of reason, you bought off the police?" I asked Theo. "I can't imagine how much it must have cost you to do the hologram of the floor, but to buy off police—that's just wrong in so many ways, I can't begin to name them!"

The policeman looked at me with suddenly wary eyes. "Are you quite yourself, madam?"

"She's fine," Theo said, taking me by the arm and gently pulling me to the door. "Just a little overset. I'll see that she gets back to her hotel."

"You're kidnapping me again, aren't you?" I asked him as he opened the door and all but shoved me through it. "You're kidnapping me right in front of a policeman, but because he's part of your horrible scheme, he's not going to stop you."

Theo sighed and gently pushed me through the door. "You need a drink."

"That's the first thing you've said that makes any sense," I agreed, looking around quickly for the best route for my escape. It was just starting to get dark, the little town in the middle of the busy hour when everyone was hurrying to the shops, then home. I shivered a little, rubbing my arms as a gust of wind hit me. It was raining slightly, more of a drizzle than a rain, but it was enough to chill me. I didn't relish running the mile through the damp night to the pub, especially with Theo on my tail, but I had no choice.

My escape plan was squelched when Theo grabbed my hand and held it in a no-nonsense grip as he started up the sidewalk. "Don't even think about it. We need to talk, you and I. And we could both use a drink. We'll take my car—"

"Over my dead body," I answered, digging in my heels and coming to an abrupt halt.

He eyed me for a moment. "As tempting as that offer is, I need you alive. We will walk if it makes you feel any better." So saying, he started up the hill to where the pub sat at the crown.

"Infinitely. Release my hand."

"No."

We marched along in silence for a few minutes, Theo looking straight ahead with a grim expression on his face, me desperately trying to catch the eye of townsfolk.

"Excuse me, could you help me? I'm being kidnapped." The man to whom I spoke glanced at Theo and hurried on his way.

I spotted a lady with her arms full of groceries. "Pardon me, but could you possibly help me? This large man next to me is kidnapping me."

"Oooh," the woman said, her eyes lighting up as she gave Theo the once-over. "He can kidnap me any day."

Theo snorted and continued to haul me up the road.

"Help—" I started to scream, feeling I had nothing left to lose.

Before I got more than the H out of my mouth, Theo jerked me toward him, both his arms coming around me in a steely grip. His black eyes flashed with irritation, the last thing I saw for a few seconds as his mouth descended on mine in a bruising kiss that drove everything from my mind.

Chapter 7

I would like to think that I'm a rational, relatively intelligent, down-to-earth sort of person, who doesn't get rattled when a handsome man plants his lips on hers. I'd like to think that, in that sort of a situation, I would handle myself with aplomb and dignity. I would like to think that, but the sad reality was that the second Theo stopped trying to shut me up by swallowing my yells for help, and started really kissing me, I was a goner.

Oh, the analytical part of my mind had quite a pleasant time examining the mechanics of the kiss. It noted that once his lips softened against mine, my breath started coming in short little gasps that had me parting my own lips. It understood that the act of his hands, sweeping down my arms, around to my back, and finally down to my butt, where they pulled me up against his body, were responsible for a sensation that left me feeling as if my entire body was tingling. It noticed that when his tongue touched mine, my knees seemed to be unable to support my weight, and deep within me, sensitive areas started to throb with an almost primal need. It made no judgment when I started kissing him back, sliding my fingers through his hair as I twined my tongue around his. It didn't even care when people walking by us giggled at the sight we made, kissing like crazy on the sidewalk.

But when Theo managed to retrieve his tongue and lips from where I was nipping at them, the analytical part of my mind pointed out that I had just been necking with a man who only the day before had kidnapped and assaulted me.

Oddly enough, that seemed to fade into unimportance in the face of what must surely be the world's best kisser.

"Sweet mother earth," I swore when he stepped back, releasing me.

"*Salus invenitur,*" he said at the same time, his black eyes mirroring my surprise.

"What was that?" I asked, ignoring the giggles of three teenaged girls as they skirted us.

"A kiss. I think." Theo looked just as disconcerted by the experience as I felt. His expression changed to one of annoyance, though. He looked upward for a moment, then frowned at me. "Stop that."

"I would like to point out that you are the one who kissed me, not vice versa."

He raised one ebony eyebrow. "Really? So that wasn't you trying to suck my tongue out of my head?"

"I kissed you back. I did not initiate the kiss. If your tongue gets sucked out of your head, it's no fault of mine," I said righteously, straightening my shoulders and ordering my knees to stop melting at the memory of the kiss.

Theo walked next to me as I continued up the hill toward the pub, taking my hand again in what was no doubt a precautionary move to keep me from bolting. The fact that escaping him had slid down my top ten lists of things to accomplish in the next half hour was neither here nor there. "I would like to think the responsibility and praise for a kiss lies with both participants, not just one. Will you please stop that? It is getting annoying."

"Stop what?"

He pointed overhead. "Stop raining on me."

Good gravy, the cloud hallucination was back, and it was following me!

I'm not ashamed to say that, for a moment, a wild irrational fear gripped me. "I'm not doing that!" I wailed, then shook my hand free of Theo's and raced up the hill to the safety of the pub.

"Portia—"

The damned cloud followed me the whole way, raining harder and harder with each step, so that when I arrived at the pub, my breath coming in big rasping gasps as I clutched the stitch in my side, I was soaked to the skin.

"Portia, stop!" Theo had been right beside me as I bolted, a look of concern on his face. "You can't out-run it. You have to make it stop."

I spun around, water flying from my sodden hair. "I cannot control the weather!" I yelled.

"Yes, you can." We stood outside the pub in the parking lot, which was thankfully unoccupied at that moment. Theo grasped my forearms and looked me deep in the eyes. "You have the Gift. You do not wish to acknowledge it, but you must in order to control it."

"It's impossible for a person—"

"Don't you have any faith in yourself?" he asked, shaking me slightly.

"Of course I have faith in myself!" My teeth started chattering with cold.

"Then prove it! Prove that no matter what situation you are in, you believe in yourself."

"This is asinine. I can't control the weather!" Overhead, my cloud rumbled ominously, the hairs on my arms standing on end with the feeling of static electricity.

"Yes, you can," Theo yelled over the noise. "You can make it stop, Portia! The power is yours. Will it to go away!"

Rain pelted down on us with such force that it stung my bare skin. I looked around frantically, but there was nowhere to hide from it except the pub itself. "I'll go inside—"

"No! You must learn to deal with this!" Theo said, pulling me back. His fingers tightened on my arms as, around us, three streaks of lightning exploded so close that my skin buzzed with the power. "Make it stop!"

"I can't!"

"You have to believe, Portia. You have to have faith!" he yelled in my face, his voice barely audible over the roar of thunder immediately overhead. My skin tingled, heralding another round of lightning.

"I lost that years ago," I screamed, giving in to the

horror and frustration that were roiling inside me. I threw myself into his arms, clinging to his rain-slicked body and wishing I could hide from it all.

"Believe!" he bellowed as lightning danced around us in a circle of blue light. "I know you can do this!"

His heartbeat was as wild as mine, and I knew instinctively that, about this, he was telling the truth. He believed I could stop this freak storm. For a moment, for the time between seconds, I considered the possibility that he was right. What if I could control the weather?

The storm overhead dissipated into nothing.

Theo peeled me off his chest, his black eyes unreadable. "That was very well done," he said slowly. "We'll make a virtue of you yet."

Water dripped down my face, down my soggy clothing, to fall with soft little patting noises at my feet. "I didn't just . . . no. It's impossible. It can't possibly happen."

He laughed and turned me toward the door of the pub. "Let's have that drink and we can talk about it, all right?"

My legs were shaking so hard Theo thought it wise to help me up the stairs to my room first. "Change into something dry. I'll meet you downstairs in a few minutes."

"You're just as soaked as I am. You'll catch pneumonia or something if you sit around in wet clothes." I wondered why I cared whether or not the man who had tried to kidnap me got sick, but I did, and since I didn't seem to be able to change that, I decided it wasn't worth angsting over. There would be time enough later, when I had life in control again, to worry over the fact that I found my kidnapper incredibly attractive.

"My things are in my car. I'll bring them up here and change." He bent forward, his lips brushing mine for a moment in a caress that promised so much. I clutched the door frame to keep upright. "I'll see you downstairs in a few minutes."

I peeled off my wet clothing, towel dried my hair, which was hanging to my shoulders in limp strings, and hesitated at the wardrobe over what to put on to meet Theo. It was inconceivable that I should be dithering over what to wear to meet a man I had tried to have arrested practically since the moment I'd met him, but dither I did. I selected and discarded a few pairs of pants, finally settling on a long crushed-velvet dress that I'd bought for visits to the theater and any publishing parties Sarah would drag me to. I twisted my hair up into an untidy French twist, wishing that it was a more attractive color than walnut. My hazel eyes peered back at me in the mirror with acknowledgment that they would never inspire anyone to write sonnets.

"You've never found yourself lacking in the looks department until now," I told my reflection with a grimace. "So let's just not go overboard, shall we?"

I tried, I really tried not to care what Theo thought about me, but in the end I broke down and dug out my bag of cosmetics, quickly applying mascara, eye shadow, and lipstick before telling myself I was completely insane.

"Sarah? You there?" I stopped at her door and gave a soft knock, in case she'd gone to bed early.

"Come on in. I'm just making some notes. I've had the most brilliant idea for a book."

I poked my head in through the door. "You OK?"

She looked up from her laptop, her face distracted. "Of course I am. Did you see Theo?"

His kiss still burned my lips. I licked them, tasting once again his masculine, woodsy taste, my nether regions throbbing heavily. "Yeah, I saw him. I'm . . . this is going to sound silly, but I've agreed to have a drink with him. Downstairs, in full view of everyone, I'd like to add."

"Silly?" Sarah wrinkled her nose at me. "Why on earth would you having a drink with him be silly?"

"Is the English water affecting your memory or something? Did you forget that we've been trying to have him arrested for assault and kidnapping?"

"You've been trying to have him arrested. I haven't done anything other than try to reason with you. He's your champion, Portia. You need him." Sarah turned back to her laptop and continued to type.

I shook my head, too tired to try to reason with her. "I'll be downstairs if you need me."

"Enjoy yourself for a change. And kiss Theo for me."

I shot her a piercing look, but her face was devoid of emotion, her eyes on the laptop screen as she tapped away.

Theo was waiting for me by the time I arrived at the pub proper. He had claimed a corner table, the one farthest away from the music videos. He had changed into black pants and a silky-looking crimson shirt that set off his dark skin, hair, and eyes. For one wild moment, he reminded me of a stereotypical pirate: deadly, dangerous, and *very* bad to know.

"There is a private room, if you would prefer to be away from all this noise," he said, standing up as I approached the table.

"No thank you. I'd rather be in full view of everyone in case you get any ideas about attacking me again." I sat in the chair he pulled out for me, the skin on my back tightening when his hand brushed the bare flesh of my neck.

He sighed. "Portia, I have told you repeatedly—"

"I know, I know, you didn't know I was mortal. But you haven't said what you expected me to be if not mortal."

"That will make up a good part of the discussion. What would you like to drink?"

"Gin and tonic, please." I sat primly while he went to the bar to place our drink orders, trying not to notice how wonderfully tight his pants were over his derriere. I didn't win the battle, but felt somewhat proud of the fact that I made the attempt.

"The opposite of a mortal would be an immortal, something that doesn't exist," I said as he returned with our drinks and took his seat. "Unless there is some definition to immortality that I'm not aware of."

"There are many concepts I suspect you are not aware of, and will probably resist accepting, but time is limited, so we will have to do this as quickly as possible. You recall the discussion we had about the Court of Divine Blood?"

"Yes. You claimed that Hope was something called a virtue, a person who controlled the weather, and that members of the Court couldn't be killed."

"They can be killed; it's just incredibly difficult," he said, sipping a glass of whisky. "More so than most immortals, and yes, Virginia, Santa Claus does exist. Or rather, immortality does. Would you care to hazard a guess as to how old I am?"

Since I was being offered the opportunity to examine him freely, I did so. Although his black hair was untouched by grey, there were faint laugh lines around his eyes that made me believe he might be older than he first appeared. "I would say somewhere in the mid to late thirties."

"If you add approximately seventeen hundred years to that, you would be correct."

I goggled at him. It's not a pretty expression, nor one I cultivate, but when someone tells you they are older than a millennium, a goggle is called for. "That's . . . very, very unbelievable. You do realize that, don't you?"

"I am a nephilim," he said simply, and went on to explain before I could ask him what that was. "A nephilim is the name given to products of the mating between members of the Court of Divine Blood and mortals. We are considered fallen because our immortal parent more or less breached the laws of the Court in order to reproduce with mortals. In the eyes of the Court, we are damned, non-beings, immortal, but not allowed any of the benefits of Court membership."

"So, you're seventeen hundred years old, but you know about Santa Claus and things like that?"

The look on his face was vaguely offended. "I'm long-lived, not an idiot. Of course I know about Santa Claus. I also know about iPods, the Hubble Telescope, and nanotechnology."

"My apologies. I didn't mean to imply . . . oh man, this is a bit hard to get a handle on. Let me see if I have it straight," I said, setting down my drink. "I'm some kind of a weather angel, and you're a fallen angel? A kind of mixed-race fallen angel?"

"I've told you—the concept of an angel is something Christianity and other religions formed based on the Court, but it is not an accurate representation. My father was a power, one of the members of the Court. Seventeen hundred and eight years ago he mated with a mortal woman located in what is now southeast India. I was the product of that relationship."

I took a deep breath. A wholly irrelevant question popped into my mind. "Why do you have an Irish accent if your mother was Indian?"

"My father settled in Ireland once he was banished from the Court. He died a few years later, decapitated during a battle. I never knew him."

I mused for a few moments on the idea of angels being able to be killed, but decided the resulting headache wouldn't be worth it.

"I know this is asking a lot of you to digest in such a short time, but digest it you must. You are a virtue, although you have yet to be admitted into the Court. You are undergoing seven trials to test your fitness for the position. If you fail three of the seven trials, you will be refused admittance, and have your powers stripped from you."

"I'm going to take a grain of salt approximately the size of Montana, and just pretend that everything you've said is true and not in the least bit impossible. That being so, where exactly do you come into this whole thing?"

He sat back, lacing his fingers together on his belly. "As I mentioned, I am considered fallen. There is only one way a fallen may be redeemed—a pardon must be granted by either a member of the Court, or by a demon lord. The latter is almost impossible to obtain, since demon lords are notoriously shy about releasing someone they consider in their domain. The former is almost as impossible, but it has been done in the past."

A light began to dawn. "You were chasing Hope because you wanted her to pardon you?"

"I have worked through all of the other members of the Court without success. Hope had always been sympathetic to me, and I believed I could persuade her to grant me a pardon." He frowned into his glass of whisky. "Unfortunately, something happened at Court to scare her, and she went into hiding. I had just tracked her down when you summoned her. She obviously used the opportunity to pass on her position to you in an attempt to escape whatever trouble she was in."

"Where angels go, trouble follows," I quipped.

Theo gave me a look.

"Sorry. So, now you want me to give you this pardon so you can be a member of heaven . . . er, the Court of Divine Blood again?"

"Yes. It is the only way. For that reason, you must

succeed at the trials, thus I must serve as your champion to make sure you pass them."

My grain of salt grew to encompass North and South Dakota. "That seems like a horrible amount of trouble. Why don't you just go the other route and talk to a demon lord?"

It was amazing how much expression could be seen in his black eyes. Amusement, anger, frustration, sincerity—they'd all been visible during the last twenty-four hours. But at my words, a screen seemed to fall, giving his eyes a dead look. "That would not be wise. Demon lords do not perform favors without exacting a steep price—too steep. I won't do it."

"Ah. Gotcha." I swallowed the last of my drink and set the glass down on the cocktail napkin, smiling as I stood up. "Thank you for the drink, and for not abducting me. It's been a trying day, so I think I'll be going to bed."

Theo slowly got to his feet. "You don't believe anything I've said, do you?"

"No. It was creative, though. You should talk to Sarah about writing it all down. I bet it would make a good book."

"You don't believe that I am a nephilim."

"Nope. I think you're an extremely handsome, quite possibly troubled man, but as for the fallen business? I'm afraid not."

I walked to the stairs that led to my room on the upper floor. Theo followed me.

"You don't believe that you and you alone have the power to save me?"

The laughter that burbled forward died in my throat at the look in his eyes. I stopped in front of my door, oddly disconcerted. "Theo, despite everything you've done to me, despite all the trouble you've been, I kind of like you. If there is something *real* I can do to help you, I would consider it, but this . . ." I waved my hands around in a vague attempt to explain. "This is beyond me."

He took a step closer to me, and his woodsy scent curled around me. "All you have to do is believe, Portia. You just have to have faith."

There was that word again. "I lost my faith when I was eight. It is long gone, never to return."

His jaw tightened. "Then I will help you find it in return for your assistance."

I did laugh that time, even though the expression on his face was one of grim determination. "Putting aside the fact that I am getting along just fine without faith of any sort, just how do you expect to do that?"

"The third trial is tomorrow." He took my chin in his hand, tipping my head back to look deep into my eyes. "It will be very difficult."

"More old ladies beating the crap out of me? I could really do without that."

He leaned closer, and for a second I thought he was going to kiss me right there, outside my room. "I will make a deal with you—if you can give me proof that the trial is mundane, I will serve as your champion without requiring you to pardon me when you are admitted to the Court. If you cannot provide proof, you will accept the truth, and will reward me when you are accepted."

"Mundane?" I asked, more than a little distracted by his nearness. Theo was an imposing presence by any standard, but when he was close enough that I could count individual hairs in his widow's peak, he was almost overwhelming.

"Ordinary. Not supernatural."

I smiled. "Oddly enough, I have a similar bet going with Sarah. I don't think taking on another comer will be a problem. You, sir, have yourself a deal."

He took the hand I offered, a light kindling in his eyes. "Shall I show you how a deal was sealed a thousand years ago?"

His lips brushed mine as he spoke, and before I could decide what I wanted to do about the overwhelming urge to kiss him, I was doing just that, my mouth opening to welcome his, my body all but melting when his fingers dug into my hips, pulling them against his. I am not the most feminine of women, but the steely, unyielding hardness of his body made me very aware that I possessed more curves than I had given much thought to. His mouth was demanding, hot, tasting faintly smoky from the whisky, insisting that I give him what he wanted. I had no qualms at all about kissing him, going so far as to jerk the back of his shirt out of his pants so my hands could slide up his back.

"*Salus,* woman, do you have any idea how good you taste," he growled into my mouth, one hand sliding around to cup my behind, the other sweeping up to my breast.

"It's the lime in the gin and tonic," I answered, unable to keep from wiggling my hips against him.

He growled again, deep in his chest, his eyes molten with sexual desire. He caressed my breast beneath the velvet of the dress, ever so slightly tweaking my nipple. "Of all the women on this planet, why do you have to be one who will fight me every step of the way?"

"Some men like the chase," I said breathlessly, arching my back to press more of my breast into his hand. I trailed my fingernails down his back, causing him to shiver as my hands dipped lower, to his oh-so-attractive derriere.

"I prefer the yielding that follows," he said just before he kissed me again, a kiss of so much blatant sexuality that I seriously considered the possibility of going to bed with him.

Luckily, Sarah chose that moment to use the bathroom next door to her room.

"Well!" Her voice was rich with amusement. I had no doubt of the picture we made—me groping his behind, while he had one hand on my breast, our bodies locked in a sensual embrace.

Theo and I parted, although he kept his hands on me as he half turned to look at Sarah.

She grinned at us both, and winked at me before proceeding to the bathroom. "I'm glad to see you're taking my advice about *something*."

Chapter 8

"It was just a kiss."

"You said that three times already. Would you turn off that light?" Sarah plumped up a pillow behind her, and tucked the coverlet firmly over her legs before sitting back.

"A perfectly innocent kiss!"

"Honey, there was *nothing* innocent about that kiss," she said with a knowing look.

I stomped over to the light she had left burning on the desk and turned it off, feeling awkward and unsure of myself. I don't know why I felt compelled to explain that the kiss Theo and I shared was not what it seemed, but there I was, wringing my hands as I tried to sort through my emotions and thoughts.

"I find him physically attractive even though he's got some issues," I explained. "There's nothing wrong with a healthy libido."

"Nothing at all, especially when the recipient of your attentions is a gorgeous angel. I looked up nephilim while you were occupied with Theo. That's what a nephilim is, you know. Kind of a sub-angel, the result of a union between—"

"Oh, I know all about that," I said, waving my hands around for a moment before I was aware of what I was doing. I am not at all the hand-waving sort of person. "It's part of this tale he spun me. That's neither here nor there—what I want to know is what is going to come of a relationship with a lunatic!"

"I thought you said it was just your libido?"

"It is!" I shoved the chair aside just because I could. "But you know me—I don't do casual sex, so if things progress beyond kissing, I'm going to end up in a relationship. With a madman!"

"Theo isn't a madman," Sarah said calmly, picking up the book she'd brought to read on the vacation.

"Well, maybe not mad by the strictest definition of the word, but you have to admit that he's not normal."

"Of course he isn't. He's immortal. Are you done trying to convince yourself that he's not handsome as sin, and twice as delicious?"

"I did not—oh, you're impossible!" I said loudly. "And speaking of that, you sure changed your tune quick enough."

"What do you mean?"

"Yesterday you were positively drooling over Theo."

Sarah looked surprised for a moment. "Don't be ridiculous—I'm happily married, which you know."

"That didn't stop you from ogling Theo yesterday." I refused to examine why it bothered me that she had ogled him. It couldn't possibly be important.

"Oh, that was before," she said, returning to her book as she waved a dismissive hand toward me.

"Before what?"

"Before Theo explained he wasn't for me."

I sat on the chair, staring at Sarah, confused by her calm acceptance of the short-lived lust she had felt for Theo. "Aren't you the least bit disconcerted about the fact that Theo interested you? Should happily married women feel that sort of thing?"

"They should if the man in question is a nephilim." She sighed at my puzzled look. "I thought you knew about nephilims? Didn't Theo tell you that they have an effect on mortal women?"

"No, he didn't." I frowned.

"Ah. Well, that's why I initially fell victim to his attractive self. He dismissed the effect once he realized I was being affected by it."

I shoved myself out of the chair and stalked to the far side of the room. "He didn't dismiss it for me!"

"That's because you weren't affected by him in the first place. That's interesting, actually. It could mean he's the real deal, at least so far as you and he are concerned," she said, looking thoughtful.

That was a thought. I considered that for a moment, then decided it was yet another distraction I didn't need in my life. I wished Sarah good night, and left her to her book.

I slept poorly, waking up roughly every hour to find myself wrapped in vague remnants of nightmares. The unease caused by the nightmares hung over me all day, leaving me feeling itchy and nervous even though we spent a delightfully normal day touring a nearby castle, during which no ghosts, ghouls, specters, or phantoms of any sort manifested themselves.

"It was nice to have a day where the oddest thing we encountered was that woman who insisted on bringing her parrot on the castle tour," I commented at dinner that night.

Sarah glanced toward the door of our private dining room, nodding. "Although I could have done without you expounding *at length* about how much force would have to be supplied to rip someone's limb off while on the rack."

"You are the one who insisted on seeing the torture chamber. I was simply answering a question of physics."

Sarah gave me a look that spoke volumes, glancing once again over my shoulder at the door before eating a bite of garlic-roasted potato. I pushed a clump of limp broccoli to the side of my plate, and rearranged a bit of hollandaise sauce more attractively around a mound of poached salmon.

Sarah looked past me again.

"For Pete's sake, will you stop that! You're making me as nervous as a cat."

"Aha!" Sarah waved her fork, bedecked with a piece of pork loin, at me. "I knew it! And you said you weren't nervous earlier when I asked you when today's trial was going to be."

"I wasn't nervous until you started looking over my shoulder every five seconds." I set down my fork and stopped pretending to enjoy the meal. "Oh, this is ridiculous. I'm letting myself get all worked up over nothing. Obviously whoever is Theo's cohort of the day has had a change of heart. So you can stop looking over my shoulder for him, because he's probably decided we're not worth what must be a sizeable outlay of money to pull off whatever scheme he's attempting."

Sarah chewed the bit of pork. "How you can sit there and deny that Theo is exactly what he says he is—"

"I deny it because it's perfectly clear he's a con man—"

"A man you think is sexy as hell—"

"Well of course I do! He is! But that doesn't excuse the fact that he's trying to pull some scheme—"

"Admit it, Portia." Sarah speared another bit of potato. "Part of the attraction he holds for you is his undeniable air of mystery, that dangerous sense of the unknown that sends shivers down your back every time he's near. No woman can turn away from that—it's a scientific fact that bad boys are completely irresistible! Give in to your inner woman and just admit he chimes your bells because of what he is."

I pushed back from the table, tossing down my napkin. "You're impossible when you're in that sort of a mood. You're sure you don't want me to go with you tonight?"

"No, you take the evening off. You wouldn't enjoy sitting in a graveyard with the clairaudients, anyway."

I smiled instead of giving her a piece of my mind about the so-called skill of recording the voices of the dead, and mentioned that I'd amuse myself instead with a walk around the countryside.

"That's a great idea—your mind will be refreshed by the walk for the next trial."

My smile turned wry. "Whatever. Have fun in the graveyard."

"Maybe we should call Theo," Sarah mused to her dinner as I headed out of the room. "Maybe he would know what's up with the trial . . ."

Once in my room, I stripped off the only other dress I'd brought with me on the trip, shaking my head at myself for dressing up just because I expected to see Theo sometime during the day. I pulled out a pair of jeans and a sweatshirt, garb much more suitable for tramping around the countryside than the bright dress I'd put on that morning, wondering as I did if Theo liked red.

I hesitated as I pulled a pair of tennis shoes from the wardrobe, glancing down at the black silk-and-lace teddy I was wearing, my mind shying away from the reason I'd put it on that morning. "Oh, for heaven's sake, it's just underwear, not a world crisis," I told myself after an indecisive minute, turning around to grab my jeans. "Just get dressaieeee!"

The floors in England seemed to be particularly prone to non-traditional behavior, for the boards that had served so solidly beneath my feet suddenly opened up into a hole, through which I fell in startled fear. "What the . . . ooof!"

"Good evening. My name is Noelle. I'm a Guardian, and I'll be acting as the proctor for your third trial." I had fallen what seemed to be a deceptively short distance, landing on a stone floor with a thump that stung my ankles, and jarred my teeth painfully. "Erm . . . do you know that you're just wearing a teddy?"

Someone had set a couple of portable camp lights on a shelf in an arched inset in the wall, the light pooling on the floor in front of me. The voice came from behind. I spun around, my eyes widening as I took in the large stone sarcophagus upon which a young, red-haired woman sat.

"I have shoes," I said, holding out my tennis shoes, wincing to myself at just how inane that sounded. "I was in the middle of getting dressed. I wasn't expected to be sucked down to . . . where exactly are we?"

"Crypt," Noelle said, giving me a rueful smile as she slid off the top of the sarcophagus. "Sorry about the bad timing, but I've had a day from Abaddon— literally!—and couldn't get to the trial until now. Oh well, it'll soon be over, and you can go back to your dressing. Why don't you put on your shoes, and we'll get started."

I walked over to her and pressed my fingers to her shoulder. She certainly felt real. Which could only mean one thing.

Her eyebrows rose. "You look confused. Is there a problem?"

There were so many problems I couldn't begin to frame them in my mind, let alone explain to her the trouble I had with accepting the fact that I'd just been teleported to some unknown crypt.

"No," I answered in what sounded like a choked

voice. I cleared my throat and tried again. "It's nothing outright insanity wouldn't explain."

"Oh, good." She smiled again, and gestured toward the center of the crypt. On the floor, an elaborate circle with several symbols had been drawn upon it. "Shoes?"

"Of course," I said, putting on my tennis shoes. "The insanity isn't going to be complete without the idea of me standing around in nothing but lingerie and tennies."

"It's a very pretty teddy," Noelle said, walking around to the back. "I like the straps on the side. Oh, it's not a thong. Good on you. I hate thongs—they're always getting places they shouldn't be."

I shook my head at myself, wondering if the rest of my life—now that I'd clearly gone quite, quite insane—would follow this pattern, or if some kind friend or family member would see to it that I got the mental help I needed.

"Ready?"

Noelle's voice brought me out of a reverie where I spent endless years learning how to write with my feet because my arms were confined by a straitjacket. "Sure, why not? I've got nothing to lose, right?"

She made a face, and looked down the room to a doorway that lurked in the darkness. "Well . . . let's just say that you really need to get this one right. Right. Champion, you may enter the room."

It didn't surprise me in the least (one of the perks of now being deranged) when Theo strolled into the room. He stopped after a few steps, pursing his lips as he looked me over from toes to head.

"That's . . . a new look for you," he finally said, having taken his time in the perusal.

"I didn't have a thing to wear," I said with a firm smile. "Besides, what does it matter? I'm just along for the ride now."

"I like it, regardless." His gaze flickered between my breasts and my face. "What ride would that be?"

"The highway to dementia. Want to come along?"

He sighed and only just kept from rolling his eyes. "You are not insane, Portia."

"No, of course not. It's perfectly ordinary to be teleported to a crypt, so I can stand around in my undies waiting to . . ." I turned to Noelle. "What exactly am I waiting to do?"

"Defeat a demon," she said, stepping backward until she was in the shadow of the crypt room. "You may begin . . . now!"

I don't know what I expected a demon to look like—probably a short, squat red-skinned beast with horns, cloven feet, and a pointy tail—but the teenage boy who appeared in the circle did not scream demon to me.

Until the little shit opened his mouth. "Nice tits," the boy leered, reaching out as if he was going to honk them.

"Stay out of the circle," Theo commanded as he flung himself onto the boy.

"Why do you get to go in it?" I asked.

The demon teen spun around screaming, trying to pick Theo off his back, but Theo was bigger and stronger, and kept the teen's arms pinned behind him.

"Just defeat it while I'm subduing it," he grunted, twisting to avoid the demon's attempt at a backward butt.

"Defeat it how?" I looked around the crypt. I had no idea what it took to beat a demon, not that they really existed except in my own delusions. "You'd think that if my mind was going to snap and go to the trouble of imagining all this, it would give me a big demon-bashing club, or a cool samurai sword, or something like that."

"Use your Gift," Theo said, grunting as the demon jerked them both forward.

"The weather thing? You've got to be kidding."

"Just use it!"

The demon suddenly kicked up his legs, twisting at the same time, pulling Theo to the floor where the two of them wrestled inside the circle.

I parked my hands on my hips. "I doubt rain is going to do anything but make him more slippery to hold. Ow. That had to hurt. Um. Noelle, can you help us?"

Her voice came out of the shadows, filled with regret. "I am the proctor. I cannot assist you in any way or the trial would be void."

"Portia, use your damned powers!" Theo demanded. He was sitting on the demon, who was pinned to the floor, but writhing with what looked like incredible strength. The demon bit Theo on the wrist, drawing blood.

I raised my hands, letting them fall helplessly. There was nothing in the room I could use as a weapon. "I don't know how!" I finally admitted, unsure of what I could do to help Theo. Even if this was all a figment of my distraught imagination, I didn't want to see Theo hurt. "How do I use weather to defeat someone?"

"Gather it up and direct it at the demon." Theo's voice was garbled as the demon slammed his head into Theo's thorax, his arms and legs thrashing wildly. Theo was holding him down as best he could, but it was evident that, sooner or later, Theo's strength was going to give out and the demon would have the upper hand.

"That's impossible! No one can do that!"

"Oh dear. I'm afraid this is getting out of hand. I am authorized to stop the trial if it's clear that the test subject is not in control," Noelle said, taking a step out of the shadows. She had a notebook in her hand and was making notes.

"You must do this!" Theo snarled, his face bloody. "Now! One more failure and it's all over!"

I took a deep breath, made an apology to what I hoped was a still sane part of my brain, and concentrated on gathering up weather.

"I'll see you in Abaddon," Theo swore to the demon as the monstrous teen used both hands to claw him, his shirt coming away in shreds to reveal long, bloody streaks. "Do something, woman!"

"Weather, weather, weather," I said hurriedly to myself, wringing my hands as the teen continued to slash at Theo, his demonic mouth open in a wordless snarl, his eyes filled with hatred. "What is weather? It's rain and wind and snow. It's particles of water suspended in the air. It's atomic elements, protons, electrons, neutrons, gluons, positive and negative charges, electrical charges . . ." The word *electrical* glowed in my mind with an intensity that blinded me to all other thoughts. "It's lightning. Lightning is electrically charged, superheated air that is released in tremendous blasts of energy—"

I closed my eyes, holding out my hands, allowing myself to feel what I was thinking. "Energy is the ability to do work."

My fingertips tingled.

"Portia!"

"Work is force times distance, which is also kinetic energy."

Around me, tiny little motes of static electricity gathered, as if I was summoning it to me.

"I'm going to have to call this," Noelle said in a sympathetic voice. "I can't let the demon get out of control. I'm so sorry."

"You've got to do something!"

I kept my eyes shut despite the plea in Theo's voice, imagining myself pulling from the stone and earth and air surrounding us the electrical charges that existed in all atoms. "Kinetic energy can be transformed into potential energy."

"Gargh!"

I opened my eyes to see the demon on top of Theo, ripping with long, vicious swipes at his arms and chest. Around me, the air glowed blue with static, the hairs on my arms standing on end.

"I'm sorry, I must stop—" Noelle started forward toward the circle.

"Now!" Theo demanded, interrupting her.

"And potential energy can be converted into the physical form known as electricity!" I yelled, slamming the power that surrounded me into the demon. As the blue light burst into the demon's body, it threw him backward against the wall, a deafening clap of thunder bursting forth in the crypt. I shouted an oath and covered my ears, throwing myself onto the floor next to Theo. The floor cracked, the walls screamed with the echo of the thunderclap, while dust and small pieces of rock rained down from the stone ceiling. I crawled over to Theo, trying to shield his head from any falling objects. He was crumpled in a heap, filthy with dirt and blood, but alive.

"Oh, that's not good," Noelle said from the other side of the room, where she'd gone to look at the demon.

"Are you all right?" I asked Theo, propping him up on my lap in order to gently wipe blood and debris from his face. "Are you hurt badly? You're bleeding a lot. I should call a paramedic."

"Erm . . . Portia . . . I'm afraid there's a situation here," Noelle said from where she squatted next to the wall.

I ignored her as I peeled back the shredded remains of Theo's shirt. "Sweet mother! We have to get you to a hospital."

Theo grabbed my arm as I was about to leap to my feet, not sure of where I was going to go for assistance, but driven to getting him help. "I'm all right, Portia. The wounds are not fatal."

"Your chest is torn to shreds," I started to say, but at that moment, Theo turned his head. I had pulled him up slightly, and his head was resting on my chest. He eyed the breast that was a scant millimeter from his mouth.

"I heal quickly." It was just three words, but my nipples tightened with the feeling of his breath on the thin silk that was the only thing separating my flesh from his mouth.

"That's . . . you're speaking into my breast," I said, oddly loathe to move.

"Yes, yes I am," he said, his eyes fixed with fascination as my nipple hardened even more, little waves of heat rippling outward from my breast across my chest before heading downward to pool in my stomach . . . and locations further south. "I'd like to do other things to it, but now is not the time or place."

The air in the room seemed to evaporate into nothing. "There's going to be a time and place?" I asked, inwardly wincing at the moronic question, but unable to keep from asking.

"I fervently hope so," he said before looking down at his own chest.

It took me a moment to wrestle my mind from the images of just what I'd like Theo to do to my breasts, but the sight of his chest healing before my startled eyes did a lot to bring me down to earth.

"That's . . . that's impossible," I said, reaching out to touch a long welt which had been a deep gash just a few minutes before. His flesh was hot, fever-hot, radiating heat that indicated a lot of energy was being used to heal his wounds. "This is . . . it's . . . it's just not possible!"

"Welcome to Wonderland, Alice," he said with a smile that stripped the air from my lungs, and left my heart racing.

Life as I knew it ceased to exist. Life as I never believed possible began.

"This is real, isn't it?" I asked, gently touching another now-healed welt. As I watched, several more scratches merged together, healing to thick, raised patches that melted away into smooth flesh after a few minutes. "All of this is real. I'm not insane."

Theo sat up as the last wound disappeared. His eyes expressed mingled pity and an unexpected sadness. "No, you're not insane."

"Then you're . . ."

"A nephilim. Immortal."

I swallowed hard. "And I'm . . ."

"A virtue. Soon to be immortal, as well, once you are accepted into the Court of Divine Blood." He got to his feet, and pulled me to mine, holding onto my hands.

It was too much, too much to take in at once. I shook my head, not at what Theo was saying, but at the fact that my brain was trying to process all this new information so quickly.

I just couldn't believe it was real . . . and yet, finally, I admitted to myself that the evidence piled up indisputably pointed to one conclusion: everything I had believed impossible, everything I knew could simply not be, now suddenly was. It was as if a whole new part of life opened up before me, beckoning me to go forth and explore all the mysteries it had to share.

It was frightening as hell.

"And that teenager, that kid who was here tearing you apart . . ."

Theo gave me a slight smile, the corners of his mouth curling up in a manner that, despite my bemusement, made my stomach lurch uncomfortably. ". . . was no teenager, but a demon, which you handily defeated."

"I hate to interrupt, but I feel it necessary to correct that statement." Noelle got up from where she had been looking at the wall, and came over to us. "Portia didn't defeat the demon."

Theo's thumbs were rubbing softly over the tops of my hands. He frowned at Noelle. "What do you mean she didn't defeat it? I saw her do it."

"No," Noelle said with a sigh. "What you saw her do was completely annihilate its physical form. I didn't send the demon back to Abaddon. I didn't have to—she so completely destroyed its human form that it was sent back by necessity."

Theo's eyes widened as both he and Noelle looked at me.

"He was hurting Theo," I told them both. "I wasn't going to just stand there and let him beat Theo up. Not to mention which, you both were egging me on to do something."

"We're not chastising you for defeating the demon," Noelle said with a watery smile. "It's the fact that you destroyed its mortal form that has us in a situation."

"What sort of a situation?" I asked, pulling my hands from Theo's. It was too distracting being in physical contact with him. My brain didn't want to think about anything but him when he was touching me.

"Which demon was it?" Theo asked Noelle.

She ignored my question to answer his. "Nefere. It belonged to Bael."

"Salus invenitur," Theo swore, rubbing his forehead.

"Do I want to know who Bael is?" I asked, rubbing the goose bumps on my arms. I was starting to get cold standing in the crypt in nothing but my teddy and shoes.

"Bael is the premiere prince of Abaddon," Noelle answered, her eyes on Theo.

"Abaddon being hell?"

"Yes," Theo answered, his face grave. My stomach wadded itself up into a dense ball, and seemed to drop to my feet. "Bael does not tolerate abuse of his legions. He will summon us before him to answer for the damage we did to his demon's form. Come, you are cold. I will take you back to the pub."

He held out a hand for me, clearly intending me to follow him out of the room.

"Wait a sec," I said, rubbing my arms again. "Why can't you just zap me back the way I came?"

Noelle gave me a rueful smile. "Teleporting is a temporary power given to the trial proctors. It summons, but does not send, I'm afraid."

"Oh great," I grumbled as I took Theo's hand and allowed him to lead me out of the crypt. His hand was warm, his fingers strong and reassuring. "Now I'm gallivanting who knows where in my teddy. This is so the image I want to remember England by. I don't understand why killing a demon is bad. They're demonic, right? So why isn't a good thing that I blasted it to kingdom come?"

"It's a bit complicated," Noelle said with genuine regret in her voice. "I must go back to the Court and submit the results of the trial. That, at least, you passed." She stopped at the doorway to what appeared to be the nave of a church, her gaze moving from me to Theo. "Good luck. I wish I could help you, but it would be a violation of Guild law."

"I understand." Theo released me long enough to shake her hand, thanking her for her help.

She gave me a brief, bright smile. "I hope the rest of the trials go well. I think you'll be a very nice addition to the Court."

She hurried off before I could respond. Theo escorted me out of the (thankfully unoccupied) church and into his car before I got too chilled. I wrapped myself up in the car blanket he kept in his trunk, and shivered the entire fifteen-minute drive to the pub, wondering the whole way there what had happened to the nice, orderly, sensible life I had made for myself.

Chapter 9

"I think I'm handling this very well," I said after a few minutes of watching the night slide by the car window. We were approaching the town and the familiar humpbacked bridge. "Mind you, the only other available option is to completely lose my mind, so I don't have much of a choice, but still, I believe I'm taking this all very, very well. I'm not screaming or laughing hysterically, or even crying, although somehow, I feel like doing all three."

He patted my blanket-covered knee. "I appreciate the fact that you are restraining your hysterical tendencies. This is a . . ." He hesitated for a moment. ". . . difficult situation."

"This prince guy, you mean? I have to tell you, Theo, I don't believe in hell any more than I do in heaven."

He drove in silence for a few minutes. "Just as the Court of Divine Blood is not heaven, so Abaddon is not hell, although it is commonly referred to as such. The prince you refer to is the head of all the seven demon lords who rule Abaddon, and I'm sorry to say that they do very much exist."

The skeptic in me wanted to argue the point, but I reminded myself that I was still in the process of coming to grips with the idea that there was more to life than I imagined, and thus such an argument could wait.

Not to mention the fact that I now had to admit to Sarah that she was right and I was wrong.

"So what is this demon lord guy likely to do? He can't hurt us, can he?"

Theo laughed a particularly mirthless laugh. It made a little chill skitter down my back. "He's likely to demand reparation for the demon's form. Such things do not come cheap, or so the demon lords would have us believe."

We turned into the pub's now-crowded parking lot. "Wait a second . . . are you saying I just destroyed the demon's body, but not the demon itself?"

"Yes. Demons can't be destroyed as such . . . their power changes into a different form, but isn't actually obliterated, if you understand what I mean."

"Of course I understand. It's the first law of thermodynamics." I wrapped the blanket tightly around myself as I got out of the car, smiling at Theo's look of confusion. "Energy is neither created nor destroyed. It can be transformed from one form of energy to another, but the sum total is always the same. What you're saying is that a demon is made up of some sort of energy, so it makes perfect sense to me that the energy of the demon is itself not able to be destroyed. I could go on to draw an analogy about what the physical form is like, but unless you're into physics, it would probably seem like overkill."

Theo laughed, a warm, deep laugh that rolled around me, filling me with an incredible light feeling that I identified with some surprise as happiness. "You have the most deliciously analytical mind."

"Well, I guess it's better to have you admire my mind over my breasts, like the other men I've dated."

A little flame of desire burst into being in his eyes. "Oh, I admire your breasts greatly, have no fear. But I do appreciate the desire you have to understand how the world works, rather than just blindly accepting it."

I shuddered despite the warmth of his gaze as I went through the door he opened for me. "Blind faith was never my forte. So what do we do about this Bael?"

The pub was just about to close when we walked in the door. I won't say conversation came to an abrupt halt at the sight of me, but the few die-hard regulars who were still there did give me curious glances.

"I . . . er . . . fell in the river," I explained to the pub owner, who walked past carrying a batch of dirty glasses.

He eyed the blanket I clutched around me, and nodded, saying nothing.

"Maybe we'd better discuss this in a more private area," I said quietly to Theo.

"Whither you lead, so shall I follow," he said with a little bow.

What a ham he was. A sexy, adorable, gorgeous ham. I led the way upstairs to my room, plopping down on the bed still clutching the blanket. My room wasn't huge to begin with, but with Theo in it, it suddenly seemed very small and intimate.

He went to the window and looked out into the night. I was very, very aware of him as a man, and no amount of reminding myself that just a few days ago he had tried to throttle me dissuaded my body from the idea of flinging itself on him right at that moment.

He kidnapped you a few days ago, I told my errant erogenous zones, all on full alert and tingling with anticipation. I touched my neck where his fingers had left it bruised and tender. He could easily have killed me.

"What's wrong?" Theo asked, turning back to me.

I felt my neck all over, then got up to look in the mirror on the inside of the wardrobe door. The blanket slid to the floor. "Where are my bruises?"

"I have no idea. Do you normally have bruises on your neck?"

"I do when people try to strangle me. The day that you did that, and tried to kidnap us, I had bruises all over my neck, and it was tender to the touch. Now they're all gone. And for that matter . . ." I flexed my arm, swinging it in a wide circle. "My sore shoulder isn't the least bit sore, and the doctor at the hospital said it would probably be a few days before the pain and stiffness wore off."

He moved closer, his warm fingers gently touching my neck. It felt so much like a caress that my knees threatened to give in. "I am sorry that I hurt you, Portia. I never meant to harm you."

"I know," I said, horrified by how breathy my voice was. With him standing so close to me, my brain was losing a battle against my emotions and bodily demands. "Now, at least. I didn't know it then. But that doesn't explain why the bruises are gone."

His thumb brushed the hollow in my throat. I swallowed convulsively.

"You are a virtue. They healed."

"I thought I wasn't officially part of the immortal Court until I pass all the trials?" My breath caught in my throat as his hand slid down to my shoulder. He pulled me close to his chest, his eyes glittering blackly.

"You're not immortal yet. But you are a virtue, which means you're . . . enhanced."

"Enhanced can be good." My breasts tightened and sent little zings of pleasure down to my belly as they brushed against his shirt, the heat from his body warming me like the blanket couldn't.

His head dipped, his lips brushing mine. "Enhanced can be wonderful. I want you, Portia."

I leaned into him, rubbing my hips against his in a wanton fashion that was so totally alien for me that for a moment, I was shocked by my own desire. "I kind of got that idea."

"Are you . . . that is, do you understand what it is I want from you?" His voice, deep to begin with, roughened, the Irish lilt more pronounced. His hands were on my waist now, holding me, but not caressing. The look in his eyes was earnest, hot, filled with carnality that I knew should have shocked me to my toenails, but instead called forth a response within me.

"Are you asking if I'm OK with the thought of going to bed with you?"

His tongue flicked across my lower lip. I wrapped my arms around him and let him see my own desire.

"Yes, I'm OK with it. I know that only a few days ago I would have moved heaven and earth to get this most fabulous butt of yours into jail. I know you're virtually a stranger, and I'm not at all the type of person to jump into bed with someone I've just met, but somehow none of that really seems to matter anymore."

"No, it doesn't," he murmured, his hands moving, sliding down my silk-covered back to my behind, easing their way under the material to stroke my bare flesh. "I've wanted you since the moment you tried to run me over. You are unlike any woman I have met before. You are strong, and courageous, and you do not suffer fools. Not to mention the fact that your breasts drive me to distraction."

I sucked in an inordinate amount of air as one of his hands suddenly cupped my aching breast, gently teasing my nipple until I thought I would spontaneously combust. "You have way too many clothes on," I finally managed to say, my hands shaking with excitement as I struggled with the buttons on his shirt.

"Yes, yes I do. Feel free to remove them."

I all but ripped his shirt off, ignoring the sound of a couple of buttons as they pinged on the floor, my eyes feasting on his bare chest for a moment before he pulled me back into an embrace.

"I highly approve of your chest. It's masculine without being overly hairy," I said as his mouth descended upon mine, the last coherent words I spoke while he kissed the breath right out of my lungs. He tasted faintly of wine, and something that was wholly Theo, an elusive masculine taste that thrilled me. His hands were everywhere, touching, stroking, teasing me in so many different places that all I could think of was how much I wanted him.

"You look as if you're hot," he said a few minutes later, when we came up for air. The desire and admiration in his eyes bathed me in a glow that raised my temperature another notch.

"Sweltering," I said, panting slightly. "Teddies are notoriously hot."

His gaze slipped down to my chest. "In so many ways. But it would be ungentlemanly of me to allow you to be uncomfortable. Would you like me to remove the cause of your discomfort?"

"You may," I said, chafing a bit at the leisurely way he drew a finger along my collarbone to the thin strap of the teddy. He paused for a moment, passion flaring deep in his eyes.

"Would this be the sort of garment that closes at the crotch?"

Warmth burst out in the pit of my stomach, quickly spreading to surrounding areas. Deeply personal parts of my body were tingling in celebration. I swallowed hard again, trying to keep my voice steady. "How do you know about that sort of thing?"

He grinned. "Just because I'm immortal doesn't mean I don't live in the here and now."

"That's a little more up to date than I imagined. But as you ask, yes, it is that sort of teddy. You're going to have to undo the snaps in order to get it off."

"I am only too happy to oblige," he murmured, his hands caressing my belly for a moment before they slid lower.

I clutched his shoulders, my eyes closed as I braced myself for the touch of his fingers on my most intimate parts.

That touch never came.

"I'm sorry if I'm a bit . . . anticipatory," I whispered, my eyes still closed. "I can't seem to help it."

Beneath my hands, his shoulders tightened. I opened my eyes to find him staring past me, his brows pulled down in a frown as he looked around the room.

"Is something wrong?" I asked, looking around as well. No one else was there.

"Don't you feel it?" He let go of me, taking a step forward, looking around us in a puzzled manner.

"I don't feel anything out of the ordinary, given the fact that I was about to jump your bones."

His back stiffened. He grabbed his shirt, pulling it on quickly. "Do you have a dressing gown?"

"Bathrobe? Yes, I do. It's on the chair behind you."

He tossed my robe to me. "Theo, is this some sort of odd English foreplay that I've never heard of?"

"Put it on. We're about to have a visitor." He stalked over to where I stood in the corner of the room, waiting for me to comply.

"All right, but this really will make me hot. It's crushed velvet and not the lightest thing in the world." He watched silently as I donned the bathrobe. Dressing gown was actually a more appropriate term—it was one of my private pleasures to have a tailor custom make the long, full-skirted robe that closely resembled a Victorian lady's dressing gown. It had a square-necked front, heavily embroidered with gold thread, which set off the crimson velvet nicely.

I had just done up the buttons in the front when Theo spun around and looked to the opposite corner of the room. To my astonishment, the wall next to the bed rippled, then tore, a horrible rending sound filling the air. A short, dark man stepped out and snarled something I didn't understand. The lightbulb in the bedside lamp exploded, followed by tiny tinkling sounds as the glass rained down onto the floor.

"You are summoned," the short man growled, grabbing for me.

Theo wrapped his arm around me, pulling me protectively to his side, putting his body between us. "Not without me."

The man smirked. It was such an oily, evil smile; I felt soiled by exposure to it. I didn't have long to fret about that, though. The man simply grabbed Theo by the free arm, and yanked him—and me—through the tear in the wall.

Chapter 10

We were falling, sinking, spinning, our insides churning outward in a soul-rending process that sank us deep into a horrible miasma of pain and nausea. Just when I thought I was going to pass out or die (I wasn't sure which, and at that point, didn't really care), the horror ended and I dropped to a yielding, warm surface.

"Ow!" grunted the surface.

I pushed myself off, apologizing under my breath to Theo. "Sorry about that. Did I hurt you? What just happened? Who is that horrible man? How did he come through the wall? And just where the blistering inferno are we?"

"Ah. There you are. You may leave, Digan."

I was insanely glad that Theo made me put my bathrobe on. The man who had spoken strolled into view as we got to our feet. My jaw just about hit my feet at the sight of him—he was one of the most beautiful men who'd ever walked the earth. Theo was handsome—almost too handsome, with his dark, brooding looks that seemed to do odd things to my stomach—but this man was astoundingly, breathtakingly beautiful. Dark blond, curly hair framed a face that was almost feminine, with high cheekbones, sculpted honey blond eyebrows, startlingly blue eyes, and full lips that quirked as I gawked.

"You like this form?" the man asked, doing a little twirl for me. The rest of him was just as impressive as his face, but as he came closer, my skin crawled. His hair suddenly turned dark, straightened, and grew about a foot. His brow broadened, his eyes narrowed slightly, and his jaw became more pronounced as his entire face morphed into that of another equally beautiful man. "Or perhaps you like this one better?"

Theo's arm slid around my waist. I leaned into him, pulling comfort from the contact. I didn't know who the morphing man in front of us was, but I didn't like him.

"No? You prefer redheads?"

He changed again, this time into a freckled, red-haired man with an angular jaw and glittering grey eyes.

Theo's arm tightened around me. "You are Bael, I presume?"

My eyes widened. This beautiful man was a demon lord, the first prince of Abaddon?

"I have that honor." The man bowed politely at Theo, then turned to me and laughed at what was probably a horrified expression on my face. "Since you have no preference, my dear, I shall go back to my normal Tuesday form."

He shifted back to the blond Adonis with no visible effort, turning to a large desk that sat behind him. I looked quickly around us. "This is hell?" I asked Theo in a whisper. "I expected something along the lines of pits of fire and a hail of brimstone."

"I detest the smell of brimstone," Bael said, pulling a sheet of paper from his desk and glancing over it. "And pits of fire make the fax machine act up. Ah, yes, the matter of the demon Nefere."

We appeared to be in the office of an affluent businessman, the standard desk with computer, phone, and assorted office-type items behind the demon lord. A comfy suede couch sat on one side of the room, while on the other a glass table held a magnificent floral bouquet. It was everything one did not expect to find as the headquarters of the most powerful being in hell.

Not that I believed in hell . . . or at least I didn't before I found myself standing before the head honcho.

"It seems that you destroyed the mortal form of my demon, Nefere," Bael said, giving me a smile that raised goose bumps on my arms. I looked away from him, unable to look into his eyes.

He propped himself up on the edge of the desk, waving us to a couple of chairs that sat before it. "Please, be comfortable."

I leaned harder into Theo, not wanting to get anywhere near the beautiful, evil man.

"We prefer to stand," Theo answered. "I admit to destroying the demon's form, but will point out that I did not summon it, and thus I can't be held responsible for the destruction."

"The one who summoned Nefere has nothing to do with this situation." Bael frowned and looked at the paper again before setting it aside. "I understood that the virtue named Portia Harding destroyed my demon's form?"

"I didn't mean to destroy him," I said quickly, earning myself a sharp squeeze from Theo. Obviously he was trying to shift the blame to himself, but I couldn't allow him to do that. "Hang on now! I am new to this whole virtue thing, and didn't know how to control the power. I will do better next time, I'm sure."

"I am Portia's champion. I urged her to destroy the demon, therefore the blame is mine. Although I deny your right to punish either of us, if there is to be punitive action, I must insist that it be dealt according to precedence." Theo held Bael's gaze steadily, not shying away from that dread gaze at all.

"You wish to martyr yourself for the lady, eh? I admit it is tempting to punish a virtue," Bael said, tapping a finger to his chin while he eyed me. I couldn't keep from fidgeting slightly. "It has been many centuries since I have had the opportunity to do so. However, current politics makes me hesitate to strike a blow against a denizen of the Court, thus I will accept your petition and recognize you as champion."

The muscles in Theo's arm, which had been as tight as steel, relaxed. I had no idea why he thought it was a good thing that he be punished in my place, but I wasn't about to debate the point. "You both assume too much. I am wholly responsible for my actions, and if there is to be punishment, I will be the only one to incur it," I said firmly, looking at a spot just beyond Bael's head.

"Don't be ridiculous, Portia," Theo growled in my ear. "You are mortal still. Punishment could kill you. I am immortal. There isn't much he can do to me."

"If his punishment isn't that bad, then I can take it," I argued back in a whisper.

"I didn't say it won't be bad. He can't kill me without violating terms of the peace treaty between the Court and Abaddon. Let me do this—it's part of my job."

I opened my mouth to protest, but Bael interrupted.

"The point is moot, virtue. Your champion has been recognized as your official representative, and to him the punishment will be dealt." Bael walked toward us, sketching a symbol in the air that glowed sickly black. "Now, how shall I punish you? Taking a few years of your life are no use—you will not miss a few years in the several thousand you will live. Physical pain, perhaps? A good old-fashioned medieval torturefest?"

I shuddered and grabbed the hand that held my waist. Next to me, Theo stood silent and still.

"No, I think that would be almost as ineffective, albeit amusing at the time." Bael's eyes narrowed. "Nephilim are notoriously hard to punish, since their very lives are penance for the sins of their fathers. Hmm. Perhaps I could simply wipe away your memory?"

"You do, and you'll have to answer to me," I said, driven to an unreasonable outspokenness by my irritation with my own fear of Bael. I've never been afraid of anything before, and it galled me to find myself almost sick with terror.

He ignored my outburst as if it wasn't worthy of his attention. "You know, really, it's a shame nephilim are protected under the treaty. We have need of your kind in Abaddon."

Theo looked utterly bored. I wanted to cheer at such a brave act in the face of the bad-ass demon lord. "Punish me, if you will, but make it quick. We were pleasantly engaged when your demon fetched us."

"Full points for such eloquent acting," Bael said, laughing, but the amusement didn't reach his eyes. They were flat, glittering, brittle blue lights, absolutely devoid of all emotions. I shivered in response, wanting desperately to be away from him. He didn't make any overtly menacing moves, but there was something around him, an aura of peril that made my flight instincts kick in.

Bael's cold gaze flickered to me. "It would be so much more fun with just the lady . . . ah, well. Another time, perhaps?"

"I would just about give anything to make sure that doesn't happen," I said, my mouth suddenly dry.

He smiled, but said nothing before turning back to Theo. "As for you—I believe I have a solution to my quandary. It is a bit extreme, but then, I've found that people learn so much better if the punishment is suitably harsh."

Theo's body tensed next to me as Bael put his hand on Theo's forehead, leaning close to say in a voice filled with so much evil portent that I had to put my hand over my mouth to keep from vomiting,

"I curse thee, Theondre North. As you spend the centuries alone, shunned, and empty, remember me."

A golden light burst forth from Theo, surrounding us until it blinded me. Theo was wrenched from my side with such force that I fell to my knees. The light was all around us, brilliant, warm, and so wonderful, I wanted to weep with joy at it.

"Theo? Are you all—"

A man screamed at that moment, a hoarse, gut-ripping sound that seemed to come from the soul. I knew it was Theo. I thrashed my arms around, desperate to find him in the blinding light. "Stop hurting him!" I shouted into the light, lunging to the side where Theo had stood. The light disappeared, leaving me unable to see.

"You are dismissed," a harsh voice growled behind me. Before I could turn around to see who it was, I was picked up and thrown into a brick wall. At least that's what it felt like, but as I shook the stars from my head and raised myself up off the ground, I realized that the demon who had yanked us from my hotel room through the tear in the wall had evidently returned us the same way.

Vision slowly returned to me. "Theo! Sweet mother of reason, are you all right?" I crawled over to where Theo lay facedown on the floor next to my bed. "Where did he hurt you? Is anything broken? Are you bleeding?"

Carefully, I pushed over Theo's unresisting body until he lay on his back. I quickly checked him over for injuries, but found none. "Theo? I can't find anything wrong with you. What did the demon lord do?"

"I'm all right." His eyes opened slowly.

I sucked in my breath, unable to believe what I was seeing. "Your eyes . . . they're grey."

Theo frowned. "Pardon?"

"Your eyes are grey. They aren't black anymore. Here, I'll show you." I helped him to his feet and opened the door to the wardrobe so he could see. He stared at himself for a moment, then turned back to me, despair and anguish welling up inside him.

"Salus invenitur," he swore.

"Latin was never my strong point. What exactly does that mean?"

"Salvation is found."

I raised my eyebrows in question.

A mirthless smile graced his lips. "It's the nephilim's equivalent to a self-depreciating 'fuck me!' "

"Ah. I like your version better. Why did Bael change your eyes?"

His jaw tightened. "That is merely a side effect of the curse."

"I heard him say he was cursing you," I said slowly, watching him carefully. So far he seemed perfectly normal, except for the profound sadness that seemed to leach from within him. "But I don't quite understand what happened. What exactly are you cursed with?"

To my amazement, Theo's eyes grew brighter until they were almost white. "He took my soul."

"He *what*?"

"That light you saw—that was my soul being ripped from my body," Theo said, his face flushed with fury. "The bastard took my soul and left me an empty shell."

"Sweet mother," I whispered, wrapping my arms around him, holding him tight against the sorrow and anger and frustration that filled him. The pain eased a little. I poured into him every molecule of comfort I possessed. "I'm so sorry. I can't begin to tell you how sorry I am that you got involved in this. I will feel guilty for the rest of my life."

"It's not your fault, sweetling," he murmured, nuzzling my neck. His anger and anguish melted away even more, and something hot and potent filled him instead. "I knew the risk when I offered myself as your champion. *Di immortales,* you smell good."

A little shiver of excitement skittered down my back as he kissed the hollow behind my ear. "Yes, but if I hadn't been so stupid about believing you, none of this would have happened. I would have been paying attention rather than fighting you every step of the way."

"Mmm. You smell sweet and spicy, like a woman waiting to be satisfied." He pulled back enough to look into my eyes, which were brimming with tears of guilt. "Portia, I forbid you to feel guilt at what happened. There was no avoiding this. Bael cannot punish you without bringing the wrath of the Court down upon your head, and he would not risk such an action."

"Your eyes are almost black again. That doesn't make any sense. How can eye color change? Never mind, it's not important. What is important is the fact that you've lost your soul because of me."

He laughed and nipped my earlobe, his hands roaming over my back and behind. "You never cease to amaze me. I'm surprised that given your skeptical nature and scientific training, you believe in souls."

"I'm agnostic, not a solipsist," I said, a familiar tension building within me at every nibble of his teeth, every touch of his hands. "Logic dictates that if there is a way for your soul to be taken from you, there must be a way to return it. I swear to you now that if it's the last thing I do, I will get you back your soul."

"Smart, sexy, and so delicious," he murmured against my shoulder as my bathrobe parted and slipped down my arms. "I hunger for you, sweetling. Tell me you still want me."

He was hungry. It was growing in him, an unnamed hunger for me, for something that only I could give him. It swelled and spilled out until I shared the hunger, shared the need for physical relief. I ripped his shirt off, heedless of the fact that I was destroying an otherwise nice shirt, rubbing my hands on his chest as he sucked the spot behind my ear that made me see stars.

"Theo, I hate to bring reality into . . . oh, yes, right there . . . but I don't have any condoms. I'm all right as far as birth control goes, but do you have any health issues I should be aware of?"

"No. So good," he said against my skin, his breath ragged. As if I wasn't aroused enough, the sound of his harsh breathing pushed me higher. "You taste so damned good, I want to . . . I don't know what I want. More. I want more."

"You can have all of me," I said in between kisses to his bare shoulder, my hands busy on his belt buckle and zipper even as his hands slid down my behind to the crotch of my teddy. His fingers brushed heat-soaked, sensitive flesh as he undid the snaps. I writhed against him as he peeled the silky teddy off, tormented not just by his burning touch, but by an overwhelming need so foreign, so different, that it shocked me.

I wanted to *bite* him.

I limited myself to little nipping love bites, nibbling his delectable ear as I pushed his pants and underwear down over his hips.

"Di immortales," he groaned when I wrapped my fingers around his incredibly hot penis, sucking on his earlobe and wishing I could just consume all of him.

He stood still for a moment while I explored the velvety hot hardness, then I was on the bed, Theo crawling up the length of my body, his eyes as black as night. "I hope you're ready for me, Portia, because I don't think I'm going to be able to last much longer."

"Ready, oh-so-willing, and as able as humanly possible," I answered, pulling him down so I could taste his delicious mouth again.

"Salus invenitur," he whispered into my mouth. I sucked his lower lip, sliding my legs around his hips, cushioning his weight and glorying in the sensation of his bare flesh on mine.

"Oh, yes," I cooed, my back arching as he sucked a hard, aching nipple into his mouth, his tongue swirling around it with velvety heat. I'd never felt any pain so exquisite as that, and almost cried out with joy as he guided himself into my body. My mind shut down at the sensation of him parting my waiting flesh, of the feel of his chest against mine, of his mouth on my shoulders, licking the spot where my neck joined my shoulder.

"Portia, I have to . . . I have to . . . " Theo groaned as his body stroked into mine, a sudden white hot pain flaring outward from the spot he was kissing. I was flooded with emotions and sensations that didn't make any sense, but were so profound in nature that I just accepted them.

Theo reared back, his eyes shocked, his lips crimson with blood. "*Per imperium,* what have I done?"

As he spoke, long canine teeth flashed white against the blood.

"I don't know, and right now, I don't give a damn! Just don't stop!"

"This isn't right. I can't . . . not like this . . ." His eyes closed, pain written on his face, so intense that it spilled out onto me. "You'll hate me."

I tried to pull him down so I could kiss him, but he resisted. "I don't hate you, Theo. For Pete's sake, I'm damned close to falling in love with you! Don't stop or you'll kill me!"

"You don't understand," he said, turning his head away. "You don't understand what I am now, what Bael has made me."

Vampire. The word echoed in my mind. I ignored it.

"I know that you need me." I turned his face so that I could look into his beautiful black eyes. "I know that there's something I can give you which will ease the pain inside. And I know that we are meant to be together, Theo."

Regret, sorrow, and sadness swamped me as he

started to pull away, but I wouldn't let him. I wrapped my arms around him, yanking him back down onto me, kissing him with a passion so deep I was left shaking.

Theo resisted, hard and unyielding . . . until my tongue invaded his mouth. The taste of my blood was in our mouths, and at it, Theo went wild. He pulled my hips up, pounding into me with a force that knocked pillows from the bed. His mouth was hot on my flesh, pain sharp and hot fading quickly into a sensation so intense, I could swear I felt the pleasure it gave him. I closed my mind to the knowledge of what he was doing, and gave in to the tension that wound tighter and tighter within me.

Theo exploded into an orgasm that pushed me over the edge, his body racking with the need to pour life into me, at the same time he took it. I gave him everything I had, gave him my pleasure, gave him my warmth, filled the empty dark spots where his soul used to be, and accepted from him pleasure that lifted me from the mortal plane and sent me flying.

I was vaguely aware of Theo's weight lifting off me as I floated down, but a great, languid sense of peace and well-being washed over me, leaving me unable to move despite the desire to comfort what I could feel was a profound sense of unease in Theo.

"Portia!"

"Mmm." I stretched a little, relishing the sensation of having been well-loved.

"Portia, you're bleeding."

"Not possible. My period isn't due for another week or so."

"Your neck is bleeding. Where I . . . where I bit you." Theo's breath was warm on my face as he leaned over me.

"It'll be all right," I said, growing increasingly drowsy. My eyelids felt like they weighed a thousand pounds each, impossible to keep open.

The bed lurched. I didn't bother to open my eyes when I heard the door open, followed by the sound of bare feet padding down the hallway. I just lay there and relived the wonderful memories of our lovemaking.

Theo returned with a cloth that he pressed to my neck. "You must make an effort to stay awake, Portia. I think I took too much of your blood."

"You're not hungry anymore," I said slowly, each word seeming to take an inordinate amount of energy to speak. I decided it wasn't worth the energy to try to talk more. *I gave you great pleasure. I liked giving you pleasure.*

"Wake up, Portia!"

My body lightened and floated upward, drifting around as if I was a mote of light. I drifted higher, no more substantial than a thought. *You gave me pleasure, too. More than I'd ever had before. You are a very good lover.*

Sweetling, you must fight this. The bleeding won't stop, and you've lost too much already. You have to help me, Portia.

I really think I'm falling for you, Theo. Which is very unlike me, but there it is.

A stinging slap on my right cheek suddenly brought me back to earth. I opened my eyes, shocked that Theo would strike me.

And that's when I realized two things: Theo and I had been speaking into each other's minds, and the word he spoke earlier was an important one.

"Vampire? You're a vampire? You can't be a vampire! You're a nephilim!"

"Don't move," he said, pushing me back onto the bed. "Put your hand here and press down hard."

"Oh, sweet sensibility. I'm bleeding? I'm hemorrhaging? Call the paramedics!"

"It's going to be a bit difficult explaining to the authorities why you're missing so much blood," he said, grabbing the phone off the tiny nightstand.

"You're calling someone? While I'm lying here bleeding to death? Oh my stars, you bit me! You drank my blood! And . . . and . . . good gravy, I enjoyed it! It was so . . . what have you *done* to me?"

The last few words came out as a wail of self-pity that made me flinch even as I spoke them.

"Calm down, Portia. Panic will make your blood pressure go up," he said, sitting beside me on the bed. He punched a few numbers on the phone, holding it between his shoulder and ear as he edged up the towel I pressed to my neck. "I'm calling someone I met a few years ago. A Dark One."

"A dark what? Not another demon lord! Is it still bleeding?"

"Yes," he replied as I goggled at him. "Not yes, I'm calling a demon lord, but yes, it's still bleeding. Dark Ones are vampires. Or they have been called such—they aren't as evil as legend has painted them. Hello? Christian Dante? I doubt you'll remember me, but we met in 1879 in Paris. My name is Theo North . . . that's right. Only I don't seem to be a nephilim any longer. Or perhaps I am, but I've—it's a long story. Can I meet with you?"

"I feel woozy. I think I'm going to pass out. Oh my god, I had sex with a vampire! I'm falling in love with a vampire! I *fed* a vampire!"

Theo covered up the bottom part of the phone. "I'll give you fifty pounds if you don't say 'vampire' again."

"VAMPIRE!" I screamed, snatching a pillow off the floor and hitting him with it. "You drank my blood!"

"You liked it," he said to me, before listening at the phone again, giving whoever was on the other end the name and direction of the pub.

I bit back an oath. He was right, damn him. I did enjoy it. I enjoyed it so much, I suddenly wanted to do it again.

"One more thing, Christian, my . . . er . . . she's bleeding. It doesn't seem to be stopping."

"I'm going to die. I'm going to bleed to death because you're a blood-crazed fiend. A sexy, seductive, completely gorgeous blood-crazed fiend." I whacked him again with the pillow. "If I die, I'm never going to forgive you!"

"Hush!" Theo commanded, frowning as he listened into the phone. "You're kidding. All right, I'll try that. Thank you."

"How dare you tell me to hush when I'm having an emotional breakdown," I said, as indignant as someone can be who is lying naked on a bed, next to an also-naked man who was so incredibly fabulous that, despite his blood-drinking frenzy, it made me want to wrestle him to the floor and have my wanton way with him.

"Lie still. You can have your wanton way as soon as I'm done here."

"Done what? What are you doing? What are you . . . oh, sweet mother of reason!"

Theo's tongue swirled over the spot on my neck that seemed to tingle in a not-unpleasant manner. His entire body froze. Mine went up in flames at his touch. He looked at me. I looked at him.

His fangs were back.

"Did it stop the bleeding?" I asked, clutching big handfuls of the bedding to keep from grabbing him.

"Yes." He seemed to have lost his breath again, his eyes ebony pools of desire, need, and passion.

"Do it again!" I demanded, pulling him down onto me.

He resisted for all of three seconds, then gave in to both our desires. I arched back against the bed as his teeth pierced my breast, his pleasure and satisfaction mingling with my own rapture as he drank.

Now I know why the ladies at work love those vampire books. Holy moly!

Chapter 11

"Here's another scone. And more coffee. Why did Theo tell me to tell you to be sure to put lots of jam on the scone?"

I accepted the plate of scones and cup of coffee, although I wasn't sure I could consume either. It was my fifth cup of coffee and fourth scone, and I was getting full. "He wants me to rebuild my strength."

"Uh-huh." Sarah sat down across from me, the tiny private dining room blissfully empty of everyone but the two of us. "OK, I've been the good friend. I didn't once smirk when Theo emerged from your room this morning. I didn't make any jokes about the fact that you obviously have the hickey to end all hickeys under that bandage on your neck. And I haven't even hinted that I'd like full details about what the two of you have been up to, even though, as your best friend, I believe I'm due some consideration in that area."

I sighed and pushed the half-eaten scone away.

"And just who is that man in the Indiana Jones hat who has been talking to Theo for the last hour?"

"His name is Christian Dante."

"Dante?" She looked thoughtful as she stirred a spoon of sugar in her tea. "There's an author named C. J. Dante, but he lives in the Czech Republic, not England. I wonder if he's related?"

"No idea. Christian is . . ." I took a deep breath and looked Sarah dead in the eye. "He's a vampire."

"A vampire?" Sarah's eyes grew huge. She dropped the spoon, chipping the edge of the saucer. "Oh my god, a Dark One? Then that has to be C. J. Dante! He writes about Dark Ones! Good god, I had no idea he was in England. We have the same publisher. I have to meet him!"

"Hang on a second," I said, stopping Sarah as she was about to rush out of the room. "There's something more."

"I have always wanted to meet a Dark One! Dante makes them sound so incredibly sexy! All dark and tormented, spending long centuries seeking their Beloved. This is wild! What is the something more?"

Dark and tormented. It didn't quite fit Theo, but who was I to quibble? "It's about Theo. He's . . . last night we . . . oh, I don't know where to start."

Sarah patted my hand in a comforting manner. "A simple, 'We had wild, sweaty bunny sex' would do."

"Well, we didn't. I mean, we did, but that's not all we did." I tried to sort out my unusually tangled thoughts. "We didn't start out the evening that way. I went to bed not long after you, and woke up in a crypt."

"A crypt? What crypt?"

"One in the ruined abbey we saw two days ago. I wasn't alone in the crypt—there was a woman named Noelle, who was some sort of demon wrangler or something. She said she was there to administer the third trial. She summoned a demon, and I was supposed to subdue it."

I thought Sarah's eyes were going to pop right out of her head. "Oh my god! A demon?" She scrabbled in her purse for the minirecorder she carried around to make notes on book ideas. "Start over again. I want to get all of this down."

I told her about the trial, how Theo had shown up, and how my experience with the demon had at last dropped the blinkers from my eyes.

"About time, too," Sarah said with no little satisfaction.

"I'm willing to concede you were right, and admit you won the bet, but any 'I told you sos' will be summarily ignored."

She grinned. "Fair enough. It's worth swallowing them to get you to admit you were wrong. Proceed."

By the time I had described our time spent with the demon lord, Sarah was taking frantic notes on a tiny notepad. "This is incredible material. I can't believe you had the balls to talk back to a demon lord! So, what was this curse he put on Theo? It can't be too serious—he looked fine a few minutes ago. And obviously, if you guys spent the night together, I take it that none of his various and sundry parts were harmed."

I looked past her, out the window. It was sunny and fairly warm. An hour earlier, Theo had stepped outside the pub to greet the Dark One who had come to see him, only to end up with a nasty burn on his arms and face. It seemed that about one thing, legend was correct—vampires and sunlight didn't mix. "No, nothing was harmed in the way you mean . . . unless you call having your soul ripped from your being and a curse damning you to eternal vampire-hood harm. Which, it need not be said, I do."

Sarah did her googly-eyed impression of a pug. "You're kidding!"

I lifted an eyebrow at her.

"Oh dear god, you're not kidding! Theo is a vampire?"

"Could you speak a little louder, Sarah? I don't think *everyone* in the village heard you."

"He's a vampire?" Her voice dropped until it was a husky whisper. "He can't be a vampire—he's an angel."

"No, he's the son of a fallen angel, and evidently there is no rule that says nephilims can't also be vampires. I am told the correct terminology is Dark One. That's why the Christian person is here—Theo's hoping to get some information from him about how to go about changing back to his normal self. Or as normal as an immortal person can be."

"This is absolutely astounding," Sarah said, her eyes distant as she poked a scone with her butter knife. "I can't believe this is really happening, but you're the last person on earth who would ever try to pull my leg about something like this. A *vampire*! You know, Portia . . ." She looked up at me. "There are some drawbacks to having a boyfriend who is a Dark One."

Theo found me five minutes later, wiping my eyes

and hiccupping with the aftereffects of laughter that was only slightly tinged with hysteria.

"I'm delighted to see you're so amused about the situation," he said, handing me the napkin that had fallen from my lap.

"It's better to laugh than go outright insane. Did you get all the information you needed?"

Theo turned and gestured to the man in the doorway. "Yes, thanks to Christian."

"We did not have the opportunity to be introduced earlier," Christian said, coming forward and taking my hand. He made an old-fashioned bow over it that should have seemed hokey, but was quite the opposite. "I am delighted to make your acquaintance. It is not often I meet a Beloved who is also a member of the Court of Divine Blood."

"Beloved?" I sent Theo a quick, embarrassed glance. "We've only just . . . that is, we're not really . . . we're not . . . oh, crap." I glared at Theo. "Would you like to tell the man that we only just met, and have not yet established if there is a relationship waiting to happen?"

The two men exchanged looks. Sarah looked uncomfortable. The silence in the room was thick with some unspoken comment.

"What?" I asked them all.

"There are a few things I need to explain to you," Theo said, taking my hand and pulling me toward the hall.

"You have my mobile number if you have any other questions," Christian said as I reluctantly followed my personal champion.

Theo tossed a thank you over his shoulder. As I closed the door, Sarah was pouncing on Christian with an explanation of who she was, and how they were related by publisher.

"I'm not sure it's the wisest thing in the world to leave them alone," I said as we went upstairs to my room. "She can be horribly fangirl about some authors."

"He'll survive. There are a few things you should know that I felt you'd prefer hearing privately."

"Uh-oh." I entered my room, sitting primly on a chair. "That doesn't sound good. Is it about you being a Dark One?"

"Yes." Theo paced to the window, spun around, and paced back to the door, one hand ruffling his hair.

"I have an awful feeling you're going to say you can't get your soul back, but I refuse to accept that. If someone can take something away, someone else must be able to put it back. I was quite serious when I said I would do whatever it takes to get your soul back, you know. I am aware such a thing won't be easy, but I am fully dedicated to doing whatever is required."

"It's not quite that easy." Theo paced past me.

"But it can be done? You can get your soul back?"

"In a manner of speaking." Theo made three more passes before he sat on the end of the bed and fixed me with a grey-eyed look. "Christian was very informative about Dark Ones. It turns out there are two types—those born of an unredeemed father, and those cursed by a demon lord."

"Unredeemed? There's redemption possible?"

"Yes." He took a deep breath. "Each Dark One has a female counterpart, a woman who is, for lack of a better word, his soul mate. This woman is called a Beloved, and she has the ability to restore to the Dark One his soul."

"Beloved. That's what Christian called me. You think I'm your soul mate?"

"Yes. I don't know. Possibly." Theo jumped up and resumed pacing. "The relationship between a Beloved and a Dark One is a complicated thing. He can take blood only from her. Their lives are linked together—if for some reason she is destroyed, he dies as well."

"That seems a bit extreme," I said slowly, watching him as I thought about the ramifications of what he was saying. "There's a flaw in that reasoning. Christian called me a Beloved, but you don't have your soul back."

"No, there are seven steps we would have to go through before you would be considered a bona fide Beloved." He walked to the window, pulling the curtain back to look out. Sunlight spilled into the room, causing him to yelp when it splashed across his bare wrist. "I gather Christian referred to you in that manner as a courtesy, rather than as a description."

"Seven steps, seven trials . . . is that the only number you people know?"

"It's a good number," he said, stalking past me. "It's a prime number. Those are always good."

I was unable to keep from smiling. "Words to warm the heart of anyone who's spent the time I did in math classes. What are the seven steps?"

"Christian gave me a list." He stopped in front of me, pulling out a small card. "First is marking."

"Marking? Like a cat marking its territory?" My nose scrunched at the thought.

"No. Evidently the fact that we can communicate without speaking is a form of marking."

"Ah." I mentally cleared my throat. *It is pretty different, I'll give you that.*

"Yes. Second is protection from afar."

I thought. "Well, you did save Sarah and me from those whatever-they-weres."

"Hashmallim."

"Yeah. Is that considered from afar?"

Theo shrugged. "Third is an exchange of body fluids."

"Body . . . oh. Well, we've done that."

To my secret delight, Theo smiled. I felt a warm little glow at the sight of it. "Actually, Christian said a French kiss would qualify in that situation."

"I see. Well, I'm happy to revisit that step as often as you like."

His eyes darkened to charcoal. "The fourth step requires me to entrust my life to you by giving you the means to destroy me."

I looked away. "Well, I've failed that one already. I've destroyed your soul—I don't know what can ever wipe clear that sin."

His hands were warm on my knees as he knelt before me. "I've told you that you are not to blame for what happened. If you continue to be obstinate, I will be forced to take action."

"What sort of action?"

His smile grew wicked. "Trust me, you will find my gratitude far more to your liking."

Images grew in my mind, erotic images that I knew were Theo's fantasies. My nipples tightened. My breath grew short. And I had the most overwhelming urge to push him backward and do all the things to him that he wanted to do to me. "All right. I'm willing to concede that your good humor is by far a better attitude to cultivate. Is it hot in here?"

"I'm always hot when you're near me," he said, his voice rich with innuendo.

I shivered at the blatantly carnal thoughts he was sharing. "I won't say I'm not interested in the things you'd like to do, especially that one with the pillows, although I'm not sure I'm limber enough to pull it off, but I do think that we should concentrate on getting your soul back first."

Reluctantly, Theo ceased thinking of ways he'd like to make love to me, and consulted the list again. "The fifth step is the second exchange of body fluids, and yes, last night would count for that."

I grinned.

"The sixth requires you to assist me in overcoming my darker self."

"Darker self," I repeated, wondering what that meant. "I suppose getting you back your soul might qualify for that, but if it doesn't, there's always getting you pardoned with the Court."

His jaw tightened. "Assuming we can make that happen."

I brushed an errant curl off his forehead. "We will. I'm not going to go through all this just to make it rain at my command. If I'm going to do this whole virtue thing, then I'm going to get you what you need for a pardon."

"I'm beginning to think I will not be able to get along without you," he said, kissing my knuckles.

My heart melted at his words. I looked down at his head as he nibbled on my fingers, wondering how I could fall so fast and so hard for a man who I was convinced was a lunatic felon a few days ago. "So far this seems very doable. What's the last step?"

"A blood exchange, followed by a sacrifice where you offer something in recompense for my soul."

"What sort of a something?"

He stood up, pulling me to my feet and into his arms. "Christian didn't say. I gather it's something unique to each couple. Kiss me."

"Oh, I don't think so," I said, squirming out of his arms. "If I do that, we'll end up spending the whole day in bed, and much as I'd like that, we have a soul to find."

A frown creased his brow, as if he was going to argue with me, but after a moment's thought, he nodded. "It saddens me to agree, but you are correct, although there is a more pressing concern than conducting the seven steps of Joining."

"The trials," I said, changing my shoes from sandals to tennis shoes. "Yes, I was thinking about that. I'm getting a little tired of having these trials sprung on us when we least expect them."

A slow smile spread across his face as I stood up. "I think one of the things I admire most about you is the way you face life head-on. It's refreshing to find a woman who doesn't play games."

"Hey now." I poked him in the chest, then smoothed over the spot with the palm of my hand. "Men play just as many games as women do."

"True, but we aren't the masters of manipulation that you women are."

I gave a faux sigh, opening the door as I did so. "Spoken like a man raised in the dark ages. Can you take me to the Court of Divine Blood?"

The retort that perched on the edge of Theo's mind faded away in his surprise. "You want to go to the Court?"

"I do." I took his hand as we walked down the hall toward the stairs, a secret part of me thrilling to the sensation of his thumb brushing the top of my hand. "It's time we take charge of this situation, Theo, and I mean to do just that. I'm going to see whoever is in charge, and have a little discussion about this whole trial thing. And while we're there, we can find out what it will take to get you a pardon."

"You think it will be just that easy?" he asked, amusement rich in his voice and face.

"Of course it won't be easy. But we can at least approach the problem in a logical manner, and that means learning enough to have a sound understanding of what sorts of solutions are reasonable. Thus, to Court we go."

Theo's lips twitched.

"We are smart people, Theo," I said as we marched down the stairs, pausing so he could don a long overcoat and a hat he'd bought off the pub owner. "We both have perfectly good brains, you have knowledge of the Court, and I have . . . well, I know physics, which I'm not quite certain how it will benefit us, but I am confident that we'll figure it all out."

Theo's laughter trailed behind him as we dashed out to his car.

It failed to reassure me.

Chapter 12

"You've got to be kidding."

"You're not impressed?"

I made a face and considered the white stone building. "On the contrary, I'm always impressed by castles. This one is particularly nice. It has a nice view of the ocean, and it's not falling down like lots of the castles Sarah has dragged me to see."

"But?"

"Portland Castle isn't really my idea of heaven," I said, waving a hand that I hoped would express all the emotions I was having difficulty verbalizing. "I know, I know, the Court isn't heaven, but it's similar, and well, this just isn't my idea of what heaven should look like!"

Theo laughed and took my hand, leading me in through the entrance, on the tail end of a group of tourists. "Would it help if I told you that the Court itself isn't in the castle?"

"Then why—"

"One of the portals is contained here. This way."

Heedless of the tour group, which was heading for the Tudor kitchens, Theo turned left and walked down a short hallway to a thick wooden door bearing a sign that read PRIVATE.

"You'll have to forgive my curiosity, but what was life like when this castle was new?" I asked as we entered a small, dark room, no doubt an administrative office. I shivered a little at a draft that seemed to be centered at the doorway.

"Dirty. Everyone had lice and diseases. And it smelled. Here we are. See this?" Theo pointed at a small niche in the outer wall of the room. It was probably intended to hold a candle or lamp. "Press the far left side, and the entrance to the portal should be revealed."

A dull rumbling noise had me turning around in surprise. The wall on the far side slid back about three feet, leaving an opening through which it was possible to enter. "Good gravy, don't tell me this castle has a secret passageway?"

"No doubt several. It was built by Henry VIII. He had a partiality to secret passageways. Left at the fork, then straight on."

The passageway was lit with soft lights, for which I was grateful considering the uneven floor. I proceeded down the narrow passage, obediently taking the left branch when the passage split into two. "What happens if you come here when someone is in the office?"

"Doesn't happen. That room is unoccupied, just made to look like an office in case someone stumbles upon it."

"Haven't the castle people noticed it?"

"I'm sure they have, but the room is warded so that they think nothing of it. All portals are created in such a way. They are visible to mortals, but made so that unless you know what the portal is, no memory of it will remain."

"That's a handy trick," I said, pushing back the skeptical thought that such a thing was impossible. "Is there anything else I should know other than what you told me on the drive here?"

"Through that misty blue doorway," Theo directed.

I stopped before the twirly bluish lights that evidently served as a portal to the Court. Despite several mental lectures, my stomach continued to churn unpleasantly.

"I told you—I've only been to the Court once, for a petition that failed. Non-members are seldom allowed in, and then only on Court business. I can't imagine they'd deny you and your champion entrance since you're undergoing the trials, but politeness will count heavily on your side."

"I'm always polite. Except to Sarah, but she's my oldest friend, so plain speaking is allowed," I said, taking a deep breath to calm my stomach. Theo must have felt my nerves, because he put his hands on my shoulders, giving them a supportive squeeze.

If you prefer, you can leave the talking to me. I might not be a member of the Court, but I'm more comfortable with the members than you are.

No, it's OK. I can do this. You're sure they won't separate us?

I won't let them.

I was comforted both by the warmth of his hands on my shoulders and by the smile that brushed my mind. With another deep breath, I pushed through the bluish haze, and entered the Court of the Divine Blood.

"OK, now I'm impressed. I can't even begin to imagine the equations it would take to explain the time and space of the Court." I stopped on the cobblestoned corner of what appeared to be a pleasant European village circa the early eighteenth century. Ahead of us was a town square complete with well. Several people in modern dress were sitting on the broad wooden lip of the well, chatting. More people strolled through the square, some carrying briefcases, others walking in small groups, a few popping in and out of the half-timbered, Tudor-style buildings that lined the square. Someone whizzed past us on a bicycle, the rider chiming happily on a bike bell that warned of his approach. An orange cat sat in a pool of sunlight, licking her paws. Three dogs chased a small, laughing child. Overhead, birds sang elaborate songs in the trees that lined the square. Above it all, tall spires of various buildings could be seen over the blue-tile roofs capping the stone and wood structures that surrounded the square. It was idyllic, pleasant, and completely mind-boggling when you considered that it was all located in a small English castle.

"As with most elements of the Court, it's best if you just accept it and not try to figure it out," Theo said, consulting a signpost with several narrow arrows on it.

"I've never been one for blind faith," I reminded him, smiling as a hummingbird flitted toward me, pausing in front of my face to give me a thorough look before flying off. "Don't get me wrong, this is really lovely, but it's not very heavenly, is it?"

Theo looked amused. "What were you expecting? Fluffy white clouds and choirs of angels playing the harp?"

A young woman walked by carrying a tray of pies. They smelled . . . well, heavenly. I sniffed the air appreciably. "Maybe nothing quite so trite. So the Court is made up of a town?"

"Yes. Or a palazzo, or cathedral, or forest. The one time I was here, it resembled a desert, complete with snakes and scorpions. It all depends on the whim of the sovereign."

I turned from admiring the clothing displayed in a shop at the edge of the square, and looked warily at Theo. "Sovereign? You mean . . . er . . ."

"No. I told you, this is not heaven. The Christian concept of God is based on the Sovereign, just as are the deities of other religions, but they are not the same thing."

"But there is one . . . er . . . deity in charge?"

"The sovereign isn't one entity."

"So it's multiple beings?" I asked, thinking of the Greek and Roman gods.

"No. The sovereign is the sovereign. Neither one, nor many. It just is."

"You refer to the head of the Court as an 'it'?" I asked, more confused than ever.

Theo shrugged. "The sovereign has no gender. It is

simply the sovereign. It presides over the Court and enforces the canon. All else is done by the mare."

"Mare? Mare like the dark area on the moon?"

He smiled, and my heart turned over. "No, in this case it's an old term that is more or less equivalent to princess. The mare are the sovereign's right hand, so to speak. It will be one of them who grants you membership to the Court once you pass the last trial."

"How many mare are there?"

"Three."

"So the mare are female, but the leader of the Court is gender neutral?" My mind balked at accepting so many impossible ideas at once, but I was firm with it. My new attitude was going to be one of "go with the flow" that held off judgment until I had sufficient information to make an intelligent conclusion.

"That's right. Ah. That looked like a messenger. Stay here. I'll be right back." Theo dashed off down one of the narrow alleys that snaked off of the square. I forced a pleasant expression on my face, and tried to look as if I frequently found myself in pseudo-European, out-of-time town squares.

Two young men in a small horse cart drove past me, the horse's hooves clip-clopping pleasantly on the cobblestone. Behind them, a young woman in a short black skirt and long pink scarf, perched on a bright yellow motorbike, whipped around the horse cart with a wave at the driver.

This place was definitely going to take some getting used to.

"Well, hel-lo there, beautiful."

I turned to face the speaker. A man wearing a

skimpy tank top and black and turquoise biker pants leaned against a light pole, giving me a salacious once-over. "You must be new. I haven't seen you around the Court. The name's Gabriel."

"Gabriel? I'm surprised to see you without your trumpet." I didn't protest when the man took my hand and gave it a rather sloppy kiss, although I badly wanted to wipe my hand afterward.

"Alas, I am not *that* Gabriel," the man said with a smile that bordered on a leer as he not-so-subtly eyed my breasts. I crossed my arms over my chest. "I am a cherub, not a vessel."

"A vessel?"

"Gabriel. He's a vessel. So, are you here alone?"

"You are *not* a cherub," I said, willing to be polite, but not made a fool of. I casually stepped to the side, to put a little space between us.

His leer got a bit brighter as he leaned closer. "Winged babies, right? In diapers, flitting around from cloud to cloud? Cupid and all that?"

"That is the standard image of cherubs," I agreed. "I'm sure I don't need to point out that you're far from that."

"It's a common misconception amongst the mortals." He suddenly touched my neck, mumbling something about a bit of lint on my collar when I backed out of his reach. "The truth about us is much more pleasant, I think you'll agree. You are new here, aren't you? You must have a tour."

"I'm actually waiting here for someone," I said as Gabriel the not-so-very-cherubic took my hand and tucked it into his arm.

"This won't take long. It's best to think of this incarnation of the Court as a giant wheel, with the main square here as the hub. There are three areas on the outer edges of the town, all reachable from this square," he said, ignoring my protest. He waved a hand toward the people at the well. "That's the equivalent of the office water cooler. Those are shops along the edges."

I had a bit of trouble coming to grips with the idea of a celestial shopping mall, but managed to get my mind to overlook the trouble spots and move on. "Shops. All right. Does the . . . er . . . does the sovereign change the appearance of the Court often?"

Gabriel shrugged, and escorted me down one of the four cobbled streets that led away from the square. "Whenever it gets the urge to, I guess. Over here is the petitioner's park, and through that archway is the library."

I caught a glimpse of a green open space as Gabriel whisked me by an arched doorway into another area. "You'll forgive my ignorance, but what exactly does a cherub do?"

"Communication, for the most part. I'm in charge of the Internet. See that building? That's the athonite. Don't go in there if you don't want to be bored to death. It's full of hermits who prose on about nothing for hours on end."

"You are in charge of the Internet? In charge how?" I asked, little warning signals going off in my mind. I stoked up my "go with the flow" intentions, and told myself I'd sort it all out later.

"Oh, this and that. It's mostly automated now, so

it doesn't take too much effort to keep running. Leaves me time to spare for more pleasurable activities, like showing a lovely lady around the Court."

"You've clearly devoted much time to flattery. It's second to none," I said with a smile I didn't really feel, gently extracting my hand from his arm as we walked through a tunnel.

"Why, thank you, sweet lady." He kissed my hand, then gestured widely as we emerged through an arched doorway into the third area. "Behold, the sanctuary."

"Is the sanctuary a, for lack of a better word, holy place?" I had tried to keep an eye on where we were going, memorizing as best I could the twists and turns through the town so I could find my way back to the main square. I gave up doing that as soon as I realized there were frequent signposts like the one Theo had consulted.

Gabriel laughed, and gave my fingers a squeeze, replacing them in the crook of his arm. I gritted my teeth against the desire to remove my hand. "I can see you're going to need some help understanding how things work here. Holy has no meaning in the Court."

Portia? Where are you?

Shoot, I keep forgetting I can mind-talk to you. I'm in another section of the Court. I'll be right there.

I do not like to be kept waiting. Where are you?

Keep your girdle on, I'll be there in a couple of minutes. Someone is showing me around.

Who?

"And here we are. The sanctuary is the area containing the offices and living quarters. No tour is complete without a visit to the grand apartments." Gabriel gestured toward a bridge leading to a square-turreted castle that, for some bizarre reason, reminded me of Sleeping Beauty's castle in Disneyland.

"Hang on one minute, now," I said, coming to a stop. "I am not going back to your apartment with you, if that's what you're thinking. I told you that I'm with someone, and he's waiting for me, so if you don't mind, I'm going to return to the square. Thank you for the tour—it was edifying in a number of ways."

He grabbed my hand to keep me from leaving. "What's your rush? Your friend will wait. My apartment is very special. I think you will enjoy it . . . and me."

I gawked at him, unable to believe I was hearing what I was hearing, but the lascivious look on his face left me in no doubt as to the meaning behind his double entendre. "I have no intention of enjoying you."

Portia?

Coming!

"Why not?" Gabriel winked at me. "You could do a lot worse than a cherub, you know. We're known for our sexual skills."

"I wouldn't be surprised to find out that you're in charge of porn sites on the Internet," I said, snatching my hand back and turning on my heel to walk back the way we'd come. *I'm on my way.*

Overhead, thunder rumbled.

"You are making a mistake, Portia Harding,"

Gabriel called after me as I stormed into the stone tunnel. I stopped and looked back at him. He was leaning against a signpost, a knowing smile on his face. I wanted to slap it off.

"How do you know who I am? I didn't tell you my name."

He laughed, pushing himself off the post to saunter over to me in a blatantly carnal manner. The air grew thick with static electricity. "Word gets around. The latest rumor is about a mortal who had the cheek to get rid of a virtue in order to pardon her boyfriend. I have to admit, I like strong women, women who are not afraid to give in to temptation. I particularly like how they struggle before submitting." He brushed a strand of hair off my face, his fingers stroking my cheek, leaping backward with a startled look on his face when two thin snakes of lightning struck the ground immediately in front of me.

"You dare!" he snarled, his face turning red as he backed up another couple of steps.

"I'm sorry. I don't seem to have much control over my little storm cloud, but it should be clear to you now that I don't intend to take you up on your . . . er . . . offer." I mentally dismissed my cloud, and was relieved when it dissipated to nothing, the air losing its charged feeling.

"Bitch! You will find that we are not as easy to fool as your lover. The Court takes a dim view of murderers and cheats, Portia Harding."

There was no reply I could make to that which didn't involved some pretty rude language, not to mention more in the thunder-and-lightning area, so I simply turned around and walked away as fast as I could. I got lost twice despite the signposts and Theo's mental threats to hunt me down, but finally arrived back at the square to confront the furiously scowling vampire of my dreams.

"You can stop looking like that—I didn't leave willingly. I was hauled off by a cherub to go on a tour of the Court."

His scowl turned blacker as his eyes lightened to a slate grey. I followed as he started off in the opposite direction. "Don't you think you have enough trouble without getting involved with that randy lot? Come along, we don't have time to waste."

"Where are we going?"

"The library. One of the mares has agreed to meet with you."

"Excellent. I have much to say to her."

"I'm sure you do."

I peeked a glance at Theo, but his face was unreadable.

"Are all the cherubs like the one I met?"

"Yes."

I bumped my hand against his a couple of times, but he didn't take the hint, so I ended up sliding my hand into his, smiling to myself when his fingers tightened around mine. "You might have warned me, you know."

"Consider yourself warned: Stay away from the cherubs. They're a heartless group."

"They certainly don't fit into the idealized vision of angelic," I said, pondering that point for a few minutes while we walked along the narrow path that ran alongside a tall stone wall. "You said this isn't heaven, but I rather expected the people who hang out here to be more or less good. If the cherubs are such bad news, why are they allowed to stay?"

Theo stood aside as I passed through a narrow wooden doorway. Ahead of us, a building dominated the area. Tall, with high, stained-glass Gothic windows, and pointy spires that seemed to stretch up to the sky, the building looked more like a cathedral than a library. "You have such a black-and-white view of the world, Portia. You're going to have to adjust that to include shades of grey."

"Meaning, everyone who resides in the Court is not good? I suppose it follows that everyone in Abaddon isn't evil?"

"As you have had proof, having visited it just a few hours ago." Theo marched forward, to the marble steps that led to wide double doors.

"Touché." It was cool inside the library, the sunlight beaming through the windows not doing much to raise the temperature. As I gazed around at shelves of books that seemed to be at least fifteen feet tall, I wondered if the climate was artificially controlled. Some of the books that lay open on pedestals appeared to be old, and no doubt fragile. There was a hushed atmosphere of subdued reverence that seemed to seep into my bones, leaving me with a slightly itchy feeling, and the propensity to whisper. "Whereabouts is the mare?"

"This way." Theo's voice was quieter than normal, making me feel a bit better about my own reaction. He led me to the left, to an area that would have been a small chapel if this had been a cathedral. We wound our way through the maze of books until we came upon a door almost hidden by a rolling ladder that allowed patrons access to the upper shelves.

Theo stopped before the door, fixing me with a dark look. "Although the sovereign does not enforce strict formality in the Court, mares are usually treated with a bit more circumstance than the rest of the officials. They are referred to as 'your grace' in conversation."

"I have no intention of being rude," I assured him. "Credit me with having some amount of tact."

"You will need more than tact," he answered rather ominously, knocking firmly on the door.

A voice bid us to enter. Theo stood aside for me to go in first. I will admit that I was beginning to have second thoughts about the wisdom of tackling someone so high up in the Court organization, but a reminder of what I'd cost Theo had me walking into the mare's office with my head high, my back stiff, and my determination immovable.

A young woman in her early twenties looked up from a laptop. She looked like any other successful businesswoman, from expensively dark brown hair, to a smart, jade green suit with matching shoes. "You are Portia Harding, yes?"

"Yes, I am." Theo, standing beside me, brushed his hand against mine. "Er . . . your grace."

"Good." The mare stood up, raising her voice. "Portia Harding, you are hereby charged with the murder of the virtue named Hope. Bailiff! Take the prisoner into custody!"

Chapter 13

"Murder? Hope was murdered? When?" I asked, backing away from the muscular young woman who bowled in through the door. "I had no idea where she went, let alone what happened to her, but I certainly haven't killed her!"

Theo, what's going on here? Murder?

I don't know, but the mare must be handled carefully. This is a serious situation.

You ain't just whistlin' 'Dixie'!

"I fear there has been a misunderstanding about my client's situation, your grace," Theo said suavely, positioning himself between me and the bailiff.

The mare stared at Theo for a moment, thawing visibly when he smiled at her.

Oh, that's subtle, I thought at him.

Subtle doesn't win the fair maiden.

I sent him thoughts of what I'd like to do to him at that very moment.

You are a bloodthirsty little thing, aren't you? You can stop mentally sharpening your neutering knife. I simply mean to win her over to our side, not seduce her.

"You are the champion?" the mare asked, giving Theo a much more thorough eyeing than I thought strictly necessary.

"Theondre North at your service, your grace," he said, bowing, charm positively oozing off him.

Just see that you don't. I like to think of myself as a generous person, but when it comes to men, I don't share.

Neither do I, but that's not the issue at stake.

I won't say the mare actually cracked a smile, but she stopped looking like she was going to have me gutted on the spot. "One moment, Mathilda," she told the bailiff before turning back to me. "Am I to understand that you did not seek an audience with me in order to turn yourself in for the crime of murdering the virtue named Hope?"

I lifted my chin and gave her a polite smile. "That's correct. I am here to discuss the continuation of the seven trials I have been forced to undergo. I also wish to discuss the process for submitting a petition. And finally, I want to lodge a complaint about two old ladies who beat me up without due cause."

The mare's eyebrows rose, her eyes chilly. "I see."

"I can reassure you that my client is not the type of person who would commit murder for her own gain," Theo said, moving closer to me in a show of faith. As a gesture, it warmed me to my toes. "She is innocent of the charge you have laid at her feet."

The mare didn't look at all like she believed him.

"And did you take on the role of her champion before or after she summoned the virtue?"

"After, your grace. I discussed the situation with her at some length—"

If you could call almost choking me to death discussing the situation.

Hush.

"—and determined that she summoned the virtue without knowing that she was doing so. The virtue assumed she wished to take on the position, and since she was desirous of leaving, she passed on her powers without Portia being aware of exactly what she was committing herself to."

"Save your defense for the hearing," the mare said, gesturing to the bailiff.

The bailiff grabbed my upper arm in a grip that would no doubt leave bruises. Above my head, the cloud began to form.

"Your grace, please, we ask that you recognize the extenuating circumstances of this situation, and grant leniency." Theo sent the mare another sultry smile.

I'd really appreciate if you could stop doing that.

Saving your life, you mean?

No, sending her those wicked smiles.

Are you jealous?

Not in the least.

There was a pregnant pause during which Theo laughed into my head.

Oh, all right, perhaps a little, but it's justified. I know you're trying to get us out of this situation, but it . . . oh, never mind. Just get it over with.

"On what grounds do you ask for leniency?" the mare asked, thawing just a bit more under the influence of his smile.

The air grew thick, but not with static. I fought to control my anger, aware that it was triggering the ministorms around me. Once I got my emotions under control, everything would be fine.

I noticed the mare kept her eyes on Theo, not paying me much attention. It irritated me that he was using his masculine wiles to sway her almost as much as it irritated me that I was bothered by that in the first place.

The analytical part of my brain pointed out that I'd only known Theo a few days, and been intimate with him only one day, all of which hardly added up to deep insight into his nature. Oh, sure, we were talking about following the steps to a formal binding, but so far, that was just talk—we hadn't taken the last couple of steps. What if he never intended us to? What if we did, and I found out he was really a jerk? Perhaps he was one of those men who felt it acceptable to flirt with every female. Perhaps he was nothing more than a tomcat, on the prowl for the next conquest. Perhaps he didn't believe in things like fidelity and honor.

Perhaps I needed to stop worrying about Theo's intentions toward me, and cope instead with more important issues, like keeping myself out of heavenly prison.

What if he didn't love me?

The air grew cold around us.

"I ask that leniency be shown to Portia due to her inexperience with Court matters."

"Ignorance is not suitable grounds for clemency," the mare said, her voice turning icy as she looked at me.

"I am not ignorant," I answered, trying to tone down the indignation in my voice.

Tiny little pitter-patter sounds followed a shower of minute hailstones.

Portia, you are not helping the situation.

I'm not doing it on purpose!

The mare looked up at my cloud, then at me, with a look that spoke volumes.

"I'm sorry. I don't seem to have very good control of this whole weather business yet," I said stiffly, trying to dissipate the cloud. "As for the other, I am simply inexperienced in the ways of the Court. I did not ask to become a virtue, but I have decided, after much thought, that I am willing to take on the job. Since no one bothered to explain to me the rules and regulations governing virtues, I'm pretty much feeling my way blindly here, and would appreciate it if you could recognize that fact."

Sweetling, you must temper your tone. It is borderline hostile. And stop the hail! It's spreading to the mare's desk.

I'm sorry about that, but I will not stand by while you prostitute yourself in order to get this woman to understand I haven't done anything wrong!

He sighed into my head. *My using a bit of charm on the mare in order that she might understand our point of view has nothing to do with our relationship. You have no reason to feel threatened by other women.*

The mare lifted her chin and looked down her nose at me. The hail was growing in size and scope, until the rug in the entire room was covered in a white blanket of ice the size of small marbles. The bailiff looked questioningly at the mare. The latter looked angry.

Portia, stop the dramatics!

I can't! I'm trying to make the cloud go away, but it won't!

I can assure you that the sovereign takes very dim views of people who treat officers of the Court with such antipathy!

The hail came down even harder.

The mare suddenly picked up a book and slammed it down onto her desk. "Cease this display!" she bellowed.

"I can't! I don't know how!" I yelled back, waving my hands desperately as if that would help disperse the cloud over my head.

"Such insolence!" the bailiff said, jerking me back when I moved forward to brush the hail off the mare's desk. "This will not be tolerated."

"Your grace, please—" Theo started to say, but the mare interrupted him.

She pointed at me, her voice loud enough to rattle the windows in the room, looking like some sort of Nordic goddess as the hail swirled around her. "You are out of control and a danger to others, as well as yourself. For that reason, and that reason alone, I will bypass the justice calendar and commit you to an immediate hearing concerning the charge of murder that has been leveled against you. You will report to Petitioner's Park at Nones. You will not leave the Court without permission. You will not discuss your case with anyone but the appropriate authorities. You will not utilize your Gift without permission. Do you understand what I have said?"

I blinked a couple of times, surprised that she didn't order me clamped into irons and thrown into the nearest dungeon, to be left to rot for a few years before someone remembered me. "I . . . yes. Thank you."

The mare took a deep breath. "Now get out of here!"

Reluctantly, the bailiff released my arm.

What just happened? I asked Theo.

I believe she realized the truth in what we were saying about you not having any experience with the powers of a virtue.

Just because I couldn't control the hail?

Yes. Anyone who intended to become a virtue would have a basic understanding of the role, and better control over those elements in her domain. This may actually be a good thing. "Thank you for your generosity, your grace."

The look she gave Theo as he made another bow was enough to raise my hackles, but I gritted my teeth and reminded myself of what Theo had said.

The cloud disappeared as I left the room.

"We really do need to get you through the rest of the trials so you can take control of your Gift," Theo said in a low voice as he hustled me out of the library.

"You're telling me. When is Nones?"

Theo glanced at the sky. "Another hour. Time enough for us to get some answers . . . and food. You are hungry."

"So are you," I said, aware of the hot need that growled inside him.

"Yes. We will seek the dapifer. This way."

A dapifer, it turned out, was some sort of steward responsible for caring for visitors to the Court. Or so Theo explained as we met with a small bespectacled man who wrung his hands when we asked for a room and food.

"We don't normally allow nephilim in the apartments, but if her grace said it was all right . . ."

I bit back the desire to state the obvious about such a ridiculous policy.

"I don't suppose there are any phones here?" I asked instead as the dapifer showed us to a room in the keep that housed the noble apartments. It was furnished in an odd mixture of old and new, with a huge, canopied bed, candles in sconces on the wall, and an armoire that contained a TV, DVD player, and popular video game machine. A small, modern bathroom led off the main room. It was comfortable, though, and I certainly wasn't in any position to comment about the eccentric decorating schemes of the sovereign.

"Gracious me, no, no telephones are allowed! Contact with the outside is strictly prohibited in the Court," he told me, looking horrified at the very thought. He gave us both a curt little bow. "I will have a meal delivered to you immediately."

I thanked him, sinking onto the bed with an exhausted sigh as he left. "I wanted to call Sarah and tell her I'd be late, but I guess that's out. Unless your cell phone . . ." I looked hopefully at Theo.

He shook his head. "Won't work here. Only certain officials are allowed access to the outside world."

"Damn. I hope Sarah doesn't worry. We were supposed to go to another haunted house tonight."

Theo stretched, pushing aside a heavy maroon curtain to look out the double-glazed, diamond-paned window. "Time operates differently in the Court than outside. We could be here for days, and only an hour or two would pass outside. Or a year. It just depends."

"Depends on what? How can the time variable be so diverse?"

"It depends on the whim of the sovereign, I suppose. I knew a man who was here for a few days, and only an hour passed outside. His wife, who was with him, left at the same time only to find three years had gone by in her absence."

"That doesn't make any sense." I spent a few minutes trying to calculate the equations necessary for such an impossible thing, but gave it up when a headache bloomed to life. "No, that can't be right. It's not logical at all."

"Shades of grey, sweetling, shades of grey."

"Oh, I've been shades-of-greying ever since we met that demon, but that is asking too much. Even here, even in this Court, there has to be an underlying, fundamental structure of physical properties upon which reality is built. To say that no laws keep the structure consistent is impossible."

"That's where faith comes in," he said dryly.

I let the matter drop. It didn't do any good to argue with Theo. I was willing to accept that a different set of physical laws applied to the Court, but exist they must. And I was just the person to explore what sort of glue held together this bizarre world I had joined.

"The only other time I was in Court, I was not allowed to stay in the keep," Theo said after a few minutes of silence.

"Why not?" I asked, pushing aside my concerns to watch him. So many emotions rolled around inside him that I had a hard time separating them.

"I was considered unworthy." He turned to look at me, a smile on his lips. "If nothing else, sweetling, you have elevated me beyond obscurity."

I made a face. "I'm willing to bet you would have preferred not being known as the boyfriend of the woman who hailed on a mare."

"Boyfriend?"

"Well . . . what's the male equivalent to Beloved?"

"Dark One."

"That's rather a general-purpose label, not one indicative of a man so completely wrapped around his woman's little finger."

"Is that what you think I am?" he asked, one eyebrow cocked in inquiry.

I smiled, kicked off my shoes, and slid back on the bed, wiggling my toes in invitation. "Aren't you?"

Hunger roared through him with such intensity it made me gasp. He started toward me, his eyes black as onyx, one hand undoing his belt. "Intrigued, yes. Impassioned, definitely. Aroused . . ." He glanced down at himself. "I don't believe that is in question. But wrapped around your little finger? I am not so easily manipulated."

"How about in love?" I asked, suddenly breathless as he knelt on the bed and started crawling up my legs.

He stopped, his face impassive, but inside him a great well of pain existed. "I have loved women before, Portia. I don't think I could have lasted as long as I have without occasionally being in love, caring for someone, and receiving love in return."

A knife twisted in my heart. It was unreasonable for me to expect that Theo could live the thousand plus years he had lived without falling in love, but my heart refused to recognize reason.

"What I feel for you is . . . different."

Different could be good. Different could be . . . oh, who was I fooling? Different was horrible. I didn't want to be different—I wanted Theo to love me just as much as he loved the other women in his life. I wanted the same place in his affections, to mean something to him other than a means to an end. I wanted him to love me as much as I was coming to love him!

"I see." My throat ached with unshed tears of self-pity. "These women you loved . . . were they immortal?"

"No. I knew when I began with them that the relationship was finite. I knew they would grow old, and there would come a time when they would die, and I would be left alone again." He sat back on his heels and unbuttoned his shirt, tossing it onto a nearby chair. With a look in his eye that warmed me despite the pain, he continued up the length of my body. "You, as I said, are different. Whether by Joining as my Beloved, or by acceptance into the Court, you will be immortal."

"Which means that when you grow tired of me, you won't be able to count on attrition to get rid of me."

His breath feathered against my mouth as he settled onto my body. "I have never grown tired of any of the women whom I loved. I mourned their passings, and felt myself diminished for a time."

"And then you got over it and fell in love again." The pain hurt so deeply in me that I wondered if there would ever be an end to it.

"Yes. But now there is you, and you, as I said, are different."

His lips brushed mine as he spoke. I wanted so badly to kiss him, to taste him, to merge myself with him that my body shook. But the pain at his confession was too much, too much for me to live with. I couldn't do it.

"I need you, Portia."

Hot tears leaked out of my eyes as I closed them tightly, turning my head to the side to avoid the torturous lure of his mouth. Oh, yes, he needed me. He needed me for sustenance. He needed me to help him achieve his greatest wish—salvation. He needed me not in the way a man needs a woman, but as a partner, someone sharing an adventure, bonded by circumstances into a symbiotic relationship.

You, my love, will be with me forever. You will be mine to love, mine to share the joys of life, mine to explore all the possibilities that lie before us.

I looked at him through eyes made blurry with tears. I wanted so much to believe him, but the pain was too deep to be erased with a few easily spoken words.

You complete me, Portia, don't you feel that? His eyes were filled with fire, but it wasn't just the head of passion that burned within him. *It is true I have loved in the past, but I know now that I was only biding my time until you would come into my life. You are life to me, my love. I could not exist without you.*

I burst into uncharacteristic tears at such beautiful words. I didn't need to look into Theo's face to know that he meant them—his emotions surrounded me, merging with my own until it was impossible to tell which were his and which mine.

His kiss burned more than just my lips; it scorched my soul with its intensity. I gave myself up to him, relinquished every last bit of me, but I wasn't in the least bit diminished. My heart sang as I drank in the sweetness of his mouth, filling me with such joy that I seriously thought for a moment that I would burst with happiness. I wanted to tell him how I felt, what he meant to me, how the warm kernel of love was growing into a feeling that lit up the corners of my soul, but the words would not come. Instead, I poured into him every emotion I possessed.

You don't have to say it, sweetling. Just as you know what I feel for you, so I can read your emotions.

Good, because it's a bit embarrassing falling in love so quickly with a man who I wanted to see in jail just a few days ago.

Theo chuckled in my mind as his tongue continued a lazy exploration of my mouth. *Kismet, perhaps? We were meant to be together.*

Do we have time for this? I asked as his mouth moved to my neck, kissing a hot trail down to my collarbone. *Don't get me wrong, I'm all for it, but if someone is bringing us food, and you said you thought there was a person whom we could talk to about the murders before the hearing, will we have time for . . . er . . .*

Wild, unbridled lovemaking?

Exactly.

He froze for a moment, his head lifted and slightly tipped to the side, as if he was listening.

"We will in a moment," he said, sighing a little as he climbed off me.

Someone knocked on the door. I leaped off the bed and straightened my shirt, hoping I didn't look like we were about to do what we were about to do.

"Your meal," an elderly woman said, giving Theo a tray of covered plates. He thanked her as she left, setting down the tray on the table and lifting the lids off the plates. The scent of roasted meat and garlic filled the room.

He sighed again. "Roast beef. One of my favorites. I miss it already."

"You can't eat *any* normal food anymore?"

"I can, but Christian cautioned against it until I

became more comfortable with the vampirism. Evidently it takes some doing to digest food, and is not recommended for new . . . erm . . . inductees."

Guilt pinged sharply. "I'm sorry—"

"Don't," he interrupted, and pulled me into an embrace. His eyes were shining with a warmth that heated me to my toenails. "I insist that you stop feeling guilty about it."

"Well, the least you can do is let me feed you," I said, tipping my head so my neck was presented to him. "Soup's on!"

"No, you eat first." He pulled away and waved me to a chair in front of the table.

"You're hungry. We'll take care of you, then I'll eat."

"You're hungry as well. You first."

The stubborn look on his face made me smile. I waggled my eyebrows at him, and summoned up my best leer. "Ah, but I'm hungry for more than just roast beef."

A speculative glint dawned in his eyes. He looked down at the tray of food. I looked as well. The tray bore two plates of roast beef, potatoes, and assorted steamed vegetables. There was also bread, and something blobby that I remembered from a previous dinner at the pub was Yorkshire pudding. To the side sat a plate with two pieces of cake, lavishly frosted.

"You wouldn't be one of those people who eats her dessert first?" Theo asked as I smiled and picked up the plate of cake.

"Not normally, but I'm willing to break the rules

now and again." I carried the cake to the nightstand, dipping my finger in the frosting before popping it in my mouth and licking it off with exaggerated laps of my tongue. "Mmm. Cream cheese frosting, my favorite." I raised my eyebrows, and waited to see if Theo wanted to play.

He looked at the bed, looked at the cake, then at me. Before you could say "frosted nephilim," he was naked, lying on the bed, his arms open for me.

"You're sure we have time?" I asked, glancing at the clock.

"For this? Oh, yes. And if we don't, we'll make time."

I laughed as I started removing my clothing, my heart swelling with love. How could life be so topsy-turvy, such a mess of confusion, and yet so wonderful?

Go with the flow, my brain reminded me. Just go with the flow.

Chapter 14

"Still with me, sweetling?"

"Barely. It was a close thing there when you turned the frosting on me."

Theo, lying on his back, a sated and very smug look on his face, waggled his eyebrows and hummed a happy little song about frosting-covered nether parts. "You certainly did seem to enjoy it."

"That, my adorable fanged one, is the understatement of the year. Are you sure you're full? You seemed to spend more time in action, to be euphemistic, rather than dining."

"I am full. I am well-pleasured. I am physically exhausted," Theo said, waving a languid hand. His eyes were closed, his face relaxed as he lay next to me on the bed, delightfully naked. I trailed a finger down one of his biceps, making him smile a drowsy smile.

"You take a nap then, handsome. You certainly worked hard enough."

"I did indeed, although it was a labor of love. And, I will admit, you helped a little." He yawned.

"A little, huh?" I pinched his nipple. He pretended to snore.

The many pleasant after-tingles that were zinging around my body were one more reminder of the powerful emotions our lovemaking created. I gently traced the planes of his face, my finger stroking the length of his long, arched eyebrows, down to his high cheekbones and aristocratic nose. His lips curled slightly as I brushed them with the tips of my fingers, leaving me to marvel again at how something so mundane as a mouth could give so much pleasure.

"Sleepy," he said, his voice thick with sleep and satisfaction.

"You go ahead and take a nap." I glanced at the clock and sighed as I got off the bed. "I'd best go wash off the frosting and other . . . er . . . residue before we have to show up at the hearing."

"A shower?" Theo's eyes snapped open. "Where you're naked and wet and soapy?"

"That's generally how a shower works," I said, pausing at the bathroom door to bat my eyelashes at him. To my surprise (and no little amazement), he showed signs of arousal. I stared at his penis, watching as it stirred, thickening before my eyes. "You can't possibly be serious. You can do that again so soon?"

"Given the proper encouragement and inspiration, yes." Theo slid off the bed and started toward me, a familiar glint in his eye. "I must admit to having a fantasy or two about taking you in the shower, your flesh satin-smooth, slick with soap and warm water."

The images that filled my head left me stunned for a second, for a fraction of a second, really, and then

I was running for the shower, intent on fulfilling the erotic images that danced before my mind.

The shower wasn't very large, one of those stall types with just enough room for the two of us to squeeze into it. But I was soaped up and ready for Theo by the time he joined me, fully aroused and filled with a hunger that seemed to echo inside me.

"You're sticky," I said in between kisses, my hands busy rubbing soap on his chest.

"It's the frosting you smeared all over me," he growled, nipping my earlobe. His hands were busy as well, smoothing a soapy washcloth over my back and lower, to my backside, before sliding around my thighs and heading straight for my personal paradise. "I'm not as sticky as you are, though. You're a dirty, dirty girl."

"Oh, yes," I gasped as his fingers danced a soapy dance that had me squirming against him. "I'm very, very dirty."

"It behooves me to clean you up, then," he mumbled against my shoulder.

"Especially since it was you who made me so dirty. Oh, sweet mother, do that again!"

He did. His fingers sank into me, curling ever so slightly until the friction pushed me to the very edge of an orgasm. I teetered there, not wanting to fall alone.

My hands slid lower, lovingly cupping his testicles with one hand while slicking soap down the length of his penis.

His eyes crossed. A sharp, pointy canine nicked my shoulder. He lapped up the blood as my hands moved up and down, quickly finding a rhythm that had his breathing ragged, his hips jerking in time to the movement of my hands. I opened my mind to him, allowing him to feel what his skillful fingers were doing to me at the same time he shared his rising ecstasy. It was a startling feeling, experiencing not only my own passion, but his as well, and it pushed us both higher until we hung with tantalizing agony at the edge of completion.

Theo's fingers stilled inside me, my flesh quivering around them. My hands stopped moving, his penis pulsing with his rapid heartbeat. Our eyes met.

I love you, I told him, pouring my love into him, chasing away the darkness that dwelled where his soul had lived.

You are everything to me, he answered with an honesty so intense it humbled me. *I could not exist without you.*

An exaggeration, but a sweet one . . . all rational thought left my mind at that moment. His teeth pierced the skin at the back of my neck, his fingers coming to life inside me. My hands tightened around his penis, and the world supernovaed around us, exploding into a million tiny, brilliant pieces.

It took a long, long time for us to come down from our shared high, but when I did, it was to find myself slumped against him, his hands holding me upright since my legs had failed me. We were both wet, no longer soapy, and as I looked into his somewhat glazed eyes, I made a vow to myself that I would move the earth itself in order to spend the rest of my life with him.

*   *   *

"The penalty for murder in the Court of Divine Blood is eternal, and irrevocable. Only intervention by the sovereign can change it, and that has never happened."

"A death sentence?" I asked, my knuckles white. I relaxed my hands, trying to take in everything Terrin was saying to us. I didn't ask how Theo had found him. I was just grateful that someone was willing to talk to us.

Slowly, sweetling. I will not allow harm to come to you.

I don't think even you can stop the people here if they wanted to hurt me. Can you?

Theo didn't answer me, but his sadness was all too evident.

"Not a death sentence." Terrin paused for a minute, looking from me to Theo. "That is, not in so many words. Your existence would not be destroyed, but you would be . . . incarcerated."

"Incarcerated here? In the Court?"

I suppose there are worse things in the world than being held prisoner in heaven.

Don't count on it.

Terrin shook his head.

"The Akasha," Theo said. For some reason, I shivered.

What's the Akasha?

It's another name for limbo. It's where banished demons go, a kind of holding cell of misery and eternal nightmare. You do not wish to visit it.

"Yes." Terrin's gaze moved to me. It was frankly assessing, as if he was weighing whether or not I was worthy of his time. Oddly enough, I wasn't offended by this. The days when I would feel outraged over the idea that someone might not consider me an equal seemed like long years ago. I sat, humbly waiting to see what information Terrin was willing to share, well aware that Theo and I were in a particularly precarious position.

Terrin seemed to make up his mind, nodding to himself. "When I conducted your second trial, I questioned your fitness as a virtue. You seemed to possess none of the knowledge, none of the skills needed to achieve success in the Court. And yet, despite the fact that you are charged with the murder of one whom you succeeded, my instincts tell me that you are telling the truth. I have seldom had cause to doubt my instincts, and I am loathe to do so now just because the evidence is to the contrary. The tale you told is unlikely, but not, I believe, impossible."

He believes us! That's a step in the right direction. I'm glad you picked him over the other seneschals.

I had little choice. He was the only one on the list of Court officials whom I recognized. I simply assumed that he must be privy to the situation regarding Hope.

"Can you help us?" I asked, trying my damnedest to look earnest and trustworthy.

"Not in any official way, no. But I can give you the information you seek." He leaned back in his chair, crossing his legs and steepling his fingers. "You are aware that the virtue named Hope has been missing and is presumed dead, given the note she left behind."

Theo inclined his head.

"Suicide?" I asked.

"No. Her note claimed she was the victim of a plan whereby her Gift would be stripped and given to a mortal—to you, Portia Harding."

Why does everyone but you address me by my full name? I asked Theo, momentarily sidetracked by something that had bothered me.

Names have power.

"One note is hardly evidence—" I started to say.

Terrin lifted his hand. "The note continues with a somewhat impassioned claim that several murder attempts have been made against her already, and that she feels the two acts are related."

"That's absolutely groundless!" I said, outraged. "I did not murder her. I have never plotted to take her power from her. I didn't even know who or what she was when I inadvertently summoned her!"

"So you have said." Terrin looked grim.

My heart sank at the circumstantial evidence that was being used to manufacture apparent guilt on my part. It was transparent and ridiculous, but I could see how people who didn't know me might imagine it could be true.

"It is only because no evidence of Hope's body has been discovered that you have been allowed to continue as you are, under supervision only rather than incarceration."

I've been supervised? By who?

I have no idea, but it wouldn't surprise me.

"This is absolutely asinine. It doesn't make any sense! Why would I want to kill a woman I'd never met?"

Terrin's gaze dropped. "The speculation is that, at some point, Hope returned to reclaim her Gift from you, and you killed her after a heated exchange." He raised his hands to forestall the objection that was on the tip of my tongue. "I am not the one you need to convince of your innocence, Portia Harding. I am simply telling you what is being said around the Court."

A dim rumbling sound warned of things to come. *Portia, control your Gift.*

It wasn't easy, but I bit back several hasty and borderline rude comments about the mental makeup of the Court, making a concentrated effort to dissipate the anger which had been transformed into thunder. "Does any of that speculation run to why I would do something so heinous?"

Terrin's gaze dropped to his fingers. "I have heard that you are bonded by blood to Theo North. It is not difficult to imagine that someone with such a tie would intend to grant him a pardon as soon as membership to the Court was approved."

I shot a quick look to Theo. He sat impassive, looking mildly bored, as if nothing the seneschal said had anything to do with us. "Everyone thinks this? Everyone thinks that I tricked Hope into giving me her powers, then I murdered her, and all to get Theo his pardon?"

"Rather starkly put, but yes, that is the explanation being given for your actions."

"I see." My knuckles were still white with strain. I made another conscious effort to relax my hands as I stood up, my head held high. "Thank you for your time and cooperation, Terrin. I hope that associating with me in this manner will not cause any problems for you."

He stood slowly, a smile warming his eyes. "I do not fear repercussion, if that is what you are concerned about."

"Good. Thank you again."

"It has been my pleasure," he said, bowing over my hand. "I have no doubt that we will meet again . . . hopefully, under less exacting circumstances."

"Why didn't Terrin worry about meeting with us?" I asked Theo a minute later, when we had emerged from the dark warren of offices that were housed in the grand apartments. The sun was hidden behind several dark-looking clouds. I shivered, but the cold seemed to come from within rather than from the dark skies.

"I'm not sure," he answered, looking thoughtful as he adjusted his hat, pulling up the collar to his coat to shield the flesh on his neck. "I suspect there is more to him than appears on the surface."

"You can say that about everyone here," I pointed out, leaning into him when his arm slid around my waist. "What now?"

Theo sneaked a quick glance at the sky. "It's almost Nones. Now we gird our loins."

I didn't like the concern I felt in him, deep and dark and destructive. "I'm an old loin girder from way back," I lied, giving him a bright smile that I hoped hid the truth that I was worried to death about the hearing.

You needn't be worried, Portia. I told you that I

would not allow anything to harm you. I have a few tricks up my sleeves yet.

What sort of tricks? I asked as we headed to the area containing the Petitioner's Park.

You'll find out in due time.

The sight of seemingly everyone in the city streaming into the narrow alley that led into the park was enough to choke any further questioning I intended to pursue.

Courage, sweetling. I am here with you.

For which I'm grateful to the depths of my being, I told him as we elbowed our way through the throng to the center of the park, where a ring of druidic stones had been arranged in a style reminiscent of Stonehenge. Stone benches dotted the inner perimeter of the ring. Four of the benches were filled with various people. The fifth was empty. In front of it stood an officious-looking man, who frowned when he spotted us.

"Portia Harding, stand forward," the man said.

I stepped clear of the crowd, into the circle of stones, Theo next to me in the shadow cast by one of the tall stones. I wanted badly to take his hand, but wasn't comfortable with such a show of affection in front of so many hostile strangers.

"Know ye all that this hearing commences in the sovereign year one thousand fifteen in the eightieth age."

Ten-fifteen? You're older than that!

The Court calendar differs from the mortal one. It is divided into ages, each of which contains roughly fifty-six thousand millennia.

I did a swift mental calculation, pleased that the years worked out to be the approximate age of the Earth.

"Behold ye now, her most gracious of majesties, the mare Suria."

A smiling, petite blonde in a gauzy green and gold sundress emerged from the crowd, laughing at a quip someone called out. She bestowed her smile on Theo and me, taking a seat on the empty bench.

"Behold ye now, her most gracious of majesties, the mare Disin."

The mare we'd met with earlier marched out, her expression grim. She didn't look at me, simply strode over and took her seat next to the first mare.

"Behold ye now, her most gracious of majesties, the mare Irina."

The last mare took me by surprise. I was expecting another woman of younger years, but the bent-over, frail woman who hobbled from the masses was clearly in the latter years of her life . . . if that was possible with an immortal. She, too, settled on the bench, her milky blue eyes searching me curiously.

"This hearing does not concern your champion," Disin said, frowning at Theo.

"With respect, your grace, Portia is my Beloved." Theo stepped forward slightly, careful not to go beyond the edges of the shadow. "I cannot allow her to stand trial alone."

Around us, the crowd gasped, little whispers hissing in the air as people digested the information that Theo and I were bound by blood.

Was that the wisest thing to say? I asked, forcing myself to relax as the clouds overhead grew darker.

The three mare consulted one another. *It seems to me that just gave more fuel to the fire.*

Theo's laugh was mirthless. *Those three women are the pinnacle of power in the Court of Divine Blood. The only one who has more is the sovereign itself. There is little that escapes their attention. The fact that I am now a Dark One may not have been common knowledge, but I assure you they were aware of it the moment we stepped into the Court.*

The mare ended their consultation.

"You may remain," Disin said, giving Theo a regal nod. "But you will not speak to the charges in Portia Harding's place. It is for her alone to do so."

He bowed, murmuring his thanks.

"You are charged with the destruction of the virtue Hope," the first mare said, her face somber. "How plead you, Portia Harding?"

"Not guilty." There were other words that wanted to burst out, such as a declaration that I do not kill people, not for any reason, and certainly not for anything so frivolous as the ability to control weather, but I pushed them down. I doubted if such an outburst would do good.

The silence that followed my statement hung heavily for about five seconds, then the whispers behind us began fast and furious.

The sky grew darker despite my attempts to keep my emotions in check.

Disin narrowed her eyes. "Do you refute the fact that you intend to grant exculpation to the nephilim named Theondre North, the same man to whom you are bound as a Beloved?"

Strangers be damned. I took Theo's hand, sucking in a deep breath as I tried to calm my nerves. "I do not deny that I have discussed the subject with Theo. I do deny the implication that I murdered Hope in order to bring such a thing about."

"Do you deny that just one night past, you sought the company of a demon lord?"

"We didn't seek him—"

"Do you deny that you had an audience with the demon lord, the premiere prince of Abaddon, the lord Bael?"

Several people gasped behind me. Theo's fingers tightened around mine. He wanted badly to say something but was bound to silence by the mare's order, an order that evidently covered not giving me advice as to what I should say in answer to the ridiculous charges being bandied about. "The circumstances of our visit to Bael are not of our doing. We were summoned there by Bael."

More gasping and a couple of outright cries of horror. I kept my eyes fixed on the three women in front of me, drawing strength from the touch of Theo's hand.

Disin leaned forward, her eyes as cold and hard as steel. "Do you deny that you have said to the nephilim Theondre North, on several occasions since taking on the mantle of virtue, that you would do anything to restore unto him that which he does not possess?"

"His soul," I said, waving my free hand in an expressive manner. Overhead, thunder rumbled ominously. "I was talking about his soul, which was ripped from him by Bael, all because he protected me from the demon who was part of the third trial. A trial, I might add, that is sanctioned by this Court!"

Theo's fingers tightened around mine. I glanced at him, nodding abruptly at the warning visible in his eyes.

"I beg your pardon if my comments seem rude," I said, aware of the hostile looks I was getting from the people surrounding us. The mare's faces were for the most part impassive, but it was evident they had come to this hearing with their minds made up. "But I dislike being asked to justify my actions when I have done nothing wrong. I did not ask to become a virtue—Hope made me one without my knowing anything about it. I did not murder her, nor do I know who did, or why. I did not seek audience with a demon lord; it was forced upon me. It's true I have sworn to restore Theo's soul to him, but that is a matter between him and me, and I fail to see how it has importance to anyone else here."

"You dare speak thusly to the mare?" The officious little man who had introduced the mare leaped up from one of the benches, his face red with anger.

Theo's fingers tightened until his grip was almost painful.

"I mean no disrespect, but I will not tolerate a kangaroo court—"

"Silence!" Disin bellowed, her voice echoing off the trees. "We will confer."

"But I haven't been allowed a chance to defend myself properly," I started to say, but was cut off when Disin barked at me.

"I said silence!"

Theo's thumb rubbed on the top of my hand, an iota of comfort in a sea of distress. The three women leaned together.

They're going to throw us in that Akasha place, I said to Theo. His fingers twitched in response. Around us, the hum of conversation was conducted in hushed whispers, but vehement nonetheless. *I know you can't answer me, but they can't stop me from talking to you. I'm sorry if I made things worse, but you have to see that I couldn't just stand here while they twisted everything around.*

He may have been bound to silence, but his emotions were mine to read, and I took some small comfort in the pride that tinged his concern.

"Portia Harding, your insolence does you no credit, nor will it be tolerated," Disin said as the mare presented a solid front.

Thunder rumbled even louder, the sky so dark it looked like twilight even though it was the middle of the day. I took another deep breath, and calmed my wildly beating heart, hoping it was enough to keep a storm from lashing out against the people who were trying us.

"Against my better judgment"—Disin glanced for a moment at the white-haired mare—"I have been persuaded that the evidence against you is not sufficient to banish you to the Akasha. However, until the matter of the virtue's murder has been explained to our satisfaction, we cannot allow you the freedom to harm others."

I bit my lip to keep from shouting that I hadn't harmed anyone, and had no intentions of doing so.

"It has been suggested that you undergo the fifth trial now in order to determine the purity of your being. If you pass, you will be allowed to leave the Court until such time as a tribunal determines the truth of the virtue's death." Disin clapped her hands, and a small boy emerged from the crowd. The boy bowed to the three mare, then turned and bowed to me. He couldn't have been more than eight or nine, but the look in his dark eyes was one of ageless wisdom. Whatever he was, he certainly wasn't an innocent child. "Proctor, begin the trial."

The boy looked at me for a moment before gesturing Theo away. "You cannot aid her in this test, champion. You must move out of her reach."

Theo's voice was warm and reassuring in my head. *I will not leave your side if you do not wish for me to do so.*

It's OK. I tried to put a lot more confidence into my words than I felt. *I doubt if they will do anything too heinous in front of all these witnesses.*

Theo moved away reluctantly, stepping back to stand with the onlookers. I bit my lip nervously, rubbing my hands together as I wondered just what this trial was going to consist of. "Er . . . forgive me for asking, but how on earth do you determine the purity of someone's being?"

"It's simple," the boy said, smiling a gap-toothed smile that did little to lighten my heart. He spread his hands wide, then brought them together so quickly that his movement was unseen. "You die."

The blast from his hands hit me with the force of a runaway bulldozer. I fell backward, the sound of my own terrified shriek mingled with Theo's hoarse roar ringing in my ears as I left everything I knew behind.

Chapter 15

"So this is limbo," I said, looking around. I wasn't much impressed.

"The word 'limbo' is a mortal term used by some religions to express the concept of the Akasha, something most people have difficulty understanding," the small boy next to me said as we walked down a rocky hillside. He waved his hand at the sparse landscape around us. "The Akasha is more than limbo. It is a place few visit, and from which even fewer return."

"Really? What sorts of things do people have to do to get sent here?"

The boy's face gave away no emotion. "The Akasha is a place of punishment, Portia Harding. The ultimate place of punishment. To my memory, the sovereign has granted respite from its confines to only three people."

"Only three in that many millions of years?" I shivered. "Right, so note to self—don't do anything to piss the mare off enough to be sent here."

"That would be a very wise policy to follow. If you would walk this way."

I obligingly followed him as he carefully picked a way through a rocky stretch that led to a faint path. "The last thing I remember before I found myself here was you saying I had to die. Are you implying that I'm dead?"

He tipped his head to the side for a moment, then continued walking. "Do you feel dead?"

"No. I feel annoyed." Ahead of us, in a shallow valley, a large outcropping of rock jutted out of the earth. The wind whipped around us, cutting through my clothing and stinging my flesh with tiny little whips of pain. "And cold. What are we doing here?"

"This is the site of your trial. As you implied, it is difficult for the layperson to weigh the purity of someone's being."

I stumbled over a clod of earth, quickly regaining my balance, but looking warily at the rocky outcropping as we slowly wound our way through the deserted valley floor toward it. "So you decided on a trial by endurance, is that it? If I make it to those rocks there in one piece, I pass the trial?"

To my complete surprise, the boy nodded his head. "Yes. That's it exactly."

I slid a few feet down a graveled slope, my arms cartwheeling as I struggled to maintain my balance. "You're kidding!"

"No, indeed I'm not." He stopped next to a spiky, stunted, leafless shrub, and nodded toward the outcropping. "I can take you no further. The rest of this trial you must conduct on your own. The circle of Akasha there is your goal. Good luck, Portia Harding."

The unspoken words, "You're going to need it," hung in the air, but I ignored them as I eyeballed the rocks approximately three hundred feet away. I decided a little mental support was in order, and reached out my mind to Theo. *I'm not so proud I can't admit that I'm a bit frightened by this. They can't do anything to permanently harm me, can they?*

The wind was all the answer I had.

Theo? Are you there?

My words evaporated into nothing. It was as if he didn't exist.

"Why can't I talk to Theo?" I asked the boy.

He seemed to know that I was referring to our mental form of communication. "Such a thing is not possible in the Akasha."

"Lovely. So, I just walk there? That's all I do?"

"Yes. Once you reach the circle of Akasha, the trial will be over."

"And I'll be sent back to the Court?" Something wasn't right here. It couldn't be this easy. Could it?

"That depends on you," he said enigmatically.

I opened my mouth to ask him a question or five, but decided that stalling would do nothing but give me a case of exposure in this horrible cold. I rubbed my hands on my arms briskly, nodded, and took four steps forward.

From the depths of the circle of stone, three shapes emerged. They were black and curiously flat as their silhouettes stood starkly against the white stones. At the sight of them, my feet stopped moving, and I found myself suddenly drenched in a cold sweat.

"Uh . . . who are they?" I asked over my shoulder.

The boy smiled, his eyes sad. "Hashmallim."

Hashmallim. The word struck a chord of dread deep inside of me. Theo had spoken of them as being a danger to Sarah and me, and now I was expected to walk right up to a couple of them and . . . do what? Talk to them?

"What do they want? Why are they there? Am I supposed to do something with them?"

"You must walk to the center of the circle of Akasha," the boy repeated. "The trial will be over if you do that."

I swallowed down a thick lump of fear. "I don't suppose there's an alternative to this trial?"

He didn't answer.

"There never is," I muttered to myself, taking a deep breath as I tried to calm my frazzled nerves. A quick glance overhead confused me—where was my friendly little cloud that rained down destruction on those who angered me?

"Your Gift has no power here," the boy answered, just as if I had asked the question out loud. "I should add that there is a time limit to this trial. You have exactly two minutes."

I opened my mouth to protest, but the sight of those three black figures standing next to the rocks dried up the complaint I was about to make. Dread and horror, sickening in their intensity, washed over me. It took some doing, but I managed to get my feet moving again.

"Let's reason this through," I told myself, my eyes fixed on the three still figures as I slowly approached them, my steps lagging noticeably as the seconds ticked by. "Given the premise that virtues exist, we must conclude that other people have passed these trials, thus they can't be lethal."

"Only mortals must pass the trials," the boy called after me. "Immortals simply apply, and are interviewed for the positions."

"Not helping!" I yelled back, my thoughts sour as I forced myself to take another step. The sense of dread increased with each footstep, swamping me with the knowledge that I was doomed, Theo was doomed, everyone I ever knew or loved was doomed. I wanted to sit down on the rocky ground and sob myself into insensitivity, that certain was I that it was all for nothing.

"Get a grip, Portia," I lectured myself, fighting with the bile that wanted to rise as I watched the three black figures getting closer. What I thought were three people standing in silhouette turned out to be partly correct—they were people-shaped silhouettes . . . but nothing more. They weren't people standing in shadow. They weren't darkened versions of people, with vaguely discernable features. No, the Hashmallim were just inky black voids, as if they were two-dimensional representations of people. They were all the more frightening for the impossibility of their appearance. "There are approximately twenty steps left. You can do it one step at a time."

I took another six steps forward, then froze into place at the sure knowledge that I was going to my death. "No," I told myself, fighting down the mass of emotions that roiled inside me. "This can't be lethal. It's just an illusion, like so many other things."

The things I'd believed to be illusions had turned out to be real, my mind argued with me, so why should this be any different?

"Time is passing."

"Yeah, yeah."

Ahead of me, the rocks with their three horrible figures loomed before me. The best offense is defense, right?

"You're not so bad," I yelled at the three presences. I wrapped my arms around my waist and made myself take several steps forward. "You may think you can frighten me to death, but I'm tougher than I look! So you can put that in your big, scary pipes and smoke it!"

The rocks loomed above me as I approached with dragging footsteps. I panted with the effort to keep from vomiting, my brain shrieking warnings about self-preservation. I ignored them, taking another couple of steps forward until just a few yards separated the rocks and the Hashmallim from me. They were vague, black shapes now, shifting in opacity and shape, occasional glimpses of haunted, pale faces flickering into view before melting into nothing.

I wanted to run as far away as possible. I wanted to cry and curl up into a fetal ball. I wanted it all to go away.

I wanted Theo.

The Hashmallim seemed to block the path through the stones.

"What do I do now?" I yelled to the boy.

"Simply go through them to the center."

"Simple, my ass," I grumbled to myself, desperately trying to keep my feet pointed toward the horrors in front of me. "There's nothing simple about this. I doubt if the word exists around here."

I took another step forward. The nearest Hashmallim seemed to swell up, looming over me, drenching me in fear, loathing, terror, and a hundred other emotions that had me seriously wishing for death.

"I may have neglected to mention that only the pure of being can pass by the Hashmallim," the boy called to me, his voice thin and reedy on the increasing wind. "Those who are not pure . . ."

"Sweet sanity, he couldn't have mentioned that earlier?" I took a deep breath, my body racked with trembling so great that my teeth chattered as I yelled back, "What happens to them?"

"They do not leave."

A thousand and one sins flashed before my eyes, things I'd done in my life of which I was not proud, starting with a favorite toy I refused to share with a childhood friend, and ending with the loss of Theo's soul. Was I now being called to account for them? The thought of remaining in that place for eternity was almost enough to bring me to my knees, but just as I was convinced I couldn't do it, that I couldn't pass by the three Hashmallim, an image of Theo came to my mind. Theo laughing at a silly joke, Theo's face tight with passion as he found his release, Theo sleepy and adorable and so endearing it made tears prick behind my eyes. If I failed, I'd never see him again.

Theo loved me. I knew he did; I felt it in the soft touches of his mind against mine. And what was more, at that moment I knew with the certainty that I knew the Greisen-Zatsepin-Kuzmin limit was 5×10^{19} electron volts that I loved Theo with every molecule in my body. Surely I couldn't love someone so deeply, so completely, so absolutely without having some redeeming qualities?

I lifted my chin and stiffened my back, holding my gaze firm on the nearest Hashmallim as I took the hardest step forward I'd ever taken. "I am not a bad person. I have done some things in my life that I regret, but I am not evil. I don't abuse animals or children. I don't steal, try not to lie, and only kill really nasty bugs that are attempting to sting me. In a world divided into shades of good and bad, I am a good."

The Hashmallim didn't move as I forced my legs to move, closing my eyes as I brushed up against the edge of one of them. I fought to hold onto the knowledge that I was myself, a person with flaws and errors in judgment, but fundamentally good at heart.

The ground slipped out from under my feet, and I felt myself falling. I opened my eyes to stare unbelievingly at the grassy lawn of the Petitioner's Park as it zoomed up to meet me. The stone benches, the people standing around watching, Theo crouching on the ground over an inert body—they all rushed up to me until I realized I was actually plummeting down to the earth.

"Aieeeeeeeee," I screamed, my arms and legs flailing wildly.

Theo leaped back from the body on the ground as it disappeared, looking up toward me. I had a moment to see stark astonishment on his face.

"Catch me!" I yelled.

He leaped forward, his arms out.

I hit the ground a foot away from him, my fall somewhat broken by the soft lawn. It wasn't so soft that it cushioned me entirely, though. I lay facedown, spitting out bits of lawn, my head spinning, my chest aching, all the air having been slammed out of my lungs.

"Portia! *Salus invenitur!* Tell me you're all right!"

I lifted my head to glare at him, spitting out another mouthful of grass. "Exactly what part of 'catch me' wasn't clear to you?"

"Woman, you will be the death of me yet," he said, pulling me up to an embrace that would have broken the ribs of a lesser woman.

"*I'm* going to be the death of *you*?" I looked pointedly at the Portia-shaped faint indentation made on the lawn.

"I'm sorry," he said, his lips twitching as he hugged me again. *I thought I'd lost you.*

I'm not so easy to do in, I said, kissing him back when his lips found mine. *Ow.*

How badly are you hurt?

I doubt it's anything major. I wouldn't want to ravish you on the spot if it was, would I?

He chuckled in my mind. *The desire is mutual, you know. What happened to you?*

I ran into a couple Hashmallim.

You what?

"It would appear you have passed the fifth trial," Disin said as Theo helped me to my feet.

I brushed off bits of grass and dirt, straightening up slowly. Other than an ache in my chest and knees where I'd struck the ground, I seemed to be relatively unharmed, which was amazing considering the fall I'd taken. "So I gather."

It was small of me, I know, but I found satisfaction in the fact that Disin looked nonplussed.

"This result is not what we anticipated," she continued. "We will discuss the ramifications."

The three mare leaned together. Around us, the crowd was oddly hushed, the expressions on most of the faces present making it clear that few people had expected me to pass the fifth trial. I took satisfaction in their surprise, as well.

"What did the Hashmallim do to you?" Theo asked, brushing a strand of grass from my hair.

"Other than almost scaring the pee right out of me? Nothing. Oh, there was the fact that they returned me to the Court a good forty feet above the ground, but that point pales in relation to the fact that I didn't die from the drop. Why wasn't I more seriously injured? I'm not immortal yet, am I?"

"Not in so many words. You bear the gift of a virtue, though, so that makes you more or less an immortal candidate. You have a bit more stamina than you had before."

"I'm not going to bicker about that," I said, pressing carefully on my ribs. Already the pain was diminishing.

"We have come to a decision," Disin said, gesturing toward me.

I took Theo's hand, my fingers twining through his.

"Child, come forward." Irina, the white-haired mare, nodded at me.

Disin had her mouth open, as if she was about to speak, but she snapped her teeth closed at Irina's words.

Theo and I walked to the old woman.

"You are too tall. Sit." She waved a hand gnarled by arthritis toward the grass at her feet.

We knelt before her. She took Theo's face in both her hands, peering intently into his eyes. I felt a jolt of surprise in him at her examination.

What is it? I asked.

Before he could answer, Irina nodded at Theo and released his face, only to take my chin in a surprisingly strong grip. She tilted my head back so she could look deep into my eyes.

The impact of her gaze on mine shook me to my toenails. If was as if she was seeing everything I was, stripping away all the layers of societal mores and pretenses, of protective layers, exposing my true core to her faded eyes.

"Child, you are lost," she said, still examining me. I felt like a squirming beetle pinned to a board. "Your path is hidden. You have much to do to find it, but I believe you will. You will be released to do just that."

Irina released my chin, using both hands on her cane to push herself to her feet. I wobbled forward for a moment, almost dizzy with the relief of having the soul-stripping ended. Theo grabbed my arm, and pulled me up to my feet.

The other two mare stood as well.

"It is decided that the mortal known as Portia Harding will be released," Disin said in a loud voice, her eyes cold as she turned to me. "The Hashmallim have deemed your being pure, thus you will not be held. Your behavior in this place, however, is beyond tolerance. You are hereby banned from the Court of Divine Blood."

A hundred whispered comments rippled the air behind us.

Thank them, Theo ordered.

"Thank you for your generosity," I said, trying hard to keep any trace of the sarcasm I felt from lacing my words. I turned to leave, but Disin stopped me.

"You may have passed the fifth trial, Portia Harding, but you have not satisfied us that you do not have some involvement in the death of the virtue named Hope."

"I haven't . . ." I shook my head, confused. "I don't understand. Doesn't passing the test prove I have a pure heart? How can I have a pure heart and have murdered Hope?"

Disin's lips tightened. "Even purity is subjective to interpretation. What we call a heartless murder, you may truly believe is for the better good. Thus, it is entirely possible that in your mind your heart is pure."

"But . . ."

"If you did not kill Hope, the onus is upon you to prove who did," Disin interrupted. "Should you fail to do so by the new moon, you will be stripped of the Gift given to you, and banished from the Court forever."

When's the new moon? I asked Theo, more than a little stunned by the mare's demand.

I'm not sure. A week, I think. Perhaps two.

Like we don't have enough to do, now we have to figure out what happened to Hope?

I'm afraid we're not going to have much of a choice.

"I am a physicist, not a detective," I told Disin. "Don't you people have some sort of a police force that would be better suited to investigate her death? Aren't those Hashmallim guys your security people?"

"If you are not responsible for her death, then you are in the best position to determine who did cause it," Disin said dismissively.

"But I have no experience finding murderers—"

"You summoned Hope and accepted her position. With that goes responsibility."

I felt like screaming. Did no one else see the error in her logic? "I understand that, but it doesn't follow that I'll know how to find out who killed her."

Portia, do not continue. It will do no good; they've made up their minds.

But I don't know the first thing about detecting!

Then we will learn. Thank the mare.

They're using me as a scapegoat, you know.

I know. But we have no choice.

He had a point.

"Thank you again for your generosity," I said,

hoping that the sarcasm which laced my thoughts wasn't evident in my words.

Disin inclined her head, and left the park with the other two mare.

The officious little man who had started the hearing bustled up to us as the remaining crowd dispersed to their various destinations. "You must leave the Court now. I will escort you to the exit."

"We can find our own way out—" I started to say.

"I will escort you," he said with a meaningful look in his eye.

We suffered his presence in silence as we walked through the cobblestoned streets to the wooden doorway that led back to the normal world. I stepped through the doorway, back to the small, unused office, and with my return, the weight of the world seemed to descend upon my shoulders.

"Now what do we do?" I asked, hopelessness welling within me.

Theo smiled and kissed the tips of my fingers on the hand he still held. "Now, sweetling, we find a murderer."

"I don't know the first thing about solving a murder . . ." I smiled as a thought struck me. "But I know someone who used to write mysteries before she switched to romances."

Chapter 16

"Right, the first thing we need to do is make a list of people who wanted Hope dead." Sarah sucked thoughtfully at the end of her pen, then quickly wrote down my name at the top of a sheet of paper.

"Hey!" I protested. "Didn't you hear a thing I've said for the last hour? I did not kill Hope, which you of all people should know."

"Of course I know it. But all good detectives make a list of all possible suspects, then eliminate them one by one until only one person remains on the list—the killer. What was the name of that man who tried to seduce you?"

I slumped across the table we had commandeered in the corner of the pub upon returning to town, my forehead in my hands. Theo sat next to me, looking wistfully at someone a few tables away who was sipping a whisky and soda. "No one tried to seduce me except Theo, and I seduced him right back. Oh, wait, you mean Gabriel the cherub?"

"That's the fellow." Sarah added his name to the

list, tapped the pen on her lips for a moment while she thought, and added the names of the trial proctors I'd had to date. "Who else have you met?"

"Sarah, you can't list everyone I've run across," I protested.

"Don't be silly; that's how it works. Let's see, so far we have you and Theo, included for thoroughness, a Guardian, three trial proctors, one demon, and the prince of hell. Anyone else?"

I sighed. "There is no cast of characters you can run down, you know."

"Yuh-huh. If you didn't murder Hope, and I agree that's highly unlikely, then someone you've met must have."

The barmaid walked past with a tray holding two glasses of wine and a couple of mixed drinks. Theo's gaze watched the drink tray with an avidity that bespoke a hunger of a different sort than we'd fulfilled before meeting with Sarah.

"This is not one of your books, Sarah. This is real life, my life, and there's no earthly reason to believe that whoever killed Hope is someone I've met."

The pub owner walked behind the bar and set a pint glass beneath a Guinness tap, the thick blackish-brown liquid slowly filling the glass. Theo moaned softly to himself.

"Would you like me to get you a beverage?" I asked him.

His Adam's apple bobbed up and down as he swallowed. It took some doing, but he managed to drag his eyes off the pub owner and turn them to me, shaking his head. "Christian said I shouldn't until I'm used to the new diet."

I rubbed the leg that pressed against mine, enjoying the flex of his thigh muscles as much as I knew he was.

"Interesting," Sarah said, watching Theo for a moment before making another note. "Can't drink anything but blood. Very interesting."

"Portia's right," he said, ignoring Sarah's note-taking to frown at the tabletop. "We don't know that the person who killed Hope is someone we've encountered in the last few days. We don't even know when or where or how Hope died. For that matter, we don't know if she's really dead. No one has found her body. What we need is solid information, upon which we can base an investigation."

My heart swelled with delight. *I love it when you are logical.*

I'm always logical!

Not always, but when you are, it makes my toes curl.

He gave me a mental eye roll that had me giggling to myself.

"I suppose," Sarah admitted, pulling my attention back to the matter at hand.

"I agree, it makes sense. Who can we go to in order to get that info?"

Theo averted his eyes as the barmaid walked past with a large martini. "Most of the people who would have access to that information are in the Court of Divine Blood. But with the ban in place, they are out of reach to us."

"I thought only Portia was banned?" Sarah asked.

"Technically, she was, but I am her champion, and thus represent her. The ban extends to me, as well."

"Assuming Hope was killed outside of the Court, there has to be someone out here who we could ask." I looked at Theo. "This is all new to me, so I'm less than helpful when it comes to naming names. Is there someone outside the Court you can think of who we can talk to?"

His eyes lightened, taking on a wary cast.

"What?" I asked him.

"There is a potential source of information," he said slowly.

"Oh? Who?"

"It's not someone you're going to want to see again."

I thought back over the people I'd met in the last few days, and shook my head. "Oh, no. I will not go to hell and see Bael again."

"Not Bael," Theo said, his fingers stroking mine.

"The demon then, what's his name—Nefere. He's almost as bad as Bael."

Theo shook his head. "Not Nefere."

A cold, sick feel crept out of my belly and slipped into my veins. "Sweet mother of reason, you don't mean . . . you can't mean . . . please tell me you don't mean them, Theo."

"I'm sorry, sweetling. The Hashmallim are the only ones who we can approach."

"No."

"They are more or less the security force of the Court, which gives them the power to come and go as they please. All we have to do is convince one to speak with us outside of the Court."

"Absolutely not."

"They seldom come to the mortal world, but if we can—"

"No!"

He gave my hand a reassuring squeeze. "I won't leave you alone with them this time."

"I know you're not, because I'm not going to be anywhere near them."

"The Hashmallim? Those creepy guys that Portia said are made up of silhouettes?" Sarah's eyes widened, a look of delight brightening her face. "Oh, I can't wait to meet them! I have so many questions! Like, why were they chasing us that day we met?"

Theo cleared his throat and studied his hands for a moment. "They weren't actually . . . er . . . chasing you."

"They weren't?" I asked.

"Er . . . no."

"But, you said at the time—"

His hands brushed off my question. "Yes, yes, I said that they were, but I couldn't think of any other way to convince the two of you to come with me."

"So they weren't even there?" I asked, hands on my hips.

"We weren't in any danger?" Sarah asked at the same time.

"They were there. Even unused to the ways of the Court, you two must have felt their arrival. They were following Hope."

"That's right," I said slowly. "She mentioned

someone was chasing her. I thought later it was you."

"It was me . . . but the Hashmallim were also trying to find her."

Sarah clasped her hands together. "What'd she do? Something horrible?"

"It's some minor point of Court politics that she avoided mentioning to the proper authorities. The Hashmallim were sent to interview her regarding it."

"Well, I don't care about that. I just want to talk to one of the big scary guys. When can we?" Sarah asked.

"Never!" I said, squeezing Theo's hand back, and not with reassurance, either.

Sweetling, I wouldn't put you through this unless it was the only way.

Theo, I know you've been around a long time, but you have no idea how horrible those guys are up close. They're indescribably awful! It made me physically ill to be near them!

The smile he gave me was sad. *I'm well aware of the Hashmallim, my love. Who do you think was responsible for throwing me out of the Court the only other time I was there?*

"You guys are doing that mind-talking thing again, aren't you?" Sarah asked, narrowing her eyes at us.

"I'm simply trying to convince Portia that the Hashmallim are our only hope of getting some answers," Theo said. *You do believe me, don't you?*

I believe that you believe what you are saying, I answered, well aware I was sounding unreasonably stubborn. The memory of my experience with the Hashmallim was too fresh in my mind, however.

"Don't mind her, she's as stubborn as the day is long," Sarah said, tucking away her notepad. "There's just one thing I'm curious about."

"Just one?" I asked.

Sarah gave me a look that said she didn't appreciate the sarcasm in my voice, turning a sunny smile on Theo when he politely asked what was her question. "Correct me if I'm wrong, but these Hashmallim guys are the same ones that you said were dangerous when we first met, right?"

Theo nodded.

"You said you were saving our lives by getting us out of their way."

"Hashmallim are more or less the police force for the Court of Divine Blood, but their job encompasses more than just policing citizens of the Court. They are also used by the sovereign to exact retribution on mortals for sins committed against members of the Court."

"We didn't do anything to anyone, let alone a Court member," I pointed out. "We were just standing around on the hilltop when Hope appeared, and she left under her own power."

"I didn't know that at the time," Theo said with a slight twist of his lips. "As soon as you said you were mortal, and yet were clearly a virtue, I reckoned something was not right. When I felt the Hashmallim on their way, I knew it wasn't anything good, so I tried to get you away from them."

"That's so romantic," Sarah said, sighing happily.

"It is?"

"Yes, it is. Don't you see? These Hashmallim people are the police in the Court of Divine Blood, and by going against them, he was risking his own reputation, if not life."

I was shaking my head even before she finished. "Theo isn't a member of the Court."

"Not yet. But when he does become one, won't that sort of thing be frowned on?"

We both looked at Theo.

"Assuming the Hashmallim know I helped you escape earlier, and that's a pretty fair assumption given their scope of knowledge, yes, it will be one of the issues we will have to overcome in order to get the exculpation granted," he said calmly. I decided if it wasn't something he was worried over, I didn't need to worry about it yet either.

"All right, then. How do we find the Hashmallim?" Sarah asked him.

"They can be summoned."

"What makes you think that even if you get one to be summoned, he will talk to you?" I asked.

Theo frowned. I wanted badly to forget all the woes of the world and kiss the frown right off his face. "There is no reason for them not to. So long as the questions are phrased properly, we should get the answers we seek."

"Great! Let's get to summoning," Sarah said, grabbing her purse as she rose. "I'll take care of our lunch bill. You guys get your coats."

"I believe she's the only person I've met who is actually looking forward to meeting with the Hashmallim," Theo said thoughtfully, watching Sarah as she toddled over to the pub counter and handed over her credit card.

"She's not normal. She was dropped on her head several times as a baby. It left her mentally deranged. We all just pretend she's sane."

"I heard that!" she shouted, glaring at me from the counter.

"She also has very good hearing," I said, sighing as I gathered up my things.

"It'll be all right, sweet. I'll be with you this time," Theo reminded me.

It took some doing, but Theo's powers of persuasion proved to be too much for the Guardian named Noelle who had previously summoned the ill-fated demon.

"Now what happens?" I asked several hours later, as we sat huddled on a fallen tree trunk that edged one side of an empty gravel parking lot for an abandoned fish factory at the far side of town.

Noelle rubbed out the markings she'd drawn in the gravel and dirt with the toe of her shoe. "Now you wait. The Hashmallim has been summoned—he will show up whenever he wants. Is there anything else I can help you with?"

"No, thank you for your time," Theo said, rising to shake her hand. "Er . . . you didn't tell me what payment we owe you for your help."

"Oh, don't worry about that," Noelle said, giving us all a bright smile. It was dark in that corner of the parking lot, long flickering shadows stretching across it from the feeble light attached near a corner of the building, but Noelle's down-to-earth appearance and cheerful personality did much to eliminate the serious case of the creeps I'd had ever since I resigned myself to the thought of having to speak with one of the ghostly Hashmallim. "I get a stipend from the Guardian Guild to be used on such cases as I deem needy. You lot look like you could use a bit of good news, so this one will be complimentary."

We all thanked her. Theo escorted her across the parking lot to where her little blue Mini sat.

"You got yourself a winner this time," Sarah said as she watched them walk away. "What does it feel like being a Dark One's Beloved?"

Theo's mind touched mine, warm and reassuring, filled with tender emotions that made my stomach flutter with happiness. "It's . . . indescribable."

She peered closer at me. "You love him, don't you?"

"Yes." I smiled, unable to keep the happiness from spilling out of me. "More than any other man. We had a less-than-sterling start, but I know now that he's the man I was meant to be with."

"That's so romantic," she said with a sigh. "Does it hurt when he bites you?"

"Just for a second, then it's really . . . well, to be blunt, it's pretty darn erotic."

"Oh, man." She pursed her lips and looked at Theo as he stood chatting with Noelle. "You have a gorgeous, drop-dead-sexy man who clearly worships the ground you walk on, you're never going to age, never face sagging boobs and menopause and grey hair, and you get your jollies every time he needs to eat. Do you have any idea how lucky you are?"

"As a matter of fact, I—holy cow!"

Some sort of a shimmering portal opened up directly in front of me, so close I felt static from the little snakes of electricity that sparked off it. I fell backward off the log as an empty black shape formed almost directly on top of me, the sudden skin-crawling *wrongness* of the Hashmallim bursting to life in my brain.

Theo! I screamed as I crawled backward, trying to avoid contact with the Hashmallim. Panic filled me, threatening to send me teetering over the edge of control. "Theo!"

"I'm here," he said, racing over to me, stepping between the still-approaching Hashmallim and myself. Somehow, his body seemed to block some of the horrible sensations the Hashmallim's presence was causing, leaving me able to dampen the rest enough so I could get to my feet.

"Wow," Sarah said, her expression a mixture of curiosity and terror. She grabbed my arm and clung on with a grip that would no doubt leave bruises. "OK, I see what you mean about them being unpleasant to be around. They look . . . *wrong* somehow. Just wrong. Like they're empty black shells of what people are. I think I'm going to forgo my interview."

I swallowed down a thick lump that made my throat ache, moving closer to Theo. I'm sure the picture we presented—the three of us clumped up together in a tight bunch—was amusing, but that was the furthest thing from my mind at the moment.

"Hashmallim, you honor us with your presence,"

Theo said in a strained voice, his usual elegant bow coming out a bit less than perfect.

"Why am I summoned, champion?" The Hashmallim's voice matched its image—flat and devoid of all emotion, yet awful at the same time.

"Oh my god, it has nothing, absolutely nothing in it," Sarah whispered in my ear as she clung to my back. "Not a face, not a shadow, not even a glimmer of depth."

I held onto Theo, silently drawing comfort from his broad, strong back.

"This is so amazing. I've never seen anything like it. It would be a bad idea to take a picture, wouldn't it?"

"Very." I struggled with the impossibility that was the Hashmallim, aware that as it had before, its very presence seemed to fill the surroundings with despair.

"We seek answers that only you can give us," Theo said, his voice steady. My awe and appreciation of him went up another few notches. "We would like information about the virtue Hope."

The Hashmallim's shape seemed to shimmer for a moment, then moved to the side to *look* at me, if such a thing was possible. Sarah gasped, and hid behind me. I knew just how she felt—at that moment, I would have just about given anything to close my eyes and hide from the Hashmallim. "What do you seek, Portia Harding?"

I swallowed down my fear, pulling strength from the comfort Theo silently offered me. "We seek the name of the murderer of Hope. I don't suppose your investigations have led you to a conclusion about that?"

The Hashmallim seemed to swell, blotting out the night sky around us.

"I think I'm going to be sick," Sarah muttered, and ran for the grassy verge beyond the parking lot. I fought down the bile that rose in my own throat, struggling to keep control of my emotions.

"That of which you speak does not exist," the Hashmallim said, its form twisting and turning upon itself in an endless dance of horror.

"Are there any suspects?" I asked, trying desperately to remember the list of questions we'd agreed to ask.

"Portia Harding."

"Other than me," I said, clinging to Theo, drinking in the warmth of his body.

"That which you seek does not exist."

That's the second time he's said that. What does it mean? I asked Theo.

It means something is up, he answered slowly, his mind busily sorting through ideas. I gave him full marks for being able to think while confronting the abomination before us.

I mentally girded my loins, and ventured another question. "Exactly when was she killed?"

"That which you seek does not exist."

If I wasn't at the point where I could quite possibly die of fear, I'd be annoyed at that.

Hmm. Interesting. Theo's words were thoughtful. "Do you mean that Hope was not murdered, that she died from other causes?"

The Hashmallim continued to face me, violating every rule of physics, its flat nothingness sucking the gaze in and holding it. "That which you seek does not exist."

An idea bloomed in my head. I could tell by the dawning enlightenment in Theo's face that it occurred to him, as well.

I cleared my throat. "Are you saying, then, that Hope has not died?"

"Confirmation," the Hashmallim said.

She's not dead, I said in stunned disbelief. *Why does everyone think she's dead if she's not?*

I don't know, but I intend to find out.

"Where is the virtue known as Hope?" Theo asked the Hashmallim.

"The answer you seek does not exist. The summoning is at an end." In front of Theo, the portal sparked to life again. The Hashmallim drifted toward it, clearly intending on returning to wherever it had originated.

"Wait a second," I said, moving around in front of Theo. The resulting wave of revolting nausea left me staggering against him. "You can't just leave like that. You're the Court police! There has to be something you can tell us about Hope."

The Hashmallim flickered for a moment at the edge of the portal. "In order to succeed, you must first destroy."

Both the Hashmallim and the portal disappeared without any further ado.

"What in the name of Stephen Hawking is *that* supposed to mean?" I asked Theo.

"I have no idea. This Hashmallim wasn't particularly inclined to give answers, it appears."

Slowly, the horror within me began to fade. Anger quickly replaced it.

"Sweet mother of sanity," I swore, looking at the spot the Hashmallim had occupied. "So help me, once I have your soul back, and this thing with Hope is cleared up, if I ever want to get involved in anything to do with the Court, you have my full permission to beat me senseless."

Chapter 17

"This is downright creepy."

"Meh." I made a half-hearted shrugging motion to accompany the word, trudging along behind the group of people who chattered in excited whispers, occasional startled gasps punctuating their conversation.

Sarah stopped to give me a gimlet eye. "Meh? Meh! This is not in the least bit meh!"

"You're talking to someone who has been to hell itself, and had a chat with the man in charge, not to mention facing down a gauntlet of Hashmallim, which in my humble opinion is a thousand times worse than the aforementioned demon lord. Something so simple as a haunted house holds no fear to the likes of me."

"I almost liked you better when you were a pig-headed skeptic," she answered, making a face.

"Oh, I'm still a skeptic . . . about most things I am. There are some I won't dispute fall well out of the bounds of what can be explained by existing science," I answered, obediently stopping when the ghost-hunting group leader waved everyone to a halt. "I haven't seen any proof yet that this house is anything other than extremely old and"—I sniffed the air—"evidently inhabited by a very large family of rodents. I wish Theo was here."

"That's the third time in an hour you've said that—ooh, what was that?"

"Sorry, that was me," one of the men in the group called out, sheepishly answering a cell phone that had made an odd buzzing noise.

"Fine, I'll take it back. I don't wish Theo was here—I wish I was with him, instead."

"We'll wait here for the two missing members," the group leader announced in a loud whisper. "They're just outside the building. I'll go meet them at the door and escort them here. While we're waiting, let's take a few baseline readings of this upper floor. Those of you on the communication team may want to get into your meditative states and see if any entities contact you."

"People in a new relationship are always so cloying," Sarah said as she sank down gracefully into a lotus position, adopting a peaceful look on her face despite the cold, damp, and rodent-infested ambiance of the three-hundred-year-old mill we were presently occupying. "You don't see Anthony and me clinging to each other."

I plopped down next to her with considerably less elegance. "You've been married sixteen years. I assume by the time Theo and I have been together that long, I won't mind if he spends the evening off

doing mysterious things that he refuses to tell me
about except to say that he hopes it will give us
some direction regarding the whole Hope situation."

"Hush. I'm meditating."

I hugged my knees as I sat next to a softly humming Sarah, shivering slightly in the cold midnight
air. We were on the top floor of one of the oldest
standing mills in England, a notoriously haunted mill
which had a checkered past that supposedly included
several murders, three suicides, and during the 1970s,
a rash of Satanic rituals. The interior of the mill
wasn't anything special to look at—for the last hundred years it had alternately been used as office
space, apartments, and, finally, storage. Although I
didn't have the paranormal radar that Theo assured
me would come with time, I didn't sense anything in
the building that felt remotely different.

"Hey, look," I said softly, nudging Sarah with my
elbow. The group leader, puffing slightly at all the
stairs, emerged from the staircase with the two late-
comers in tow. "It's Milo from the séance."

"Mmmhmm. They belong to the group, I believe."

"I'm going to say hi." I got up and went over to
the newcomers with a smile. Milo introduced his
wife, who gave me a curt nod before exclaiming that
she wanted to spend a few minutes communing with
the spirits of the mill.

"The wife is a believer," Milo said to me in a quiet
voice. We moved to the other end the room, perching
ourselves on a rickety metal table that lurked in a
corner. "I've tried to reason with her, but . . ." He
shrugged.

"I know how that can be. I'm not saying I can't accept that there are some things that seem to escape logical explanation . . ." That was pretty much a given now that my life had become something outside of logic. ". . . but most people don't even try to look for a reason that things happen. If they see a light in the sky, it must be an alien."

"Exactly," Milo agreed, watching the group as they sat in a circle for a group meditation. "Logic, that's the key to it. You seem like a very logical person."

I smiled. "It goes with the territory. I'm a physicist, you see. Logic is more or less my forte."

"Really?" He turned an interested face on me. "You don't happen to like puzzles, do you? The brain teasers? I am mad for them, but seldom have anyone to share them with, since the wife doesn't like that sort of thing."

"Logic puzzles, you mean? Car A leaving Los Angeles at thirty miles an hour, and a train leaving Chicago at sixty, that sort of thing?"

"Well . . . somewhat. I used to belong to a logic puzzle group in university, but have lost touch with most of the members."

"Ah. I'm not much of a puzzler, but those things seem to me to be set up to be easily solved if you just take the proper steps."

"That they are." He looked thoughtful for a moment, then a smile spread across his face as he nodded toward the group in front of us. "Would you like to try one out?"

"A puzzle?"

"Yes. One to do with this group?"

I looked at the six people in front of us. "You're kidding. Logical ghost hunters?"

"Something like that," he said, laughing. "Look, there are five members there, plus your friend Sarah. That's the makings of a logic puzzle."

"I'll take your word for that." I sat back on the table, pleased there was something else to do other than watch ghost hunters communing with spirits. "I don't know if I can match someone who used to make puzzles, but I'll give it a shot."

"That's the ticket! Let's see . . . you know their names, don't you?"

"Actually, I don't. I missed the introductions because I was in the restroom when everyone met at the local restaurant."

"Perfect. I've known these folks for the last eight years, and I can tell you that each of them—this is excepting your friend, of course—live in different towns. Now, let me see, we need a third element, something you can't tell by looking at them . . . hmm. Ah, got it. Each one of these teams has members with a different supposed psychic specialty."

I raised my eyebrows, looking them over again. With my newfound knowledge of things paranormal, I didn't see any signs in them that they were also "in the know," so to speak. "OK. So I'm supposed to guess who has what psychic ability?"

"*Supposed* psychic ability," he said with a wink. "Name, psychic ability, and town, how's that sound?"

"Better than being bored," I laughed. "Let's do it."

"Right, then. The psychometrist and Mr. Brand

both like their tea without milk. The telepathist from Newberry and Mrs. Floring, the medium, don't get along well. The mind reader comes from St. Bartleby."

"Wait, wait, wait," I said, scrabbling around in my purse. "I need some paper to write this all down. Telepathist and Floring, medium, don't get along . . . St. Bartleby . . . OK, go on."

"Now then, Susannah, Mr. Bitters, Michael, the Ouijist, and the person from Learing-on-Bent all usually arrive together. Mrs. Lee and Timothy are always late. Daniel the channeler and Carol sing in a local choir."

"Oh man, this is getting good," I said, writing it all down. "It's just like a logic class I had eons ago in college."

"Daniel Richings doesn't live in Bartleby. Carol doesn't live in Leewardstone."

"England has the best town names . . . got it. Any more?"

"Just one. If you asked Mrs. Lee if she had been with the club longest, she'd say no, that was her friend from Edmonds, with whom she'd grown up in her town of Newberry."

"Hmm. OK. Let me see here . . ." I eyeballed the info I'd written down, decided it was nothing more than mathematics disguised as words, and assigned each bit of information a numerical value, then began to arrange them in equations that made sense.

"Take as long as you need, although it looks like the meditation is about up," Milo said, one eye on the group.

"I almost have it . . . no, wait, that won't work . . . hmm . . . she can't be there and there at the same time . . . aaaaah." I looked up with a smile.

"Figured it out, did you?" Milo asked, a twinkle in his eye.

"I think so. I am cheating a bit in that I can see there are only two women in the group, but even so, it makes sense that since the telepathist is from Newberry, and Mrs. Lee claims the town of Newberry, Mrs. Lee must be the telepath. Since she doesn't arrive with Susannah, then by the process of elimination, Mrs. Lee's first name must be Carol, which means that Mrs. Floring, the medium, is Susannah. She can't come from Newberry, St. Bartleby, or Learing-on-Bent, but could live in Leewardstone or Edmonds."

Milo smiled. My confidence rose.

"Since Mrs. Lee's friend is from Edmonds, and Mrs. Lee and Mrs. Floring don't get along, that means she's from Leewardstone. Daniel Richings doesn't live in Bartleby, nor can he live in Newberry or Leewardstone. Thus he has to live in Edmonds or Learing-on-Bent."

"What on earth are you doing?" Sarah frowned at me. "You're playing games while we are trying to conduct a very serious scientific investigation?"

"Just passing a little time," I said hastily, shoving my sheet of paper at Milo. "Are you all done with your humming?"

"It isn't just humming, it's opening ourselves up to . . . oh, why do I bother? Honestly, Portia, I'd think you could display a little more respect for what we're doing here, given the fact that you are what you now are," she said with a vehement whisper as she pulled me after the assembled group.

I tossed Milo an apologetic smile. He read over my paper, and gave me a thumbs-up, which I interpreted to mean I'd figured out the rest of the puzzle correctly. "Milo and I were just amusing ourselves while you guys were opening up and such. He's some sort of puzzle enthusiast. Did you know that his wife and the other woman don't get along?"

Sarah rolled her eyes and grabbed my wrist, hauling me along after the group. "Come on, we have a room to investigate. Mr. Richings says he has recorded a temperature drop of eight degrees there on three separate occasions."

"Probably just a draft," I muttered, but kept my voice low. I had promised Sarah I'd spend the evening with her temporary ghost hunting group in exchange for her help finding out what happened to Hope, and despite my wishes to be elsewhere at that moment—Theo's arms came to mind as a good alternative—I'd do what I could to see to it that Sarah had an enjoyable evening.

Why do I sense a profound feeling of martyrdom from you?

I smiled at the voice in my head. *I'm feeling particularly saintly tonight.*

Is it that bad?

Nothing I didn't expect. A bunch of people running around with equipment measuring drafts and electromagnetic flux, and jumping at every creak and pop.

It's only for a few hours. I'm sure you will triumph over such exacting circumstances.

Indeed. Why are you talking to me, not that I'm complaining? I thought you didn't want me bothering you?

Sweetling, you never bother me. You do, however, distract me from matters at hand. It's your breasts. And thighs. And lips, and legs, and all the other bits in between. Theo's words were accompanied by such erotic mental images that I found myself getting aroused right there in the middle of a cold, mouse-riddled mill.

If you don't want me running out of here, hunting you down, and wrestling you to the ground to have my way with you, you'd better stop sending me those sorts of thoughts.

Would you really wrestle me to the ground? he asked, sounding intrigued.

Absolutely. How goes the info-hunting?

He sighed. *Not so good. The nephilim I contacted knew nothing.*

Crap. So we don't have any leads?

No, we have one. My nephilim friend mentioned a vessel who evidently was very tight with Hope. But I can't find the man—he seems to have run to earth just like Hope.

A vessel is a person?

In this instance, yes. Vessels serve mortals, under the direct rule of the principalities, who in turn take their orders from powers, and the powers, as you know, are directly beneath the mare.

Sounds very much like the little old woman who swallowed a fly.

Pardon?

Nothing, just a joke, and not a very good one. So what now?

I'm going to continue to try to locate the missing vessel. I'll meet you at the pub after your ghostly group is finished, all right?

I suppose so, although I'd be happy to help you—Sarah would be hurt.

"Portia?"

It was my turn to sigh. *You're right. Saint Portia it is for the night, then.*

His laughter was warm and made me smile despite my cold, uncomfortable surroundings. *You're no saint, sweetling. But we can discuss that later tonight.*

You're on. Take care of yourself, all right?

"Portia!" Sarah shook me, her face suspicious. "You look all moony-eyed again. You must be talking to Theo. Did he find Hope?"

"Not yet, no. He's trying to find some Court member who supposedly is friends with her."

"Ah. Smart man." She flashed me a smile, waggling her eyebrows. "In more ways than one, eh?"

"Absolutely. So what's up with the cold spots?"

Her face lit up. "Oh, it's so exciting! Mr. Richings has measured a drop of eleven degrees in the corner! Come see it!"

I admired the cold spot, keeping the thought to myself that the lack of insulation and patchy repairs in the wall were more likely to contribute to the chilly air than an unseen ghostly presence. While the group excitedly took more measurements and made furious notes, I sidled over to Milo.

"So, is your name Lee or Floring?"

He smiled, holding out his hand. "I don't think we ever were properly introduced, were we? It's Lee, Milo Lee. And Carol, my wife, is over there, but you've already deduced that. It must be all that work in physics that gives you an analytical mind, eh?"

"Oh, I don't know, I think people tend to be born left- or right-brained. You're pretty left-brained yourself. What do you do? As an occupation, that is."

"Customer service for a large corporation. I live to serve," he said, with a hint of an eye roll and a mock bow.

"Ah. That must be challenging. I don't think I could deal with unhappy people for long."

"It's horrible. I've hopes to advance very soon, though, so it's an evil I'll bear a bit longer."

"Good for you. So how long did you say you and your wife have been ghost hunting?"

We passed the next hour chatting about minutiae, both of us watching with indulgent eyes as the ghost group moved from room to room. By the end of the second hour, with nothing to show for their work but some numbers written down from instrument readings, even Sarah's enthusiasm was beginning to drag. We drove back to the pub in relative silence—her in contemplation of the meager proceedings of the evening, and me in anticipation of seeing Theo again.

I went to bed alone, my errant vampire-cum-nephilim still out on his vessel hunt. When I found he wasn't back at the pub, I offered to help him hunt for the Court member, but Theo insisted he was almost done. Even separated by some thirty miles or so, he seemed to sense the exhaustion that was making it hard for me to think. I didn't argue when he ordered me to bed, just sent him an image of what I intended to do to him when he made his way back to me.

My dreams were confused, but much more vivid than I remembered in the past. I woke frequently at little noises in the pub, but, sadly, remained alone. I slipped into a nightmare where giant wasps stung me repeatedly. Slowly it melted into something much more pleasant, the stings of the wasps morphing into little fluttering brushes of wings as the wasps changed into brilliant blue hummingbirds. I writhed with pleasure on the ground, naked, warmed by the sun that shown down with such intensity that I could feel its heat deep inside me, in dark, hidden places that only came to life when Theo was around. The soft, gentle touches of the birds' wings didn't soothe me, however—they made me squirm even harder, leaving me wanting to both escape their oddly erotic touches and pull them tighter to me. One of the birds landed on my belly, giving me a long look with its dark eyes before dipping its head and stabbing at my hip with a long, sharp beak.

"Sweet mother of reason," I gasped, suddenly awake. Theo's head was bent over my hip, his dark curls brushing against my skin as the pain of his teeth piercing my skin was already melting into something so pleasurable I never wanted him to stop. His fingers fluttered for a moment against aroused, sensitive flesh, then plunged inside me in a move that had me arching back into the bed, my hips rising to meet the movement of his fingers.

Salus invenitur, Theo moaned into my mind as he drank deep from me. *You taste sweeter than nectar, Portia. How can something so wonderful hurt so bad at the same time?*

My body tightened around his fingers, blinding me to everything but the need I felt within him, and the answer that lay within me.

"It's too much," he said, lifting his head from my hip. His eyes were black as polished ebony, his face hard with hunger and passion and want.

"No," I said, feeling as if my guts had been strung tight. I pushed him onto his back, and climbed over him. "But this may be."

He tasted as I knew he would—hot, male, and incredibly wonderful, the firm flesh of his penis both silky soft and as hard as steel. He moaned aloud, his head thrown back against the mattress, both hands clutching the sheets beneath us as I took my time exploring him, reading his mind with ease, noting what drove him into a frenzy.

His rising passion and arousal fed mine. The knee I was straddling while I pleasured him jerked beneath me, pressing tight into my own sensitive flesh. The bolt of ecstasy that ripped through me as a result took me by surprise, but not as much as Theo suddenly grabbing my hips and hauling me up his body, thrusting upward into me as he pressed me down. Existence ceased to be, my world, the entire universe, narrowing to the man beneath me who urged me, with little cries of pleasure, to ride him faster.

How did I exist this long without you? Theo asked as his mouth closed over my breast, his teeth sinking deep into my soft flesh at the same time he exploded into a tremendous orgasm, the strength of it pushing me over into my own. His body pulsed and pumped into me while I quite simply ceased to be me, the Portia I'd known for thirty-eight years, and became instead the Portia who was part of Theo. I'd never believed that a woman needed a man to be complete, but this was different. This wasn't a matter of social mores or gender issues, or even the biological need for a mate. I knew to the depths of my soul that Theo enriched me in ways that no other human could, and that knowledge shook me.

It's strange, isn't it? Theo's hands stroked gently up my back as I lay on his chest, my heart thumping wildly in my chest, my breath ragged and jerky against his shoulder. *One minute we're going about our business in life, and the next our beings are so tightly intertwined with someone else's, there's no way to separate them again.*

I don't want them separated, I said without thinking, then realized that what I said sounded weak and cloying.

His hands stilled for a moment. *I could never think you weak, love. You are the strongest woman I know.*

I lifted my head to look into his eyes, half fearing there would be pity or something just as painful in them, but to my relief they were filled only with satiation and an unabashed love that made me want to sing with happiness. *I'd say I was sorry this happened, but I'm not sorry. I regret that your soul has been lost through my ignorance, but even that can't dampen the joy you bring me.*

Silly woman. He pulled me back down onto his chest, his body still buried deep inside me. His lips were sweet against mine, his words sweeter still as they brushed gently against my mind. *What's a soul compared to this?*

Chapter 18

"What are you doing?" Sarah asked, pulling out a chair and sitting down with a smile that was shared between Theo and me.

"Plotting out a battle plan. Good morning, Darla. I'm not feeling myself, so I'll just have toast. I believe Theo wants a traditional breakfast, minus the tomato."

Theo nodded at the waitress. "Indeed I do. With lots of preserves, please."

"Since when do you not eat like a horse at breakfast?" Sarah asked when Darla had toddled off to bring us our breakfast orders.

"Since Theo prefers to appear perfectly normal, right down to eating food. Besides, I'm eating for two," I answered, pushing a piece of paper across the table at her. "This is our plan, so far. What do you think?"

I thought her eyes were going to pop out. "You're eating for two? You're not—"

"No, I meant I'm eating to keep my blood up, so Theo can eat as well."

"Oh. You scared me there for a minute." Sarah sipped at her tea while she read over the list. When she got to the good part, she choked. "You can't be serious!"

"Perfectly. It was Theo's idea, actually, but I think it makes a lot of sense."

"You're going to break into heaven?" She gawked at us, a good old-fashioned, mouth-hanging-open gawk. "You're going to *break* into *heaven*?"

"We're going to enter the Court through a different entrance," Theo corrected. "Everything I heard last night pointed to the vessel I sought deliberately covering his tracks. Presumably, he's running from the same thing that Hope hinted about to Portia. Since we don't know what that threat is, we're going to have to find the vessel first."

"But why should we go to the Court if he is in hiding from someone or something?" she asked. "He's hardly going to be there, is he?"

I smiled at her. I loved it when Sarah used the logic I knew she possessed. "No, he won't be there, but something else is—it's the only place we can access the Akashic Records outside of the Akasha itself, and there's no way I'm going back there, thank you very much."

"Akashic Records?" Her brow furrowed. Darla came in with our breakfast, conducting polite chitchat while she doled out the plates, freshened Sarah's teapot, brought me more coffee, and sent Theo a number of somewhat vapid looks. I brushed a speck of non-existent lint off his shoulder, and cocked an eyebrow at her.

She left with a polite murmur.

Very subtle, sweetling.

I strive for excellence.

"I've heard of the Akashic Record," Sarah said slowly, spreading jam on a scone. She looked deep in thought. "Isn't it supposed to be some sort of record that God keeps about everything that everyone does?"

I plopped my two pieces of toast onto the mound of food before Theo, swapping our plates. "Evidently that's the mortal definition, which has been skewed over the centuries."

"The Akashic Record is simply a listing of all beings in the Court of Divine Blood, the Akashic Plain, and Abaddon, respectively," Theo said, leaning toward me. "That bacon smells good."

"Want a bite?" I asked, offering him a forkful of egg and bacon.

He looked at it with such avidity that it reminded me of what he'd lost. His Adam's apple bobbed as he swallowed, silently shaking his head. "I'd better not."

Would it make you sick?

I don't know. Christian just said it would likely take my body a while to adjust to the blood diet, and I shouldn't confuse things by trying to eat as well. I dearly love bacon, though.

My heart contracted at the regret in his voice.

"Dark Ones can't eat at all?" Sarah asked, her gaze likewise sympathetic.

"They can, but not for sustenance, and I gather it's only done in situations where it can't be avoided,"

Theo answered, his eyes following the path of a piece of bacon as I popped it in my mouth.

What if you just try a little bit? A couple of bites? Just to see how it does?

I don't relish spending the day vomiting, or cramping, or however it is my body would react to solid food.

I felt so guilty that the food turned to dirt in my mouth.

I'm not hungry, sweetling. You satisfied all my hungers earlier this morning, he said, his mind warm and reassuring in mine. *It's just that I miss the taste of certain foods.*

I swallowed the bacon still in my mouth, wiped my fingers on a napkin, and grabbed his head with both hands, pulling him into a kiss. His tongue danced around my mouth, tasting me, teasing me, his moan of pleasure swallowed with my own.

"I'm delighted you've both found each other, happier than you can know, and I'm the last person I think anyone would call a prude, but I am trying to eat here, and it's a bit disconcerting to have people making out on top of my breakfast."

Theo slowly pulled his head from mine, giving my lower lip a couple of quick nibbles before our mouths separated.

Better?

Much. Although walking is going to be uncomfortable for a bit.

My gaze dropped to his lap. He was clearly aroused. *I hope that is due to me, and not the bacon.*

Sweetling, I have yet to be aroused by pork prod-

ucts, he answered. His eyes grew even blacker. *Unless I'm eating them off of you.*

Sarah gave an exaggerated sigh. "Can we get back to the matter at hand?"

It was difficult to dismiss the images Theo sent to me, but I managed, by dint of concentrating on my eggs, to keep from flinging myself on him. "Sure. I take it other than the objection about us sneaking into the Court, you have no other comments?"

"Oh, I have many comments, but I respect you both too much to make them," she said, waving her fork at the paper. "Where are the Akashic Records?"

"In the library, the same building where the mare have their offices," I answered, pouring more coffee and holding it out to Theo. A blissful look stole over his face as, his eyes closed, he breathed deeply of its scent.

"In their offices? Well, now I know you're crazy! Just exactly how do you expect to get to the Records without being seen? Won't anyone who sees you know who you are? Won't the mare do something terrible if they find you there?"

"Theo thought of that," I said with a proud smile at him, sipping my coffee.

"Disguise?" she asked.

"No, the only disguises we could don that would effectively mislead a mare would need to be created by a demon, and we will not go down that path," Theo answered, taking the lid off the jam pot to smell it.

"Then what—"

"Shall I show you?" I asked, waggling my eyebrows.

Sarah looked confused. "Show me what?"

"We tried this last night, in my room. It's pretty slick, really." I closed the door to the pub area, striking a dramatic pose in the middle of the room.

"You're not going to make it rain again, are you?" Sarah asked, looking worriedly at her raw silk blouse.

"Nope. This is even better than my own personal rain cloud." I closed my eyes, imagining the humidity creeping up until it was a hundred percent, followed by the temperature dropping below the dew point. Moisture from the surface of the earth was drawn forth and began to evaporate, condensing, moving upward to cool.

"Oh my god," Sarah said, her voice rife with awe.

I opened my eyes and smiled. "I'm a fog machine!"

"This is incredible," she said, batting at the billows of fog that filled the small room. "I can't believe you can control this!"

"It's an art," I said modestly, admiring the dense fog that began to obscure the objects in the room.

"And you're going to fill the Court with fog in order to sneak in? Oh, this I have to see!"

I opened a window and began to dissipate the fog.

"Erm . . . Sarah . . . I don't think the Court would be the best place for you," Theo said, looking uncomfortable.

"Why?" she demanded.

"Well, for one, mortals aren't allowed in it except by special dispensation."

She frowned. "Portia's mortal."

Theo glanced at me. "Yes, but she's a virtue. That

means she's on the road to immortality, and can conceivably have legitimate business in the Court."

"That's splitting hairs, and you know it," she said, waving away his objections. "I think I should go with you. No one will see me if it's all foggy, so no one will know I was there."

"She has a point," I said, watching Theo. "We're not supposed to be there either, so what's the difference in her sneaking in along with us? Is there any reason she shouldn't come?"

"Well . . ."

"Excellent! I'll go get my things," she said, cramming in the last of her toast before dashing from the room, scattering promises to be back before we knew it.

"If she gets caught—" Theo started to say.

I interrupted him. "If we get caught, we're going to be in a whole lot more trouble than she will ever be in. So let's go with the thought that we're not going to get caught, and instead focus on the end goal."

Theo smiled, took my hand, and began nibbling on my fingertips. Little zings of electricity skittered through me at his touch. "You are so delightfully single-minded. Very well, we will hope for the best."

There was a faint echo of unease in the back of his mind, but it was too vague for me to pinpoint. Regardless, I was a bit worried as we drove down the coast to the castle in which the entrance to the Court of Divine Blood was located. What if I couldn't perform when the time came? What would happen if Theo and I were caught? Would Sarah be in any trouble if she was seen? What if the Akashic Record didn't help us?

"Too many ifs," I said to myself.

"What is too manieeee!"

Sarah's screech filled the car, causing me to lurch forward, my hands over my ears, and startling Theo to such extent that the car jerked off the road, bounded over a small hill that ran between the road and the marshy coast, and hurtled down a slippery slope toward a large log which had been washed ashore.

Theo swore, yanking at the steering wheel, pumping the brakes to get the car to stop without flipping.

"Bloody badgers, what's going on here?" a gruff woman's voice asked from the backseat.

"Merciful heaven! Stop!" another woman cried, grabbing Theo by the shoulders and shaking him.

The car fishtailed, hit the rocky shale that merged into the soft, mucky, marshy shore, and finally crashed to a halt in a huge mountain of discarded oyster shells. Seabirds, which had been picking through the shells, rose in a cloud of squawking protests. The screaming from the backseat stopped. I turned, shaking and no doubt white from shock, to look at Theo, asking him at the same time he asked me, "Are you all right?"

"I'm OK," I answered him, craning around to look behind us. Sarah was nowhere to be seen, but two horribly familiar—if disordered—faces stared back at me. "What are you two doing here? And where is Sarah?"

"On the floor. Stop stepping on me." Sarah's head

emerged from behind the seat, her hair mussed, her face flushed with emotion. "Ow. I hit my head. What happened?"

"That's what I'd like to know," Theo said, un-snapping his seat belt so he could turn around and glare at the people in the backseat. "Who are you two, and why have you materialized in my car?"

"They are the two women who administered my first trial," I answered, adding my own glare to Theo's. I pointed at the smaller woman. "That's Tansy. She's the one who beat me up."

"I didn't mean to," Tansy answered, wringing her hands. Both women were dressed just as they were a few days ago, Tansy still appearing like someone's beloved grandmother. "But you simply wouldn't de-fend yourself."

I ignored that. "The other woman is named Letty, I believe."

"Leticia de Maurier," the Dame Margaret woman answered, her voice stiff. She looked down her long nose at us. "We are trial proctors, nephilim. You will not question the ways of those of the Court of Divine Blood."

"We'll question whoever and whatever we want," I said grimly, watching Theo as he forced the car door open and got out. He half slid down the slope of oyster shells, fighting his way around to my side of the car. "You could have killed us!"

"Don't be silly—we're all immortal here. Well, almost all immortal," Dame Margaret said with a sour look at Sarah. "We are here to administer your next trial, naturally. Shall we commence?"

"Here?" I asked, allowing Theo to help me out of the car. We'd stopped at the bottom of a huge mountain of oyster shells, the back wheels of the car sunk deep into the mucky, muddy marshland. Overhead, the gulls and shorebirds we'd dislodged cried out their objections. The stench of rotting seaweed and brackish water in small, stagnant tidal pools was enough to trigger my gag reflex.

"No time like the present," Tansy said cheerfully as Theo held her arm while she slid her way down the oyster shells to a small spar of solid ground. "Thank you, dear boy. So handsome!"

"And very much taken," I said, grumbling as I picked my way down the shells. As I reached the bottom of the slope, I lost my footing, my arms cartwheeling like crazy as I fell the last couple of feet, rolling into the same muck that held the car's back tires prisoners. The mud was black, and smelled of decomposing matter, fish, and other unsavory odors I refused to identify.

"Oh, Portia!" Sarah cried from the safety of the oyster mound.

Theo lifted her and plopped her down onto the same solid piece of land that both Tansy and Dame Margaret occupied before starting toward me.

"No, stay back," I said, trying to rise. "You'll just sink in up to your knees. I'm not hurt, just filthy."

The mud was thick and dank, and made horrible sucking noises as I struggled to my feet. I lost my summer sandals somewhere in the muck as I sunk up to my knees, my linen pants soaked through with the horrible mess. The entire front side of me was black with sodden detritus, reeking with such a horrible odor that my eyes ran.

"Well, so long as you're all right, we shall commence with the trial," Dame Margaret said, marching over to a sun-bleached piece of tree-trunk driftwood and taking a seat on it. She pulled out a notebook. "As you are no doubt well aware, this is the trial for grace."

I took one step forward, lost my footing again, and fell facedown into the muck a second time.

Dame Margaret pursed her lips.

"Letty, perhaps we should wait," her companion said, watching as Theo pulled me to solid land.

I tried not to touch him with the stinking, filthy mess that covered me, spitting out bits of foul-tasting dirt and mud.

"No time to wait," Dame Margaret answered. "We've a schedule to keep to. Now, let's see . . . during this trial, you will demonstrate to us your grace, that innate sense which separates you from the mortals, and by which you will be known as a member of the Court of Divine Blood."

One seagull, braver than the others, evidently enjoyed the aroma I'd stirred up and tried to land on my head. I beat it off with a profanity that made Theo grin, Sarah cover her face with her hands, and Tansy gasp in horror.

"Indeed," Dame Margaret said, raising both eyebrows and making a note in her ever-present notebook.

I scorned Theo's offer of a hand, stomping my way over to where Dame Margaret sat. She rose as I approached, bits of mud falling off me to hit the ground with unpleasant splatting noises.

"Really, I must protest," Dame Margaret said, pulling out a handkerchief to hold at her nose. "Your stench is quite offensive."

Mud covered me from the top of my head to my bare feet, squishing out from between my toes, ground into my hair so deeply I'd probably have to wash it at least five times to get it all out. My clothes were ruined, soaked through to my skin. I stunk of dead fish and sewer through no fault of my own, the blame for my condition standing squarely in front of me, gently fanning the air with a pristine white handkerchief.

"Step away, Portia Harding. Your audacity in standing near me knows no bounds. We are offended."

Tansy gasped again.

My eyes narrowed at her. It would be so easy.

Sweetling, do not do what I know you are thinking of doing, Theo warned. *No matter how much she goads you, she is still a member of the Court, and your trial proctor.*

She caused the whole thing! She popped into the car without warning, and her buddy grabbed you and kept you from steering properly! It's all her fault that I'm a walking, fishy cesspool!

No good will come of you seeking revenge.

Oh, I beg to differ. A whole lot of good will come from it—it will do my spleen tremendous good to see her as filthy as I am.

"You are delaying us unnecessarily," Dame Margaret said, holding the handkerchief to her nose

again. "I will make note of your attempts to deprecate this trial."

"Deprecate!" I stared Dame Margaret in the eye,
my hands itching to grab her and toss her into the
mud. It would only be fair, after all.

Sweetling . . .

I took a deep breath, choked on my own stench,
and turned around, stumbling away with my head
held high. *Don't worry, I won't do it, no matter how
much I'd give to see her as filthy as me.*

"If you leave now, it will be so noted on the trial
records," Dame Margaret yelled after me. "Do not
expect another chance, for there will be none!"

I muttered profanity after profanity to myself as I
fought my way up the grassy slope to the road.

"Does she know that if she fails this trial, it will
all be over?" Tansy asked her companion.

"She knows," Dame Margaret trumpeted. "She is
simply too cowardly to face us! Her attitude is rep-
rehensible! She is not worthy of the virtue name!"

Damn the trial. Damn everything and everyone . . . except Theo.

One of the gulls crapped on me as it flew over my
head.

Chapter 19

"I'm in so much trouble."

The hum of the air-conditioning in the car was the only noise.

"I wonder how much groveling it's going to take to get the mare to give me another shot at that trial?"

Outside the window, gulls cried overhead. I flinched as we passed the area where earlier we'd skidded off the road, averting my eyes from the sight of Theo's car, still half-buried in the mountain of oyster shells.

"I hope your car will be all right. When are they coming to tow it?"

"Soon."

I sighed, slinking down into my seat. *Are you still mad at me?*

I have not been mad at you, so there is no "still" to it.

Then why aren't you talking to me? You haven't said a word since we went back to the pub so I could take a shower and change. I know you have to be

*angry, or at least disappointed, that I've messed up
the trial so much that I won't be a virtue, and won't
be able to pardon you, but I really don't believe the
situation is as hopeless as you no doubt think it is.*

*I don't think anything is hopeless, sweetling, nor
am I in the least bit angry. I think you showed re-
markable restraint in not acting rashly with Leticia.
I know how much you wanted to treat her in kind.*

"Can I ask a question?" Sarah leaned forward so she
could be heard in the front seat of the car she'd rented
for our trip, now serving as our primary mode of trans-
portation while Theo's car was out of commission.

"Since I'm delighted to know you're still talking
to me, by all means, ask away."

"I wasn't not talking to you, silly. I was taking notes
on what happened. This is so incredibly fascinating!"

"I'm glad someone is getting enjoyment out of it.
What was your question?"

"Why are we going to the Court if you're now out
of the running as a virtue?"

A headache was building behind my forehead. I
rubbed it, not for the first time, wishing I could
rewind my life and start this section over. "Because
I'm hoping that if I bring proof to the mare of what
happened to Hope, they will excuse the last trial and
give me another shot at it."

"Yes, but if you're no longer a virtue, how are you
going to make with the fog?"

I glanced at Theo. His jaw was tight, his eyes a light
grey that indicated he was not a happy camper. "Evidently, even though I failed the three trials, I am not de-
virtued until someone strips the power from me."

"I hope so, otherwise you'll be in even hotter water than you are. So, we're just walking in the front door?"

"There is more than one entrance to the Court," Theo answered. "We will take the one nearest the library, so Portia's talents won't be overly taxed."

"Good thinking." Sarah sat back to make a few more notes. I spent the rest of the way to the castle mentally sorting the events of the last few days, looking for something we might have missed. I had an uneasy feeling that something significant had happened that I'd failed to acknowledge, but a quick survey of the last three days didn't come up with anything to assuage my uneasiness.

"Someone is bound to notice this fog isn't normal," I murmured to Theo forty minutes later, as we stopped just beyond a small doorway cut into the stone wall that surrounded the Court. Ahead of us stood the building we'd visited earlier, the library where the Akashic Record was held.

"We will be gone before they can trace the source." Theo's voice was muffled, oddly contorted through the heavy fog that now rolled through the area surrounding the library. Even though he was just a few feet away from me, I could barely see his silhouette. "Just a little more, sweetling, then we can go in."

"I resent being put on watchdog duty," Sarah hissed from somewhere behind us. "I won't be able to see anyone until they are right on top of me."

"No one knows who you are," I whispered back, taking Theo's arm. His fingers closed around mine, reassuringly warm and strong. "All you have to do is distract anyone who comes to the door. It's not rocket science, Sarah."

"Hrmph."

Theo guided us to the main doors of the library, opening them wide. I summoned more fog, and sent it into the building, thick white rolls of it slowly filling all available space. We crept along the now-fogged hallways, hands outstretched to avoid colliding with obstacles. There were a few exclamations of surprise from people who found themselves caught in the fog, one person shouting for someone to find the mare.

We don't have much time, Theo said. I clutched the back of his shirt, my other hand holding Sarah's arm, so we wouldn't get separated.

I know. "Sarah, this is the doorway to the archives. Stand here and keep anyone from coming in."

"Will do."

I released her arm and followed Theo into a small, dusty-smelling room, shutting the door behind me to keep the fog out. Theo flipped on a light switch, and stood considering the cases around us. The room was, thankfully, empty of people.

"We can split up and search for it," I said, moving to the nearest glass archive case. "What does it look like?"

"I have no idea, but since it is one of the most valuable records in existence, I assume it will be found in one of the more elaborate cases."

I quickly examined the books contained in the climate-controlled case in front of me, but nothing had a title even remotely similar to Akashic Record.

I skirted a giant library-sized dictionary opened on a book pedestal, and started for the next case.

Something tickled at the back of my head. I looked back at the dictionary, giving it a closer examination.

> *Ofaniel, also known as sefira Wisdom. Primary residence: Court of Divine Blood, Grand Apartments, second floor. Mundane residence: Marseille, France. Mundane name: Clementine Massier.*
> *Oglien, demon third class, servant of Bael, twenty-second legion. Mundane residence: none. Mundane names: Will O'Bannon, William Bannock, Will the Decapitator.*

I closed the dictionary to read the title. *The Akashic Record: Being a List of All Immortals Possessing Membership in the Court of Divine Blood and Abaddon.*

"Theo, I found it. It's very large."

He hurried over, frowning slightly. "They keep it out here in the open?"

"Evidently. I thought it was a dictionary. F, G, H . . . ah. Here it is: *Hope, originally internuncio, later designed virtue by request of holder. Primary residence: Court of Divine Blood, Grand Apartments, third floor. Mundane residence: Seaton.* Seaton?"

I looked up at Theo.

"That's near Newton Poppleford."

"That would explain why she was around the faery ring, then. *Mundane name: Hope Campbell.* Is that ink blotch covering another name, do you think, or is it just a blot?"

Theo bent over the book, squinting at the black area next to Hope's name. "It's hard to tell. It could be either."

"Hmm. I'm willing to bet she covered up her mortal-world name on purpose."

"She could have." Theo looked thoughtful as he tapped his chin. "If she thought she was in danger, she might have destroyed any proof of her name as a safety precaution."

"That's lovely. Is there anywhere else we can go to find out what name she is using now?" I asked, miffed that our lead had fizzled out.

"Not that I know of."

I sighed. "Well, at least we have one of her names and a town to go on."

"Indeed you do. That was very clever of you to think of consulting the Akashic Record."

I spun around at the sound of a man's voice coming from the doorway.

Terrin leaned against the door, a slight smile on his face. "I particularly liked the fog. Very effective. Hello again. Is that your friend guarding the other side of the door?"

"Yes, she is. She wasn't supposed to let anyone in," I said, trying to come up with an excuse for being in the Court when I'd been forbidden entrance.

"Good morning," Theo said, giving Terrin a little bow. "You have us at a disadvantage. It is somewhat disconcerting to be caught breaking and entering into the Court."

Terrin's smile widened. "And yet you managed it with such ease. A very admirable feat."

"Is my friend all right?" I asked, a bit nervous about Sarah.

"She is right where you left her. I'm afraid I had to obscure her vision for a moment or two while I slipped past her, but she is unharmed."

I relaxed a little bit. I was willing to take responsibility for my own actions, but I hated for anyone else to suffer on my behalf. "I suppose you'd like to know why we're here when we were told to leave."

"I assume your purpose is two-fold: to consult the Akashic Record, and to conduct your final trial." Terrin strolled over to the window, looking out at the still-dense fog. "Yes, a very clever use of your Gift. Quite effective."

Theo and I exchanged glances. "You're partially correct: We did come here to see the Akashic Record. But as for my trials . . . well, even if I hadn't been disqualified, I would only have been on trial number four, not seven."

"No, that cannot be correct." Terrin frowned, walking over to a desk on the other side of the room and sitting down to access the computer there. "You have completed all the trials but the last one, I'm quite sure."

"I'm afraid not. Trial number four got put off. I skipped ahead to five, which I did when I was in the Akasha. The two women who did my first trial came back earlier this morning for the fourth trial, but I . . . er . . . I failed it."

"How very odd." Terrin's fingers tapped out a few

words on the computer's keyboard. He perused the resulting screen, a puzzled look in his eyes. "That's not what it says here. According to the official records, you have completed all trials but the last one: four of them successfully, two failures."

"How could I pass the fourth and sixth trials? I didn't do them!"

"What elements did the fourth and sixth trials test?" Theo asked, looking even more thoughtful.

Terrin consulted the monitor. "The fourth was logic, the sixth grace."

"Now I know your records are at fault. I was the least graceful person alive this morning," I said, shuddering at the memory of my muck-covered self.

"Grace," Theo repeated, his eyes on me.

Why are you looking at me like that?

I was thinking that grace doesn't necessarily indicate physical adeptness. Perhaps it is another type of grace for which you were being tested.

What other sort of grace is there? I asked. *A blessing?*

No, I was thinking more the quality of forgiveness, or mercy, if you will.

Mercy? To whom have I been merciful? . . .

A vision rose in my mind of Dame Margaret taunting me, baiting me to throw her into the mud. I hadn't given in to that almost overwhelming desire, though. I'd walked away from her with as much dignity as I could muster.

"I didn't throw her in the mud," I said slowly.

"You did not. You demonstrated grace sufficient to pass the sixth trial," Terrin said.

"So Leticia deliberately caused that accident, arranged it so I would be put into a position where I was covered head to toe in the worst sort of muck, then baited me to see if I would retaliate?" I nodded. In an odd sort of way, it made sense. "That explains the sixth trial, but not the fourth one. I haven't done it at all."

"According to this, the trial was conducted last night at"—Terrin peered at the screen—"ten minutes to midnight. You successfully completed the trial seven minutes later. That was rather pushing it as far as time goes, but all ended well."

"That can't be right," I said, shaking my head. "Last night at midnight I was in a haunted mill, watching my friend and a ghost hunting group as they examined the building. There was no logic trial . . ."

Goose bumps crawled up my arms.

"Didn't you say you played a logic game with someone last night, while you were waiting for Sarah?" Theo asked.

"Milo," I said, more confused than ever. "Milo gave me one of those logic puzzles to solve, but it wasn't a trial. Milo is a person, a normal person, not someone from the Court . . ." My voice trailed away again as Theo and I both turned to look at the large book sitting on the dictionary stand.

Theo beat me to it, hurriedly thumbing through the book as I peered over his shoulder.

"*Milo, originally archon, later banished from the Court of Divine Blood for abuses of power,*" Theo read. "*Cleared of charges, and removed to vessel of mortality at request of mare Irina. Mundane residence: Newberry, England. Mundane names: Milo Lee, Miles Leighton.* Miles Leighton is the man I was trying to find last night, the one who had disappeared, the man who is known to be one of Hope's friends, and supposedly the one she sought shelter with."

"This is wild. Milo is a . . . a . . ."

"Vessel," Theo said grimly, his jaw tight. "In other words, a servant to mortals."

"Ha! That's what he meant about being in customer service. He deliberately hid his connection with the Court from me. But why?"

"I think it's time we had a few words with him to find that answer, and a few others as well."

"Agreed. Er . . ." I glanced over to where Terrin sat watching us, a pleasant expression on his face.

"Hello there. I wondered when you'd remember me."

"We hadn't forgotten," Theo said slowly, eyeing Terrin. "I'm curious as to why you haven't raised the alarm about us, though. And why, for that matter, are you here now?"

"Life possesses so many questions, doesn't it?" Terrin leaned back in his chair, his hands behind his head. "Since I am a tidy person by nature, I will answer those I can. I am here, my good nephilim, because this is one of my offices—I have three. And I have not turned you in because I am one of those people who are somewhat offensively labeled cockeyed optimists. A reverse Cassandra, if you will—rather than no one believing what I say, I believe most of what people tell me."

"You believe I didn't have anything to do with Hope's disappearance?"

He nodded. "It's been my experience that life is often full of irony. Your story is very ironic, thus I am inclined to believe that you inadvertently summoned Hope just as you described, that she bequeathed her Gift to you without your knowing it, and that you subsequently not only accepted these facts, but determined to triumph over the adversities that have met you face-to-face."

I slumped into a chair, relief easing my jangled nerves. "Then you'll help us find Hope?"

"Oh no, that would be quite unacceptable." His lips quirked. "Giving aid to someone banned from the Court would be a serious matter involving repercussions I would prefer to avoid."

"I'm sorry, I didn't mean to sound so selfish. Of course we don't want you to get into trouble on our behalf—"

"I am, however, willing to risk the censure that might follow should the blind eye I'm about to turn to your presence here be found out."

"Portia? I think you both had better get a move on. I just heard someone say that the mare were on their way over to investigate the odd fog." Sarah's voice was hushed and muffled as she opened the door a smidgen to speak to us.

"On our way." I stood and offered my hand to Terrin. He looked surprised for a moment, then rose and shook it. "Thank you for believing us."

"And thank you for not turning us in," Theo added, giving Terrin a wary look.

"It has been my pleasure. I do hope you find the answers that you seek."

We slipped out of the door, leaving Terrin standing in the middle of the room, a benign expression on his face. Outside the room, the fog was beginning to thin.

I concentrated a moment on bringing it back to full denseness, but it continued to disperse despite my efforts.

"Something wrong?" Theo asked as we hurried down the hallway, averting our faces whenever a foggy figure loomed up. "Are you not able to control this any longer?"

"No, I'm not. Let's get out of here before it's gone completely."

We made it to the side entrance of the Court without being seen, but rather than follow Sarah and me through the door to a dank, empty subbasement in the castle, Theo stopped and looked back through to the stone wall that represented the outer boundary of the Court.

"Theo? Shouldn't we get out of Dodge while the getting is good?"

"We're safe here for a minute or two. Have you ever felt as if you were being manipulated?" he asked, turning toward me.

"Frequently. I'm a woman in a traditionally male-dominated workplace. I'm always being manipulated into taking less-than-desirable projects, or taking on extra work, or covering for someone when I'd rather not—it's part of the job, unfortunately. Do you think someone is manipulating us now?"

"I'm not sure. It just seems to me..." He frowned at the door. "I am going back. You and Sarah take the car back to the pub."

"No!" I said, unhappy with the thought of separating. "You can't go back in there!"

"Sweetling, I haven't survived as long as I have by being reckless. I know a thing or two about getting around unseen." He gave me a quick kiss and turned back to the door.

I grabbed his arm to stop him. "My fog is gone. You can't stealth around the Court in full daylight!"

"It'll be no different than running from a building to the car. I have my hat—I'll be careful."

"Fine, if you insist on going, then we'll go with you. Let me yell for Sarah—"

"No, I will do this alone. You two go ahead without me."

"Why?" I asked, hurt by his exclusion.

He took my face in his hands, kissing the frown between my brows. "Because there is a slight, a *very* slight, chance I will be caught. The Court can do nothing to me, but you have too much to lose to risk visiting there again. I will speak with Terrin, then leave immediately."

"We just talked to him. Why do you want to see him again?"

His eyes were a light shale grey. "Because I dislike being made to act the puppet, and I think he knows who's behind that feeling. Portia, you must trust me—I am not going to put myself or you at risk. I simply want to ask a few more questions."

"But—"

"Go," he said, giving me a push toward the door that led out of the subbasement. "I will be with you shortly."

"And just how do you expect to get back if we take the car?" I asked, my hands on my hips. Theo could be the most fabulous man alive, but he was also one of the most frustrating.

"There's a magical thing known as a taxi," he answered, his lips curling into a smile. "You just call them up, and they take you to wherever you wish to go."

"Oh, very funny. Fine. Go off on your own on mysterious errands, and don't include me. See if I care, you incredibly annoying man!"

I love you, too, he said, his laughter soft in my mind as I made my way up out of the bowels of the castle.

"If he wants to be that way," I said, slamming the car door shut on the questions Sarah had been peppering me with as we left the castle, "then so be it. We'll just go ahead and solve the whole thing while he's off doing his lone-wolf act."

"Atta girl," Sarah replied, pulling a U-turn to get us onto the road back to our town. "What's next?"

I pulled out the packet of maps given to us by the local auto association. "I believe a little visit to the town of Newberry is in order."

Chapter 20

"That's it, number twelve. Boy, that's a mess, huh?"

"Very." I examined the outside of the small house that sat across the street. A black wrought-iron fence lurched drunkenly around a small garden that was more weeds than flowers, tall grass sheltering what appeared to be a rusted wheelbarrow. Butterflies provided brilliant spots of color as they flitted about the yard. "It's not exactly what you'd expect from someone who used to live in the Court, is it?"

"I don't know," Sarah answered thoughtfully as we got out of the car. "I suppose once you'd lived in heaven, anything else would be . . . crap."

The battered gate screeched painfully as I pushed it open, making my way through cast-off garden implements and boxes of unnamed refuse to the dirty front door.

"You're not just going to knock, are you?" Sarah asked as I raised my hand to do just that.

"Of course I am. What did you think we were going to do here?"

"Well, I don't know." She clutched her hands together in an agitated manner. "I thought maybe we'd stake out the house for a bit, and watch to see where Milo goes, and who he meets, and things like that. That's what I'd do, anyway."

"This isn't one of your books, Sarah, it's real life, and we don't have the time to play private detectives." I knocked on the door, taking a deep breath to calm my suddenly twitchy nerves.

"Yes? What is it?" The door opened, Milo's wife visible as she frowned out from the depths of the entrance. For a moment, I thought I saw a flash of surprise in her eyes, and I was overcome with a sense of similarity, a déjà vu that sent a skitter of goose bumps up my arms.

"Hello. You probably don't remember me, but my name is Portia Harding. My friend Sarah and I were at the ghost-hunting event last night."

She didn't so much as bat an eyelash. "Yes?"

I trotted out my friendliest smile. "I wondered if we could have a word with your husband?"

"Milo?" She frowned, giving us a look that expressed all sorts of suspicions. "I suppose so."

"Thank you—" I started to walk to through the door, jumping back when she closed it literally in my face. "Well, damn!"

"She isn't the friendliest person in the world," Sarah said behind me. "Wouldn't chat at all during our time at the mill. Mr. Richings told me he thought she was just shy, and that she'd probably loosen up once she started making regular runs with the group."

"Shy isn't quite the word I'd use to describe her," I said, rubbing my nose where it had bumped into the door. I turned back to Sarah, puzzled by something she'd said. "Once she started—"

"Hello, ladies! What a pleasure it is to see you both again, although a bit unexpected." Milo smiled at us, shaking our hands. "To what do I owe this honor?"

"You'll have to forgive us for stopping by without calling first, but to be honest, I wasn't sure if you would see us, and I really would appreciate the chance to talk."

"Of course," he said, stepping back and gesturing toward the door. "Please, come in and make yourself at home. Would you like a coffee?"

"Coffee would be lovely, thank you."

He escorted us down a dimly lit hallway to a small room that was clean, but had an unused feel to it, as if it was the room saved solely for company. "I'll just tell the wife that we've got visitors," Milo said, making a quick escape.

"Quaint," Sarah pronounced after making a cursory examination of the room. "Very English. Do you think Milo knows that we know who he is?"

"I'm not sure. He's a difficult man to make out." I sat in a flowery gold and scarlet chair, making a mental list of things I wished to ascertain.

"Oh, I don't know, he seems pretty straightforward to me." She shot me a quick glance. "With the exception of the obvious, that is. You know I don't like to make snap judgments, but I'm not sure I like his wife. What did you say her name was?"

"Carol. Sarah, does she remind you of anyone?"

"Milo's wife?"

I nodded, trying to pinpoint what it was about her that seemed so familiar.

"No. Unless you're talking about someone back home, and then I'd have to say Janice Del Rio. She used to come in and clean for me when the twins were little, remember? I caught her one day trying on my best dress."

"That's not it. I can't quite put my finger on it, but she reminds me of someone. I just can't think of who."

"Whom." Sarah went to the window to look out. "Do you want me to ask him about Hope?"

"No. I can ask my own questions."

"Portia, honey," Sarah turned, her hands spread wide. "You know I love you like a sister, but if you have a failing, it's that you're invariably blunt when you want information."

I lifted my chin and looked down my nose at her. "I am not blunt. I'm straightforward. The difference between which you are clearly unable to appreciate."

"Call it what you will, it seems to me that this situation is going to need careful handling. Since I am the soul of tact and subtlety, why don't you let me handle it?"

"I would be insulted except there's not time for me to argue with you. Suffice it to say, I will be the personification of the word subtle. All right?"

She sighed, and looked out the window again. Silence filled the room, no sound at all penetrating from the rest of the house.

My mind, normally organized and orderly, squirreled around, randomly hopping from thought to thought, giving me an uncomfortable, unsettled sort of feeling. But behind all that, there was a nagging sense of having missed something again, something important that, if only I could concentrate, I could see. It was at the tip of my awareness, just beyond my focus . . .

"Here we are, then." The door opened for Milo, bearing a small red plastic tray adorned with coffee mugs, a milk jug, sugar bowl, and small yellow bowl filled with the tea cookies so beloved by the English. "Sorry for the wait. How do you take yours?"

"Black is fine, thanks." I took a mug from him, and waved away the offer of a cookie. "I apologize again for barging in like this, but I'm in a bit of a bind, and I was hoping you could help me."

"Certainly," he said, offering Sarah a cookie. His eyes were the same smiling brown eyes of the man who'd amused me the night before, but I was wise to his ways now. "Anything I can do to help."

"We're looking for a virtue named Hope, and I was told by someone in the Court of Divine Blood that you knew her."

"Oh yes, that's subtle," Sarah murmured.

We both ignored her.

"Hope?" Milo asked, his eyes mirroring the surprise on his face. "The Court?"

"Look, I know you used to be an archon there, and were later kicked out, only to have the charges against you dropped," I said, setting down my mug. "So, although I appreciate the fact that you don't like a couple of relative strangers poking around in your past, you don't have to pretend you don't know what I'm talking about. I've seen the Akashic Record."

Milo slumped back in his chair, one hand rubbing over his face before he opened his eyes and gave me a short nod. "It seems I don't have a choice. If you've seen the Record—but what was it you wanted from me?"

"Let's start with, why didn't you tell me you were a trial proctor last night, when you conducted the fourth trial?"

"It's a bit complicated," he answered, his elbows on his knees as he leaned forward toward me. "I'm going to tell you the truth because you're a nice person, and I quite like you. It's true I concealed my position with the Court from you. I didn't want to, but I was told by someone high up in the Court that if I didn't, I'd lose my job."

"Someone didn't want me to know that I was undergoing the fourth trial?" I frowned when he nodded. "That doesn't make any sense. All the other proctors have announced who they were, and that a trial was about to start. Why wouldn't someone want me to know I was doing the fourth one?"

Milo stared down into his coffee, his thumb rubbing along the thick edge of the mug. "I wish I could tell you, Portia, I really wish I could. But I have my wife to think of. I've been banned from the Court before—I can't risk that again. All I can say is that someone doesn't want you to succeed as a virtue."

"Who?" Sarah asked.

"I can't tell you that," he said, giving her an apologetic smile.

"Well, can you narrow it down somewhat?" she asked. "Can't you give us some clue about who this secret enemy is? Surely Portia deserves that much consideration."

I sent Sarah a look of gratitude.

"Of course she does," Milo answered, rubbing his chin as he continued to gaze into his coffee. "I suppose it wouldn't be breaking any confidences if I was to tell you the person who wishes you ill is someone you've met here in England."

"Hmm. Someone I've met. Let's see, the first person who has Court ties whom I met is Theo."

Milo gave me a long look.

"There was Mystic Bettina," Sarah said, her eyes narrowed in thought. "And Milo and Carol, but obviously you're excluded from the list of suspects."

"Obviously," he said, smiling for a moment.

"Tansy and Leticia," I continued the list.

Milo's expression didn't change.

"Who did your trial after that?" Sarah asked. "I've got them in a muddle. Was it the demon woman?"

"Noelle the Guardian? No, she came after the second trial. That was done by Terrin. Following him was the demon—"

Milo's shoulders twitched. I stopped, mentally backing up. "Do you know Terrin?"

His face became as smooth as a mask. "Would you like more coffee?"

Sarah's gaze met mine. It was clear what Milo was trying to tell us between the lines. Which was very interesting, considering all that Terrin had told us.

"No thank you, I'm fine." I took a sip of the coffee before continuing. "I do have another question for you, if you don't mind my apparent nosiness. Do you know the virtue named Hope?"

"Hope!" His face brightened for a moment, then he shot a hunted look over his shoulder toward the door, his voice dropping to a near whisper. "Yes, indeed I do know her. She's been a stalwart friend for several centuries. She stood by me when I went through my black time."

"Black time?" Sarah asked.

"Excommunication," he answered. "I lost a great many friends then, but Hope wasn't one of them. She spoke out on my behalf, and almost lost her own position because of that. Fortunately, I was exonerated before any action could be taken against her."

"I see. Do you happen to know where she is now?" I sat back, my hands on my lap, apparently at ease, but oddly nervous, as if some secretive thing lurked in the shadows.

He chuckled. "I'm glad to see you don't put any stock in that ugly rumor that she's dead. I knew you would see through those murder charges sooner or later. Unfortunately, I can't help you find her. I haven't heard from her since before you summoned her."

I opened my mouth to tell him I didn't knowingly summon her, but decided that point wasn't relevant to the conversation. "Do you have any idea where I can find her? We stopped by her flat just before we came here, but the janitor we talked to had no idea where she was. Obviously, I need to find her to prove to the Court that I didn't kill her."

"No idea, I'm afraid," he said, shaking his head. "I wish I could help, but I haven't a clue where she's gone to, although if she was feeling threatened by someone . . ." He paused a moment, his gaze dropping to his hands. "If she was feeling that her life was in danger, she would take steps to make sure no one found her. I'd guess that she would leave the country, go somewhere no one would think to look for her, and lay low until she felt it safe to emerge again."

My disappointment must have shown on my face.

"I'm sorry," he said again, patting my hand. "I wish I could help you—"

"Milo!"

He jumped and looked around guiltily. His wife stood in the door, giving us a cold-eyed look. "Hello, dear. I was just chatting with our visitors."

"You said you were going to do the shopping before tea," she said pointedly, giving Sarah and me an even colder nod.

"Oh, yes . . ."

"Thank you for the coffee," I said as Sarah and I stood up, gathering our things. "I appreciate the opportunity to talk with you."

"It's been my pleasure." He escorted us to the front door. I swear waves of coldness rolled off his wife as we scooted past her in the narrow hall. As we reached the door, I paused for a moment, looking straight at his wife. She met my gaze without flinching, one of her eyebrows arching in an unspoken question. The penny dropped at that moment, my mind suddenly wonderfully organized again as the missing piece of the puzzle snapped into place. I forced a smile to my lips, and continued out the door.

"Please don't hesitate to give me a ring if you have any other questions. And thank you for . . . er . . . understanding my little deception. I assure you that it was not by my desire," Milo said, waving good-bye.

"Well, that was hardly more than useless," Sarah said as we carefully picked our way down the broken-tiled path to the street. "All we learned was that this Terrin person has it in for you, and that Milo knew Hope well. There's not a lot to go on."

"You don't think so?"

I opened the car door, glancing over the top of the car to look at Milo's house. A curtain in one of the front-facing rooms twitched, as if someone had been peeking out. "I'd have to disagree. I thought the conversation was very enlightening. Very enlightening indeed."

"Really?" She shot me a fast look before pulling out into traffic. "Enlightening in what way?"

"I'll let you know as soon as I talk to Theo."

"Oh, for God's sake . . . Portia, you're a big girl. Just because you're madly infatuated with Theo, doesn't mean you have to be a doormat. You can talk to me about things before checking with him first."

"Have I ever been a doormat?"

She pursed her lips and didn't answer.

"That's right, I haven't. I'm not waiting to clear the subject with Theo. I simply need to determine if my proof will support the supposition I believe fits the circumstances."

"I hate it when you talk in that horrible empirical way," she grumbled, but knew me too well to do more than voice the complaint.

We drove along in silence for a few minutes before she asked, "Well? Did you discuss it with Theo? Does he agree with your supposition or not?"

"Hmm? Oh, no, I can't talk to him right now. He's in the Court, remember?"

"What does that have to do with the price of tea in China? I thought you guys could talk even if you weren't physically near each other?"

"Normally, we could, but there's something about the Court that inhibits mind-talking."

"Well, isn't that just fine and dandy! Now I'm going to have to wait—"

"Turn left at the intersection."

"—until Theo comes out so you two can discuss whether or not to reveal to me this supersecret insight you seem to have?"

"Left again, please."

"I may be just a normal person without special powers or anything, but that doesn't mean you can treat me like . . . hey. Isn't this taking us around the block?"

"Yup. There's a parking spot right over there."

Sarah looked to where I was pointing, shooting me a curious glance before pulling in behind a large panel van. "You want to tell me what we're doing back on the street where Milo lives, or is that, too, a big secret?"

"Actually," I said with a grin, "it's probably better if you don't know. That way it can't be said that you were an accessory."

Her mouth made an O for a second, then her curiosity—almost as great as my own—got the better of her. "Dish, sister."

"Taking a leaf from Theo's book, we're going to become kidnappers. Can you see the front door of Milo's house from here?"

"Yes. Why are we kidnapping Milo? I bet if you asked him to come along with us—not that I know where we're going—he'd be happy to do whatever you wanted. He seems like a nice man."

"Yes, doesn't he?" I rubbed my chin, trying to decide on the wisest course.

"I know you're almost a member of the Court of Divine Blood and all, but you still have to live in this world, and here it's illegal as all get out to kidnap someone." Sarah had a familiar pugnacious expression on her face. I just broadened my grin.

"I hate it when you do that," she told my grin.

I sighed and decided it wasn't fair to involve her in something so potentially dangerous. "You're right. It annoys me to admit it, but you are right, Sarah. What I'm about to do is very illegal, and I think that it probably would be best if you weren't involved. I know it's asking a lot, but would you mind leaving me the car? I don't think I can get another one at short notice, and I'm sure there are taxis that can take you back to Newton Poppleford."

"Oh, no, you're not getting away with that crap," she said, taking a firm grip on the steering wheel. "We're in this together, if you recall."

"Our original plans did not call for kidnapping," I pointed out.

"No, but I'm your friend. A friend's place is at your side when you commit felonies. Oooh! Look! Milo! How do we get him into the car?"

My lips thinned as I watched Milo leave his house, walking around the front to the other side, where I assumed a detached garage sat. "We don't."

"I think he's going to get his car. Are we following him?" Sarah asked, her hand on the ignition key.

"No. Duck!"

I doubled over in the passenger seat, having seen a white car emerge from the area behind Milo's house. Sarah hunkered down as well, waiting until the sound of the car passing us had faded.

"All right, now I'm confused . . . Where are you going?" she asked as I got out of the car.

"To get our victim." My heart was racing as I approached the door to Milo's house, my palms suddenly damp with sweat. "I hope I do this right."

"Do what?"

"I'm going to Taser Milo's wife Carol."

Chapter 21

"You're going to *what*?" Sarah grabbed my arm as I was about to knock at the door. "Are you crazy? Oh, what am I saying? You don't even have a Taser . . ."

"No, but I do have a handy little skill that allows me to control lightning."

Her eyes widened. "You're going to strike Carol Lee with lightning? That could kill her!"

"Not if I can control it properly." I took a deep breath, pushing aside the doubting thoughts, focusing on what I needed to do. "A Taser is a device which uses a high-voltage pulse of electricity to momentarily shock its target, thereby disrupting the neurotransmitters, and effectively overloading the nervous system. Carol will be temporarily immobilized, but not permanently harmed."

Overhead, my little cloud formed. I spread my hands about six inches apart, mentally envisioning a concentrated electrical charge pulled from the surroundings. My fingers began to tingle, the sensation spreading up my arms, reminding me of the time I'd touched a low-voltage electrical fence. Sarah watched with open-mouthed horror as a small blue ball of light formed between my hands. The tingling intensified as the ball shrunk into a small blue orb between my palms.

"Knock on the door," I told Sarah, my attention focused on holding the charge where I wanted it.

"Portia—"

"Please, Sarah. I don't know what will happen if I stop focusing on this."

"I hope to god you know what you're doing," she said, shaking her head, but knocking on the door.

It took about sixty seconds, but the door finally opened up a few inches, with Carol Lee's white, expressionless face visible. "What do you want?" she asked.

"The truth," I told her, flinging the electrical charge directly at her. Her eyes widened for a moment before the charge zapped her, knocking her backward a few feet.

"I knew it! You've killed her!" Sarah pronounced as I pushed open the door and knelt down by Carol's supine figure. My hands were shaking as I checked her pulse.

"No, she's alive. Her pulse is a bit rocky, but fine." Carol's eyes were open, unblinking, and flat. "Go get the car. We'll get her into it and restrained before she comes out of this."

Sarah stood above me, her hands on her hips, a warning note clearly evident in her voice. "Portia, I never thought the day would come when I'd find you, the most passive of pacifists, disabling and kidnapping an unarmed, innocent woman—"

"Innocent, my ass. Get the car quick," I said, hurrying into the kitchen to look for some twine or duct tape I could use to bind her arms.

To my relief, we managed to get Milo's wife securely bound and bundled into the rental car before she came out of her shocked state. After five minutes of non-stop abuse hurled from where she lay on the backseat, the noise abated once we applied a scarf in the form of a gag. She continued to mumble behind the gag, but, thankfully, it was subdued enough to ignore.

"Where are we going?" Sarah asked as I returned to my seat after gagging our victim.

"The Court of Divine Blood."

Sarah made a soundless whistle, saying nothing more but shooting me frequent questioning glances. Silence and occasional outraged gurgles from the backseat filled the car as we drove to the castle. I knew Sarah was as uneasy as I was over the potentially damning act of kidnapping, but I saw no other solution available to me. The silence bore down heavily on me as I ran over a mental checklist, hoping that I hadn't missed anything important.

"You don't think anyone is going to notice this?" Sarah said twenty minutes later as a huge billow of fog filled the courtyard of the castle.

I prodded Milo's wife forward, ignoring her glare of pure venom, keeping one hand on her wrists bound behind her back. "I'm sure someone will notice the localized fog, but I don't really care. It's difficult enough kidnapping someone—getting them where you want them to go without interference from the public is tantamount to impossible. I'm just taking the easiest way out."

The fog, my lack of familiarity with the castle, and Carol Lee's repeated, abortive attempts at escape made it take a good three times the normal amount of time it would have taken to find the room that opened into the portal to the Court, but at last we arrived at our goal.

I saw Carol eyeing the windows and grabbed onto her shoulders with both hands, shoving her toward the entrance to the Court.

"Portia, are you sure—" Sarah started to say, doubt evident on her face as we approached the fuzzy portal.

"Reasonably sure. I've examined the evidence and can't come to any other conclusion. Deep breath, everyone. It's showtime!"

"I can't believe the only time I'm visiting heaven is in the pursuit of some crime or other," Sarah grumbled as we marched to the center of the town square. The usual business prevailed: people talking in small groups around the center well, the shops doing their brisk trade, other people busily hurrying hither and yon. At the sight of us materializing in the center of their activities, everyone froze.

"Hello, again," I said, recognizing a few (albeit startled) faces from the hearing. *Theo?*

An equally startled silence filled my head. *Portia? What are you doing in the Court?*

Doing what you asked—resolving one of our problems. Where are you? I think I'm going to need a little help in getting my prisoner to the mare. The

*people in the square seem to be stunned into some
sort of a fugue state.*

Theo seemed to share their reaction, at least for a
few seconds. *Prisoner?*

*Yes. I kidnapped Milo Lee's wife and brought her
here.*

A soft sigh echoed in my head. *Portia, do you
have any idea how the Court is going to react to you
kidnapping a mortal and bringing her here? As if we
weren't in enough trouble—*

Carol Lee took advantage of my distraction with
Theo to twist herself out of my grip, racing toward
the doorway that led back to the land of reality.

"Oh, no you don't!" I took a leap that would do a
broad jumper proud, flinging myself at Carol, just
catching the heel of her shoe as I fell. She went down
just as my head cracked the cobblestones, but I
didn't let go of her despite the stars that seemed to
weave around in front of me.

"Such an entrance you apparently desire to
make," a male voice drawled as I got to my knees,
shaking my head but keeping a firm grip on Carol's
kicking foot. "I could almost imagine you were trying to get my attention."

"Think again," I ground out as I got to my feet,
hauling up my still-struggling prisoner.

Gabriel the cherub pursed his lips as he eyed first
the woman bound with silver-grey duct tape, then
me. I blew back a strand of hair that was sticking to
my lip, and lifted my chin, trying to look poised and
in charge of the situation.

"I see you've added abduction to your resume,"

he said, the corners of his mouth crooking upward. "As if murder wasn't enough?"

"Portia didn't murder anyone," Sarah said, coming forward to give me a hand with Carol as she continued to fight her bonds, her eyes wild. "If you knew her, you'd realize that she's incapable of something so immoral."

Carol flung herself backward, her head knocking into mine as she tried to kick my legs out from under me. I sidestepped the back kick, yanking her bound arms up and hissing in her ear in as mean a voice as possible, "You try that again, and I'll break both your arms."

Gabriel's eyebrows rose.

"There are, naturally, different interpretations on the word 'immoral'," Sarah said, looking as if she was about to explain the whole circumstance to Gabriel.

"Don't bother trying to make him understand," I interrupted. "Gabriel has his mind already made up about me."

"Gabriel?" Sarah's face took on an awe-struck cast. *"Gabriel?"*

"Not that Gabriel," he said, looking annoyed. "What is it with you mortals? Is there only one Gabriel you know?"

Sarah nodded, disappointment rife in her eyes.

"This Gabriel is a cherub," I said, catching sight of a familiar form skulking along the edge of a building, staying well into the shadows. "And not a particularly nice one. Come on, Carol, we have a little business with some friends of yours."

"I could make a comment about your niceness as

well, virtue," Gabriel called after us as we left him. "But I am too much a cherub to do so!"

"What's his problem?" Sarah asked in a whisper, glancing over her shoulder at him.

"He's a bit pissed that I refused to let him seduce me. Or so I gather—honestly, it could be just about anything. I may have breached some sort of Court etiquette or something, and offended him. I've never felt so out of my depths in my life."

"I wouldn't worry about it." Sarah gave me a reassuring pat on the arm. "Gabriel may be a handsome devil, but he's no Theo."

"Indeed he isn't."

Theo's eyes were shaded by the brim of his hat, but I could see the light color of his irises even before I got up close to him.

Not a good sign.

"I don't suppose you'd care to explain just why you felt it necessary to kidnap someone when we're attempting to clear your name of a murder charge?" Theo asked.

"I told her it wasn't a good idea," Sarah piped in. "But you know how Portia is—once she has a goal in mind, she moves heaven and earth to achieve it. It must be all that science stuff—she's so linear in the way she thinks."

"She can be," Theo said, his gaze darkening into something expressing less displeasure and more thoughtfulness. "Which leads me to believe that I might owe her an apology after all. It's been my experience that Portia doesn't look before leaping, so to speak."

"Thank you, I will graciously accept your apology. Is there a mare or two around we can speak with? I think they're going to find Carol very interesting."

Theo gave the bound woman a long look. *Who is this?*

Milo's wife, Carol Lee.

Theo waited for more. I smiled into his head. *Don't you recognize her? She's an old friend of yours.*

His eyes narrowed as he looked her over more closely. She jerked convulsively, trying to break my hold on her bound arms, her eyes all but spitting hatred at us.

I knew the instant Theo recognized her. His eyes widened as he took a step toward her.

"I think we should let that wait for the mare," I told him. "Are they in the library, do you know?"

"I have no idea where they are, but we will find out," he said, stepping past us, careful not to leave the shade of the building as he hailed a young girl passing on a brightly colored bike. He had a few minutes' discussion with her, then gestured to us to follow him. "The messenger says that two of the mare are in the sanctuary."

Carol flung herself on the ground, shrieking behind her gag. Theo simply hoisted her onto his shoulders and carried her to the area of the Court containing the offices and grand apartments.

"We have an audience," Sarah said as we marched along. I glanced back to where she was looking. Just about everyone who had been in the town square was following behind us, with others streaming in to swell their ranks as we proceeded to the other section of the city.

This should prove to be interesting, Theo said as we waited for the same dapifer who had taken care of us a few days before to determine if the mare would see us. *Added to what I found out while you were so industriously occupied, I believe we may have a solution.*

Oh, I can't believe I didn't ask you about that! Did you talk to Terrin? What did you find out?

"Their graces the mare Irina and mare Disin have granted you an audience," the dapifer said, his lips moving soundlessly as he eyeballed the gathered crowd behind us. "I believe the ballroom will be best. This way, please."

What did Terrin tell you?

Have you ever heard of renascence?

Renaissance? Sure.

No, renascence. He spelled it for me. *The concept is similar to renaissance in that both essentially mean rebirth, but in this instance its usage applies solely to the Court of Divine Blood.*

In what way? I asked as we were led to an entirely different area of the keep from where we'd been before.

It is the method by which the entire Court hierarchy is remade. The sovereign allows one renascence per millennium.

What happens to the people who are remade? I asked, my skin crawling as thoughts of concentration camps and ethnic purging danced through my head.

*They take new positions under the reformed hier-
archy. It is not a mass extermination, sweetling . . .
although the results can be nearly as devastating.*

"Do we get to see the sovereign?" Sarah asked in
an awe-hushed voice, drawing my attention from the
dark path my thoughts had taken.

I looked around us as we made our way into the
depths of the castle, noticing the surroundings with
growing amazement. The word "grand" was an understatement when applied to the reception rooms.
Rich ebony-edged lapis lazuli furniture jostled for
room with crimson and gold chairs, settees, and op-
ulent drapery. The walls looked like something out
of an art museum, with objects adorning almost
every free space: everything from chunks of rocky
walls bearing faded cave paintings, to wooden trip-
tychs depicting the medieval idea of religion scenes,
to icons, both old and new.

The dapifer leading the way stopped before a pair
of rococo double doors. He turned back to us, giving
Sarah a frown. "The sovereign is never seen."

"What do you mean, never seen?" Sarah looked
confused. "Not seen without an appointment?"

"No, I mean that the sovereign is never seen. That
is, the sovereign does not appear in the Court of Divine Blood. Their graces are waiting for you," he
continued, giving Theo and me a nod.

"Wait a second," I said, stopping him as he was
about to open the door. "Are you saying that the person running the Court doesn't bother to put in an appearance once in a while?"

The dapifer's face reflected mild annoyance. "The

sovereign does not choose to make its physical form known."

"How incredibly convenient," I said, shaking my head. "Why?"

"Why?" The dapifer's eyebrows went up. "Why what?"

"Why does the sovereign choose to not make its appearance known in the Court, its own home, if I understand the premise correctly. Is it afraid of something?"

The murmur of conversation that had accompanied the crowd following us hushed into a pregnant silence.

Portia, you are treading on very thin ice, Theo warned as the dapifer's eyebrows rose in startled surprise at my question. *I urge you to discontinue this line of conversation. It can do no good to you, nor does it have any bearing on our situation.*

No, but surely I can't be the only one here to find it more than a little suspicious that the almighty sovereign, the supreme being of everyone here, doesn't bother to pop in now and again and see how things are going.

I turned to the people filling the hallway as far back as the eye could see. "Doesn't anyone here wonder about the fact that sovereign has never been seen? Doesn't anyone question that policy?"

Sweetling, you must stop before this goes further.

So free thought isn't allowed here? Is no one allowed to question the existence of a supreme being that no one has ever seen?

The existence of the sovereign is not in doubt by

any members of the Court, he answered, and I could feel how carefully he picked his words.

"Is there any empirical proof that the sovereign is even here now?" I asked, amazed that something so basic had escaped everyone. "Does no one even wonder if the whole idea of a sovereign is . . . untrue?"

"No," the dapifer said, his face once again bland and emotionless. "It is a matter of faith."

"Faith? Because you believe the sovereign exists, it follows that such a being must be?" I shook my head again.

Theo turned so Carol's foot whapped me on the arm. *Sweetling, cease. We have more important things to take care of, and you arguing the logic of faith will not help our case.*

He was right. I had met fanatics before—I'd lived with them for eighteen years—and I knew well that such people were not often open to logic and reason. This would be a battle for another time.

Sarah was watching me closely, concern in her eyes. I gave her a weakly reassuring smile and waved a hand at the dapifer. "Sorry to hold you up. We're ready if the mare are."

The dapifer opened both doors with a grand gesture, sweeping in to make a bow to the dais at the far end of the room.

"Hol-ee cow," Sarah said, her eyes huge as she spun around looking at the ballroom.

I had to admit, it was a pretty impressive sight. The walls were paneled in a warm, amber oak, with two rows of long windows running the entire length of the room. Sunlight poured into the room, leaving bright pools dappling the glossy, polished parquet floor. More pictures were on the walls between the windows, portraits this time, beneath each of which sat a silver and blue upholstered chair.

"They're going to need a whole lot more chairs than that," I said softly as we proceeded into the room, Theo carefully making his way around the pools of sunlight.

"Will you look at those chandeliers?" Sarah's mouth hung open just a smidgen as she ogled the ornate silver pieces of art that hung from the ceiling. "Are those swans in them?"

"Looks like a whole mythology theme going on in this room," I answered, unable to keep from looking at the mural on the ceiling. Although at first I thought it was the sort of allegorical painting one normally found on a castle ballroom ceiling, closer inspection showed elements of mythology rather than religion. Satyrs and fauns romped with sylphlike women clad in gauzy gowns in a sylvan setting, while on the far side of the room, nearest the dais which we were approaching, the scene changed to one of black and red, with figures of leering men, and small brown humanlike beings that I took to be some sort of demon.

Clustered to one side, between the woodland paradise and the fiery depths of Abaddon, but part of neither, stood a small cluster of men and women with downcast eyes, their expressions and body language depicting shame and remorse.

"Those are the nephilim," Theo said, nodding at them.

"Right. It's brass-tacks time," I said, squaring my shoulders as we stopped in front of the raised dais. Three chairs sat on it, two of which were occupied by the elderly mare named Irina and the acerbic Disin.

Theo set the struggling Carol down. I moved around to her far side, keeping a possessive hand on her arm. Theo bowed to the mare. I thought fleetingly of curtseying, but the fact that I had no idea how to perform such a move, coupled with an independent spirit that rejected such notions as someone being "better" than me, left me with the decision that a head bob would be sufficient to show respect.

"Good afternoon," I said, nodding to both the mares. "I am sorry to disrupt you without warning, but—"

"Portia Harding," Disin interrupted, her voice booming like thunder as it rolled down the room. People were still filing into the ballroom, but at her bellow they froze, a good half of the large ballroom filled with a solid mass of apparently lifeless bodies. "You have defied the judgment of the Court of Divine Blood by returning here without first being summoned to do so."

Theo moved closer to me. Overhead, a small dark cloud formed. I willed it away, taking Theo's hand instead.

"I am not aware that the hearing you held constituted a legal trial, complete with judgment," I said, keeping my voice as non-confrontational, while still firm, as possible. "As I recall, you ordered us to find the murderer of Hope the virtue by the new moon."

I waved my hand to the bound woman next to me. "We have done so."

The crowd moved forward a few feet. I recognized a few familiar faces: the nameless boy proctor who'd taken me to the Akasha, Gabriel, the messenger Theo had stopped. Probably another two hundred people had joined them, filling half the ballroom. Each and every one of them turned to look at Carol Lee.

"Your cruel and callous treatment of this woman is yet another slap in the Court's face," Disin said, her voice flinty and hard-edged. "Release her immediately."

"I realize that kidnapping someone is an extreme action, and one I do not undertake lightly. However, given the circumstances, there was no alternative. I could not have convinced her to come to the Court on her own. If I release her now, she will simply escape."

The crowd made murmurs of disbelief. Disin drew herself up until she seemed a good three feet taller than normal.

It began to snow inside the ballroom.

"Your impertinence is beyond all bounds. Release that woman immediately, or I will have you jailed for contempt."

She looks mean enough to do it, I muttered to Theo as I pulled out a small pair of nail scissors from my purse. *Keep an eye on Carol. She's going to bolt the second I have her hands free, I just know it.*

Have a little more faith in the security of the Court, sweetling. Despite appearances, the mare will not allow anyone to leave if they do not desire it.

I cut the duct tape on Carol's wrists while Theo untied the gag. The second her hands were free, she attacked me, knocking me down to the ground, both hands clutching my hair while she banged my head on the ground.

Theo pulled her off me while Disin yelled for order.

"I told you," I said softly as Sarah helped me up to my feet.

"There will be order," Disin yelled, her hands gesticulating wildly toward us. "You will, all of you, display the respect due the Court, or I will take such measures as to ensure you will not darken our presence again!"

As a threat, it had sufficient punch to calm Carol down. She jerked her arm out of Theo's grip, but limited herself to a couple of murderous looks my way.

The snow moved to fall only on Carol.

"You will cease with such unseemly dramatics," Disin ordered, pointing at me.

"I would if I could, but I don't seem to have a very good grasp on weather control," I said.

Irina shook her head, her all-seeing eyes on me. "Child, child. This is not worthy of you."

I cleared my throat as a little blush warmed my cheeks. "I hope that once I am formally accepted as a virtue, I'll be able to learn how to control the weather effects a little better."

Sweetling, you will never be an actress.

I smiled at the soft brush of Theo's mind.

"Such an event is not yet in your grasp," Disin answered with a distinct threat in her voice. "Nor will it be, if your present actions continue."

I made an effort to dismiss the cloud, arranging my expression to be something a little less antagonistic, folding my hands together and waiting for Disin to continue.

"I'm sorry, I'm so sorry, I'm late I know, but I was held up in the mortal world. Goodness, is it snowing? How interesting." Suria, the third mare, pushed her way through the crowd, giving the snow-covered Carol an interested look before taking her seat on the dais. "What have I missed?"

"Portia Harding has effected an act of violence against an outsider, and brought her to the Court without either permission or the knowledge of the mare." Disin's glance flickered over to Sarah for a second. "Two outsiders. Such an inconsiderate disregard for the laws of the Court of Divine Blood is not to be tolerated!"

"Portia has little knowledge of Court etiquette and laws," Theo said, moving closer to me. "We ask your graces to show the leniency for which you are so well known in regards to her accidental violations."

"Accidental?" Disin asked, her face tightening. "Do you consider kidnapping a woman accidental?"

"It would, perhaps, be prudent to allow Portia Harding to explain her reasons for conducting such an . . . extreme act," Irina said softly.

Suria nodded, her normally sunny face pinched and worried. "I will confess that I, too, am curious as to why Portia would go to such lengths. Who exactly is this woman you have abducted?"

"She goes by the name of Carol Lee, and is wife to Milo, who conducted the fourth trial."

Immediately, a buzz of conversation started up behind me.

"And you say that she is responsible for the death of the virtue Hope?" Suria asked.

"In a manner of speaking, yes." I slid a glance toward Theo. His face was expressionless, but his warm presence gave me much comfort.

Go ahead, sweetling.

You speak with much more of a Court flair than I do. Maybe you should be the one to explain.

No. The honor goes to you. You figured it out—you should be the one to explain.

"You will explain your actions, child," Irina said in her soft voice. The undertone of steel was enough to warn me that she wasn't going to be supportive if I didn't offer up enough proof.

"What do you mean, in a manner of speaking?" Disin asked, her words lashing the air with whiplike accuracy. "Did she kill Hope or not?"

"No."

The buzz grew in volume.

I raised my voice to be heard over it. "She did not kill Hope for the simple fact that she *is* Hope."

Chapter 22

She is Hope. The last of my words echoed eerily from the back of the ballroom.

I licked my lips, nervous now that I had to lay the facts—such as they were—out before everyone.

You are doing fine, Portia.

Disin frowned at Carol, who stood as frozen as a statue. "You claim this mortal is a virtue? Do you think us so ignorant that we can't tell the difference between a member of the Court and an innocent mortal?"

"I don't quite understand how she can appear to be someone else, nor do I know about the mortal business, although I thought someone told me that you had to be a member of the Court to be immortal, and it follows that if she isn't a virtue anymore, she would no longer be a member, and thus lose her immortal status."

The three mare gaped at me.

"I could be wrong on that, though," I said, squirming slightly under their combined looks of disbelief. "I'm not very current with all the intricacies of Court life."

"You are correct, as it happens," a man's voice said behind me. We turned en masse to see Terrin at the door, a rumpled Milo beside him. He bowed to the mare, shoving Milo forward. "Your graces, please forgive me for this disruption, but I found this man sneaking into the Court, and felt it might have some bearing on a recent conversation I had with Theo North."

"You are welcome here, scholar," Irina said, bowing her head graciously. "Bring forward the one who was banned and readmitted into our grace."

"Your grace," Milo said, stammering slightly as he stopped in front of the mare. He shot his wife a look out of the corner of his eye as he bowed to them. "There has been a gross injustice done to my wife. She is, as you can see, mortal, and not in the least bit like the late virtue Hope as Portia claims."

I nibbled on my lower lip. Carol's appearance was my one weak point. I was too unfamiliar with the denizens of the Court of Divine Blood to know if it was possible for someone to change their appearance.

"But you are a vessel," Theo said slowly. I took his hand, drawing strength from the contact.

"It is true," Milo said, squaring his shoulders as he looked out at the people gathered. "I have the honor of holding the position of vessel. Even a nephilim, however, must be aware that it is not within my powers to change a mortal's appearance."

"This is so," Disin said, turning to me. "You say that the mortal Carol Lee is really the virtue Hope, but you offer no proof for such a supposition. How do you answer this discrepancy?"

A smug look replaced the one of hatred in Carol's eyes. I knew I was right about her, I knew without a shred of doubt that she was Hope, but how did she do it? How did she morph into someone else?

"I . . . uh . . . that is . . ." I bit my lip again.

There has to be some way he can change her appearance. Is there a magic spell or something that would fool everyone?

A glamour? It is possible to confuse another mortal with a glamour, but not members of the Court, and certainly not the mare.

"Can you explain it, Portia Harding?"

"Er . . ."

There has to be some way, something we've missed, someone who has the power to change her in a way that would fool even the mare.

Theo's eyes opened wide at my words.

"It is evident that you cannot." Disin waved her hands toward Milo and Carol. "You may leave, mortal. Portia Harding, I order you taken into custody, to await arraignment on the charge of gross abuse of power—"

What is it?

He smiled. Two Hashmallim suddenly appeared, wafting over to flank me. One person shrieked, while the others backed up a good ten feet. Sarah scooted over until she was near Terrin, who stood on the far side of Milo and Carol. Only Theo stood firm, apparently not at all concerned by the Hashmallim.

I really, really hope it's good.

Oh, it is. He turned to Milo and asked in a deceptively mild voice, "Is it not true that one of your charges as a vessel is to serve as a conduit between the mortal and immortal worlds?"

"Yes," Milo answered, his eyes confident. "But the ability to go between mortals and the Court of Divine Blood is not sufficient to change the appearance of one of them. All I do is act as a courier, someone who passes along communication, and arranges for meetings."

Theo's smile got even wider.

What is it? What do you know?

Shhh. All in good time, sweetling.

Theo! How would you like a head full of snow?

His laughter echoed in my head. "And what of Abaddon?" he asked, and instantly, I knew what it was I had missed.

Oh, you're brilliant.

Thank you. You're not so bad, yourself, you know. I'd never have thought to look at a mortal for Hope.

"Abaddon?" Milo's confidence faded. "I suppose that technically it is possible, but not very likely—"

"Is it not, then, within the scope of your powers to arrange for a meeting between a mortal and a demon lord? Someone who, I need not add, has the ability to change the appearance of a minion such as a demon, or imp . . . or mortal servant."

The gasps of surprise from the crowd were loud, as was the resulting torrent of conversation.

"Silence!" Disin shouted, jumping to her feet. "There will be silence here!"

Irina smiled slightly, leaning back in her chair. I

had the feeling we had just won her over, and smiled back.

"Such a thing is against the laws of the Court," Milo protested, his face pale. A light bead of sweat broke out on his forehead, and I knew we had him.

"Far be it from me to cast stones from the sanctity of my glass house, but you haven't been horribly concerned about following the laws of the Court in the past, have you?"

The look he gave me could have stripped cement.

"My past situation with the Court has nothing to do with this." His lips tightened. "To imply that just because it's theoretically possible for me to contact a demon lord for the purpose of changing the appearance of a mortal, I have done so, is not only ridiculous, it's damned near obscene. I am a member of the Court of Divine Blood! It would be impossible for me to conduct any act in such opposition to the tenets of the Court."

Is there any way to tell if he's been in contact with a demon lord?

Theo rubbed his chin. *Not here. A Guardian might be able to, but I doubt if it would be possible to tell if Milo has been near a demon lord lately.*

"Your graces, I beg of you, please allow my lady wife to leave. She has suffered much trauma by the abduction and resulting indignities, and I fear for her well-being if she should be made to stand here while this person throws her smoke screens and misdirection." Milo's head bent solicitously over that of his wife, the very picture of husbandly concern.

"Oh, for reason's sweet sake . . . smoke screens

and misdirection. Like I'm the one trying to pull something on the Court." I didn't even try to temper the disgust in my voice.

"Everyone here knows the true reason you summoned and destroyed the virtue Hope," Milo said, his voice ringing clear and loud as he turned to confront me. He gestured toward Theo, whose fingers tightened around mine in warning or anger, I didn't know which. "You are the only one here who has an ulterior motive, not me."

"Hey now," I protested.

He continued before I could say anything more. "It is an established fact that Theo North has for centuries sought someone who would present the Court with an order of exculpation, thankfully to no avail. Until you agreed to help him by granting him the exculpation the moment you were made a member, his cause was lost."

"I did not agree to anyth—"

"Do you deny that you intend to ask for a pardon?" Milo shouted, the entire ballroom silent but for the echoes, just as if everyone was holding his or her breath.

Theo's eyes were a light slate grey. His muscles were tight, as if he was poised to spring. I cleared my throat nervously, and looked at the mare. "I do not deny that I intend to speak to the Court about Theo's situation, but that was not my plan when I came to England, nor did I ever agree to take on the duties of a virtue. I didn't even know why Hope showed up when she did! I thought she was a hallucination at first!"

How distant those days a week ago seemed.

"You lie," Milo drawled, his face hard. "You knew exactly what you were doing when you spoke the spells of summoning. Why else would you so conveniently have the spells upon you when you breached the sacred ground?"

"I told you that faery ring was real," Sarah said in a whisper, nudging the back of my shoulder.

I was about to refute Milo's ridiculous accusations when something occurred to me. "How did you know that Hope was summoned by a spell?" I asked, wondering if at last a glint of luck was turning our way. "The only people to whom I explained what happened are my friend Sarah, and Theo, and I'm sure neither of them have spoken about it to anyone here."

Both of them shook their heads.

"I heard of it from Terrin the scholar," Milo said, crossing his arms over his chest as he nodded toward Terrin. "We had a discussion regarding your trials, and he told me the far-fetched tale you'd spun him."

"I don't believe the method of summoning the virtue was ever broached," Terrin said thoughtfully. "All Portia said was that she had inadvertently summoned a virtue, and received the Gift without understanding the importance of the act."

"How is it you have such insight into the method of summoning Hope if you did not hear the details from the woman herself?" Theo asked, his voice as smooth and rich as milk chocolate.

We have him.

Possibly.

"I . . . it's only common sense," Milo sputtered. "Virtues can only be summoned by spell, thus it was safe to assume that Portia Harding used such a method."

"That's not true!" Sarah startled me by bouncing forward, apparently ready to battle Milo on our behalf.

"Sarah—"

"Who is this mortal?" Disin asked, giving Sarah a narrow-eyed once-over.

"My name is Sarah Wilson," she answered, making an incredibly graceful curtsey. "I am Portia's oldest friend. I also happen to be an author, and am the one who gave Portia the spells. I thought they had a slight chance of working, but Portia was absolutely skeptical, disbelieving there even was such a thing as a faery ring."

"This is all very interesting, but hardly has relevance—"

Sarah shook her head and interrupted Disin before she could continue. "It does have relevance. Once we discovered that Portia had inadvertently become a virtue, I did some online research into the history of virtues. One of the things I discovered was that, although virtues are rarely summoned, it can be done, most commonly by means of an invocation."

There were a few snorts of disbelief, but out of the corner of my eye I saw several people nodding.

"What Portia used was a general summoning spell, not an invocation pleading for a virtue. According to my research, the spell could have summoned anyone in the Court."

I gaped at my friend. "Why on earth didn't you mention that to me?"

She shrugged. "It didn't seem important at the time."

"It didn't seem . . . good gravy, woman!"

The mare leaned their heads together.

Theo took advantage of their inattention to drive home the relevant point. "All of which brings us back to the point whereby you knew that Portia had used a general summoning spell, rather than the more common invocation. How do you explain that?"

"We are curious as to that point as well," Disin said as the mare sat back in their respective chairs. She pinned Milo back with a look I was thankful wasn't, for once, turned upon me.

"Yeah!" I said.

Disin's gimlet glance descended upon me.

"Sorry," I murmured, folding my hands and going for a contrite look.

"You will now explain how you knew in detail what method Portia Harding used to summon the virtue Hope."

Milo looked decidedly nervous. I sent Theo a private smirk, and watched as Milo squirmed under the combined attention of the mare.

"I . . . that is, we . . . I . . ."

Carol leaned into him, whispering furiously. Milo's gaze was shifty, but he nodded a couple of times before straightening up and puffing out his chest. "By virtue of my role as vessel, and as a member in good standing in the Court of Divine Blood, I demand a renascence!"

There was a collective stunned gasp behind us, then utter silence.

He can't do that, can he? Overthrow the hierarchy like that?

I think he just did.

The mare got to their respective feet, all three standing in a tableau that reminded me, for some inane reason, of the three furies.

"On what grounds do you demand the renascence?" Disin asked, her voice deceptively soft.

Milo pointed at me. "The Court has been compromised. A non-member mortal holds the title of virtue, which is against the laws to which the hierarchy of the Court is bound."

"Portia is not yet a virtue," Theo argued, his arm sliding around my waist. I leaned into him, more than a little sick that everything had spiraled so far out of control. That I could be used as an excuse for the overthrow of the Court was unthinkable . . . wasn't it? "She will not claim that title until she completes the seventh trial."

"Which I am certainly not going to do now," I added.

Milo smiled. It wasn't a nice smile.

Uh-oh. What's he smiling about?

I have a bad feeling it's about something Terrin was about to tell me when you showed up with Carol in tow.

"You are unfamiliar with our laws, nephilim. When a renascence is called, all scheduled business is completed before the Court is disbanded and remade."

My stomach tightened into a small wad of unhappiness.

"The seventh and final trial of the mortal Portia Harding is scheduled for today, if I am not mistaken," Milo continued. "Once she has completed it, the grounds for renascence will be satisfied, and by the laws that govern the Court, it must be destroyed before reformation."

"Well then, I simply won't do the seventh trial," I told him, relief filling me at this easy way out of the situation.

"You cannot stop the trial from commencing," Milo said. "As it is scheduled, it must be enacted."

"Fine. Enact away. I will simply do the opposite of whatever it is. Er . . . what is the seventh trial?"

"Faith," Terrin answered, his eyes unreadable. "It is a trial of your faith."

I laughed without the slightest shred of mirth. "Displaying a lack of faith is not going to be difficult for me." I turned to the mare to explain, wanting to make sure they understood that my feelings were grounded in a lifelong battle rather than a slight against the Court itself. "I grew up in a religious cult, one that required its members to show absolute, unbreakable faith in the leaders and religion itself. Anyone questioning the religion was severely punished. I believe I spent more time during my childhood locked in a closet, ordered to examine my sins and renounce my disbeliefs, than I did out of it. Faith is not a commodity I have in abundance. Because of this, I can just about guarantee you that I will fail the seventh trial."

"If you do so, then you throw away all chances of an exculpation for Theo North," Milo pointed out. "He will never be a member of the Court of Divine Blood. He will remain a nephilim, an outcast, tainted by the sins of his father, for the rest of his life. He will never have a soul."

I opened my mouth to say that we'd be just fine without Theo being a member of the Court, but stopped, stunned at Milo's words.

What was that about a soul?

Theo's sigh echoed through my mind. *I wasn't going to tell you this, since it puts more pressure on you to obtain my exculpation, but members of the Court of Divine Blood cannot be soulless. If a member lacks one, it is granted when the membership is made official.*

You knew this and you didn't tell me? I wanted to whap Theo on the arm, but now was not the time. *Well, this makes everything so much easier. Instead of waiting around for an opportunity for me to make some big sacrifice on your behalf, I can get your soul back just by becoming a recognized virtue!*

It's not quite that simple, sweetling, he said, his thoughts rich with emotion.

Theo, I know what it means to you—

No. You know what it meant to me. That was before I found you, before our lives were bound together. An exculpation is no longer as desirable as is a future with you, my love.

The world as I knew it rocked, shifted slightly, and settled back, but it was changed. *I* was changed. I stared at Theo, stunned by his words, by the feelings he had shared with me. My mind struggled to cope with the revelation he laid open for me—it was as if I'd spent my whole life waiting for that exact moment in time, the moment when I knew what it was to truly be loved above all else . . . and the knowledge that I would literally move heaven and earth for the man standing next to me.

That is, without the slightest doubt, the nicest thing anyone has ever said to me. I just can't believe how much I love you, Theo.

As much as five to the tenth power? he teased.

Oh no, my darling, my love for you can only be described in terms of equations containing complex numbers. My tone was light, but I shook with emotion as, deep in the back of my mind, an idea was born.

"It would be within Portia Harding's rights to refuse to participate in the seventh trial," Disin said after a brief consultation with the other mare. "Furthermore, we feel it important to point out that even if she does successfully complete the trial and is accepted as a member of the Court, any exculpation she seeks is not automatically granted."

I gathered my wits together and tried to regain control of myself. *We still have the Beloved path of soul redemption. How would you feel if I ditched the virtue business? Could we get along just fine without the Court?*

More than fine, he answered, and allowed me to see the truth in his words. *It's you I want, Portia. Not reparation, not even my soul, is as important as a life with you.*

My knees turned to jelly under the look he gave me. I didn't think it was possible, but I fell even more in love with him. I knew then what Irina had meant about being lost. Theo had shown me the path that I needed to take.

I looked at Milo. "Theo has decided not to pursue his exculpation. I will pass on the position of virtue. The seventh trial will be conducted without my participation, and given my failure, I assume I'll be booted out of the program."

Suria and Disin nodded.

"So nice try, Milo, but your little scheme to use us for your own evil plans isn't going to fly."

Milo's laughter rolled with sickening intensity down the length of the ballroom. "You have chosen not to pursue exculpation . . . do you hold Theo's soul in so little value?"

"On the contrary, I'd do just about anything to retrieve it . . . just about anything, but not this."

Milo stopped before us, his head tipped to the side as he looked at me. "Consider this, Beloved . . . you have completed the seven steps of Joining, but you have yet to finalize it by making a sacrifice. You look surprised that I am so familiar with the rules governing Dark Ones, but this plan has been a long time in the making. Do you think I would go to the trouble of arranging for Bael to curse Theo if it was not important to gain leverage for just such a situation as this?"

"You bastard," I screamed, lunging forward to throttle him. Only Theo's restraining hold kept me from strangling Milo . . . that and the sense of calmness and love he poured into me. "You planned this?"

"Of course. The downfall and subsequent complete restructuring of the Court is not something to be undertaken without some thought."

"Well then, you've gone through a whole lot of trouble for nothing," I spat, still wanting badly to attack him for what he'd done to us. "There is another way for me to get Theo's soul back. I will not become a virtue."

Milo heaved a mock sigh. "You still don't understand, do you? Even if you refuse to become a member, thereby saving the Court, you will have damned Theo to an eternity without his soul."

"I'm his Beloved. All I have to do is make a sacrifice on his behalf, and I'll get it back—" I started to say.

"Exactly." Milo smiled, and my stomach turned over. "You see it at last. You can save the Court of Divine Blood, or you can save Theo's soul—but only the act of sacrificing the former will grant the latter."

Chapter 23

Tell me that Milo is insane.

The silence that met my question was disconcerting.

Tell me he isn't right.

Theo looked thoughtful. Everyone else, myself included, looked stunned to the point of insensitivity.

Tell me I don't have to choose between your soul and the continued existence of the whole, friggin' Court.

The existence of the Court is not your responsibility. The present hierarchy, however . . .

There has to be some other sacrifice I can make. This can't be the only thing.

Theo's silence was incredibly unnerving.

Theo? Surely there must be something else?

I don't know, he said at last, sorrow filling my mind. *I don't know enough about Dark Ones to know if just any sacrifice will work, but I suspect . . .* His sigh wrung my heart. *I suspect, sweetling, that it is that which would cost you the most that will be the act necessary to fulfill the last stage of Joining.*

The weight of the world seemed to descend upon me, pressing me down into the earth until there was little left of me.

Portia, I meant what I said. Just having you in my life is more important than anything else. You are a smart woman. Do not allow Milo to manipulate you into something you will later regret.

I sent Theo a sad smile, and straightened my shoulders.

"This is ridiculous," I said, watching the mare. They were consulting each other, but the looks on their faces didn't give me much hope that their game plan was to clap Milo in irons and dismiss his troublemaking attempts with nothing more than an airy wave and an amused laugh.

Terrin glanced my way. I focused on him as a relatively sane person, someone who made a lot of sense when I'd spoken to him. "I may not be an expert on the social structure of the Court, but I can't believe that all it takes to bring the whole thing down around your ears is the antics of two people."

"This is an unusual situation," Terrin said slowly, his eyes guarded. "That's not to say it's without precedent—the Court has survived several renascences in its history."

"What was it you were going to tell me when I was called away by Portia?" Theo asked him.

Terrin's face grew dark. "I wished to explain to you the dangers I felt Portia was in. I didn't imagine that things would come to a head quite so quickly, or I would have warned you earlier."

"I don't understand," Sarah said, joining our little

threesome. "Milo wants to remake the Court? Why doesn't the sovereign simply say no?"

"The sovereign will uphold the laws of the Court. Technically, Milo Lee is within his rights to call a renascence—traditionally, such things have been achieved by use of a demon in place of a Court member, but the laws are such that a mortal, too, could be considered sufficient grounds for beginning the unmaking."

"But why does he want to remake the Court?" Sarah asked. "What does he get out of that?"

"Milo is a vessel," Theo answered, his eyes on the man in question. "Hope was a virtue. Both are on the bottom of the hierarchy. Vessels serve mortals, while virtues have little purpose but the occasional control of weather when ordered by a superior."

"Milo said he was looking for a new job," I said, suddenly remembering the conversation we'd had while he administered the trial I didn't know about. "Why doesn't he just try to get a different one? Why does he have to destroy the whole Court first?"

"It is tradition that the Court members who instigate a renascence have a role in restructure. It is one way the sovereign ensures that only those members who have the quickness of wits, intelligence, and general fitness desirable for the upper positions claim those positions."

"In other words," I said, disgusted by the thought of Milo in a position of power, "it's a system that rewards anarchy."

"The sovereign, I believe, prefers to think of it as survival of the fittest," Terrin said mildly, craning his head when one of the mare gestured for him. "You will excuse me, please. I believe their graces wish to consult me on a point of etiquette."

"So what do we do?" Sarah's voice was little more than a whisper.

What will the mare do? I asked Theo at the same time.

His eyes lightened a couple of shades. He pinched his lower lip, a sign, I was coming to realize, that he was troubled. *I am not sure. They are bound by the laws of the Court just as we are.*

I will not be used in this way, Theo. I will not allow Milo to use us for his own greedy purpose.

His arm around me was almost as warm as the admiration and love he poured into me. *I believe we have few choices at this point, sweetling.*

"What are we going to do?" Sarah repeated.

I kissed Theo's chin, trying to instill order in my confused mind. "Let's take this from the beginning. If I complete the seventh trial, I will be made a virtue, correct?"

"Yes." A tiny little smile turned up the corners of his mouth. *You're incredibly cute when you get logical.*

Then hold onto your cute meter, because I'm about to continue. "But if I'm a virtue, and still mortal, then Milo has grounds to dismiss the current Court and demand a new one be reformed, with himself at the head of the restructuring committee."

"That is more or less true, yes."

"I assume there's some sort of rule that states he has to be here to see the renascence enacted, though."

Theo shrugged. "The study of Court canon has

never been one of my hobbies, but I am fairly certain that a member cannot call for a renascence, and then disappear."

"Hmm."

"Is there any way the mare can make you immortal?" Sarah asked.

Theo shook his head. "Terrin said that once a renascence has been called, only current business on the dockets can be completed. Inducting a new member into the Court is considered new business."

"If I do not complete the seventh trial, then you lose all chance of being made a member of the Court, and thus, your soul will not be returned to you."

Theo was silent, but I didn't need to look into his beautiful eyes to feel the emptiness inside of him. Despite his protestations to the contrary, leaving him in that situation for the rest of eternity was simply not an option.

"As I see it, the equation Milo has created is unsolvable by the terms he has set. There is simply no way we can work a solution given the limitations of Court law."

Sarah clutched my arm. "Does that mean it's hopeless? He's going to win?"

I looked at Theo, my beautiful Theo, the man whom I'd given my heart to, a man who had suffered the deepest sort of pain possible for a human without complaint. There was one solution in my mind, a way to fix all the problems, but it required so much from me. For a few seconds I wavered, not sure if I could make the sacrifice needed.

Sweetling, why have you shut me out of your thoughts?

I knew what I had to do. A lump grew in my throat, painful and constricting as I contemplated what the course of my actions would mean, what the result would be.

Portia, I don't care for this silence on your part. You're up to something, aren't you?

What it required from me wasn't going to be easy. It was, without a doubt, the hardest thing I'd ever done in my life . . . but Theo was worth it.

Portia! I demand that you talk to me! We are in this together, woman. I dislike the sense of martyrdom I feel beginning inside you.

I love you, Theo, I said simply, filling him with all the love and happiness and joy he had given me.

Stop that. Stop looking at me as if this is the last time you will see me. You must have faith that we will see this through together, sweetling.

Oh, I do have faith, Theo. I have faith in you. I have faith in our love. I will love you until the day I stop living, and I have faith that no matter what happens, you will always love me.

Portia, stop—

"I love you," I whispered against his lips, kissing him with every atom of love I possessed. "I found my faith again, and it's you."

Somewhere far away, a deep bell sounded.

"It's the seventh trial," Milo crowed, leaping forward to thrust a finger at me. "She completed it without knowing! She has proven her faith before the entire Court! Now the renascence must begin!"

"Yes," I said, my soul weeping at the pain of realization in Theo's eyes. "I have proven my faith. I accept the position of virtue."

Before Theo could voice the protests and suspicions I knew were building within him, I stepped back, closing my eyes and opening my arms wide, the better to pull in the elements needed from the environment.

"Portia, what are you doing?" Sarah asked, her voice worried. "Theo, what is she doing?"

"She is throwing herself away in the foolish belief it will solve everything," he answered, his voice a deep growl that reverberated through me. I gently pushed him out of my mind, unable to do what I needed to do and reassure him at the same time.

"The mare regret that you acted without consulting them," Terrin said behind me. "They hope to mitigate the damage your actions have done, but request that, effective immediately, you cease any further attempts to deal with Milo Lee. They are quite serious, I'm afraid. If you continue, you risk banishment from the Court, from which there is no return."

Portia, do not—

"I owe you this, Theo," I said, ignoring everything as I narrowed my attention to a razor-sharp focus. "Wind is a mostly horizontal flow of air. It is caused by a pressure gradient force generated by the uneven heating of the Earth's surface."

Around me, wind whipped past us with sufficient force to surprise everyone present. I opened my eyes when a woman shrieked, running after a scarf that had been ripped from her neck. The crowd backed up en masse, their faces frightened as black clouds formed against the mural on the ceiling, thunder rumbling ominously through the ballroom.

"Portia, this is not the time for a demonstration of your Gift," Theo yelled over the howl of the wind, which continued to pick up in intensity.

Terrin met my gaze for a moment, nodding briefly before running to the mare.

"Get out while you can," I yelled to Sarah, then turned and focused on the two people who were huddled together, backing slowly away from me. "You can't leave now. You haven't yet seen the grand finale!" I flicked a finger, releasing the stored energy I'd gathered, smiling at Carol's shrieks of horror as lightning struck around them in a circle of blue electricity.

"Hashmallim!" Disin's voice rose over the noise of the fast-building storm, a storm that I felt in every inch of my body. "Seize her!"

Two flat black silhouettes wafted toward me, the familiar horrible sense of wrongness that trailed after them filling the room. Several people ran out the door, while others huddled in the back, evidently too intrigued with the nightmare about to happen to leave.

Portia, I refuse to allow you to do this! Theo's mind was horrified as he realized my intentions.

There's no other way, my sweet Theo. I love you.

"Hashmallim, do your job!"

Sweetling, my soul is not worth banishment—

Draperies from the far end of the room were ripped from the walls, twisting through the air, flashing brilliant blue streaks as the tornado I'd summoned gathered itself and burst into being.

Milo must have realized at that moment what I intended to do. His face was white and twisted with terror as he shoved his wife aside, leaping over her to race toward the nearest window.

The windows in the ballroom shattered inward with a noise that sounded as if it came from the depths of Abaddon itself. Milo screamed as I directed the tornado on top of him. I ran forward as the Hashmallim reached me, eluding their grasp just as I eluded Theo's.

"I won't allow this!" Theo bellowed at me, lunging forward.

"I can't allow anything other than this," I answered and, for a moment, our being was one. It was a moment of the brightest love, the worst pain. I wanted it to go on forever.

Carol screamed, a high, wailing noise that was sucked up by the tornado, her body consumed by the vortex. Milo tried to get away, but it had him before he could do more than bellow my name. I directed it back toward me as the Hashmallim descended.

"I will always love you," I told Theo as the nearest Hashmallim grabbed me. I threw myself forward, into the screaming wind and cloth, the Hashmallim behind me jerking all of us, the whole twisting vortex, into the black abyss of nothing that was the Akasha.

Chapter 24

Time passed. I don't know how much because consciousness returned slowly to me, but when I regained my senses I was aware of the sound of a woman sobbing and a man screaming his fury at the top of his lungs.

I smiled even without opening my eyes. My plan had worked. I hadn't been sure if the Hashmallim would be able to extract me alone from the maelstrom of a powerful tornado, counting on the probability that they would just suck the whole mess out of the Court and into limbo. "Welcome to the Akasha," I said.

Strong hands jerked me off the ground, holding my neck in a vise of pain. Spots danced before my eyes as Milo's contorted face swam in and out of focus.

"You! You did this to us! You have destroyed everything!"

"Yes, I did. I'm just glad it worked," I croaked, kicking him in the groin at the same time I slammed the palm of my hand into his nose. There was a delightful crunching sound from his face that I fervently hoped was a bone breaking. Milo screamed again, dropping me to clutch his genitals, blood streaming down his face.

"It's over," I told the pathetic man rolling around on the ground. I spread my arms to indicate the rocky black landscape that spread out in an endless plain of misery. "And this is all you have to show for your evil plans. It's worth having to spend the rest of eternity here knowing that you're never going to step foot in the Court again."

Milo spat out some names for me that I felt were best ignored.

"I just have one question," I said, looking around. The Akasha looked the same as when I'd been here for the trial. Carol was draped over a nearby mound of earth, her sobs raw and painful on the ear. I strolled over to her, stopping just beyond her reach. "Why me? Why did you come to me when I inadvertently summoned you? Surely you hadn't been waiting around for me to do so?"

She looked up, her face blotched red and white with a combination of tears, agony, and fury. "Such arrogance! You think this was about you? *You* were nothing more than a convenient scapegoat, mortal. Long ago we had settled on Theo North as the means to demand a renascence—but when you thrust yourself in the way, we decided the two of you together would do just as well. You were both dispensable."

She spat with the last word. I jumped back, smiling at her. I'm sure she thought her words were cutting, but I took immense pleasure in the fact that their wicked plans to use us had failed.

She collapsed in another wave of sobbing.

"Well, then." I wandered away, trying to get my bearings. Beyond the small raised area we inhabited, a faint path cut between the scrubby vegetation and boulders that littered the plain floor, a trail twisting through it to the plateau. The same cluster of rocks was in the center, the faint shapes of the Hashmallim visible in between sharp upthrusts of rock. "I guess it's time to get to know the neighbors. I trust you two will be fine on your own?"

"You'll never leave here either," Milo screamed at me, pulling himself onto his knees. "You'll never again see your Dark One. You have damned him to an eternity of hell, just as you have yourself."

"No," I said, touching my chest. "Theo is a part of me. He will always be here, inside me. Nothing can change that, not even banishment to the Akasha."

"Fool," Milo snarled, his face twisted with rage and hate. "He will forget you."

I shook my head as I started down the path. "You really should learn to have more faith. I've found it's worth the effort."

He raged after me, hurling invective, rocks, and bits of the scraggly black shrubs that dotted the landscape. I dodged all of them, feeling it preferable to spend the rest of my existence talking with the Hashmallim over indulging in Milo and Carol's company. The sooner I got used to them, the better for all of us.

The familiar sense of impossibility grew the closer I got to the Hashmallim, their flat, two-dimensional voids seemingly sucking in surrounding light. The air around us grew darker as I began the climb to the crown of the rock formation.

I took every ounce of strength I had to push myself up the path, but what else did I have to do with my time?

"Hello," I said, looking up into the terrifying black nothingness of the nearest Hashmallim. "I'm Portia Harding, and if you don't mind, I'm here to tell you about the man I love. His name is Theo, and he's a nephilim."

"Dark One is the preferred term. Nephilim cannot be members of the Court of Divine Blood, and as I am, in fact, a member, I must abandon my claim on that particular title."

My heart leaped at the familiar deep, softly Irish voice that rumbled around inside me until I felt it in my blood. The Hashmallim moved to reveal Theo standing with his arms opened wide.

I sobbed his name as I threw myself on him, merging myself body and soul with him. "I didn't think I'd ever see you again."

"I know." He kissed me once, a kiss that spoke volumes, yet left me wanting so much more. "My sweet little virtue. Are you through being a martyr? Would you like to go home?"

"I can leave?" I clutched him even tighter, overjoyed to find the darkness inside of him was gone. "You've got your soul back. It worked?"

"Of course it worked. You are my Beloved," he said dryly. "Your selfless act completed the Joining, returning my soul. In addition, your brave—albeit foolish, and never again to be attempted without first receiving approval from me—act saved the Court. The mare have a few things to say about the method of your madness, but after a little pressure by the sovereign, they have rewarded your bravery by granting you full membership in the Court, as well as anticipating the exculpation you would present on my behalf."

"The sovereign?" I gazed into his eyes, basking in the glow of love and happiness that shone there. "The sovereign who never makes an appearance showed up?"

"Yes. The mare weren't going to grant you a full reprieve, but the sovereign pointed out that you had earned it with your selfless act."

My jaw dropped a little. "You saw the sovereign? What does he . . . she . . . what does it look like?"

Theo laughed, gently closing my mouth as he pulled me after him toward a bright portal of light that sat in the very center of the rocks. "Yes, I saw the sovereign. We were all sworn to secrecy, though, so I can't tell you any details."

"Theo!" I smacked him on the arm.

"Well . . . I suppose it won't hurt to tell you that the sovereign has been known to keep an eye on things by pretending to be someone holding a minor position in the Court."

"Who?" I asked, my mind rapidly going over every face I could remember there. "Is it someone we know? Terrin? Gabriel? No, they're not minor. How about the dapifer? Oh! I know, it was that officious little man who introduced the mare. I'm right, aren't I?"

Theo just laughed, and kissed me.

"It's not him? What about the messenger girl, the one who rode around on the pink bike? The woman selling bread in the square? One of the people who sat around the well and gossiped?"

Theo didn't answer, just pulling me into the portal.

"Dammit, Theo, I insist as your Beloved that you tell me!"

"No."

"Well, at least tell me why the sovereign, evidently completely out of the blue, decided to make itself known and intervene."

"Think of it this way, sweetling—you have all of eternity to use your womanly wiles to persuade me into telling you about it," he answered, a wicked glint in his eye as he pulled me into a kiss that I knew would melt my socks off, not to mention drive all thoughts from my mind but the joy he brought me.

I was right. As his mouth took possession of mine, his tongue swept aside my irritation to send me spiraling into the familiar well of ecstasy.

You're hungry, I said, feeling the burning need inside of him.

Yes. For you.

It took an effort, but I managed to pull my mouth from him, looking around with wonder. We were in a familiar room, the one we'd been sent to while waiting for the hearing.

"You're a man of many talents," I said, my voice muffled as he pulled my shirt off.

"Oh yes, and you've just begun to tap the surface

of them." He paused in pulling off my clothes when my stomach gave a rude growl. "Would you prefer to eat first?"

"Yes," I answered, kicking off my shoes, pants, and underwear before striking a seductive pose on the bed. "I'd like to eat you first, then you can nibble on me. Sound fair to you?"

"Oh, yes." His eyes burned black with desire as he ripped his own clothes off, his body positively burning as he lowered his length to me. "I couldn't have survived without you, you know."

"That's a sweet sentiment," I murmured between kisses, my hands busily stroking his back and sides, reacquainting myself with his deliciously silk-covered steely muscles, my toes all but curling with ecstasy as his kisses moved to the spot behind my ear that had me shivering with anticipation.

It's also the literal truth. Dark Ones—even redeemed Dark Ones—cannot live without their Beloveds. So you see, sweetling, I just couldn't allow you to sacrifice yourself that way. Something had to be done.

His penis nudged those parts of me that were pleasurably anticipating its arrival, the tight burn of arousal causing my knees to slide up around his hips. His teeth pierced my flesh at the same time he penetrated me, our bodies, minds, and souls merged into one burning conflagration of love.

The meaning of his words sank in as I drifted down from a climax that went beyond the merely sexual. Theo had flipped us over so that I was resting on him, my heart beating against his, sharing one rhythm. I lifted my head from his damp chest to look up at his face, propping myself up on an elbow to look at him. "Are you saying that you got the sovereign to intervene? You managed to not only figure out who the sovereign was pretending to be, but you convinced him . . . her . . . *whatever*, to help us? You faced almost insurmountable odds to do all that, and you seriously believe you are not going to tell me everything about it, in the most excruciating detail?"

His smile was lazy, filled with smug masculine satisfaction. "You haven't sufficiently persuaded me to tell you, sweetling."

I sat up on him, pulling one hand behind my back, the other tracing a line down his damp chest. His eyes opened, the banked fires of desire beginning to smolder again as I slid down his legs.

I smiled as his penis twitched in anticipation. "Then I guess I'll just have to try harder, won't I?"

The fingers of the hand behind my back grew cold from the snowball that was forming in my palm.

Tired of waiting for the next *Aisling Grey, Guardian* novel? *Holy Smokes* will be in bookstores in November 2007, but you can read ahead for a glimpse of what's been going on for Aisling and her demon dog, Effrijim. Aisling is a Guardian and demon lord with her hands full. . . .

To: Amelie@grimoirefrancais.com
From: demonsdoitbetter@dragonsepts.com
Subject: My love!

Dearest Cecile,

I long to suck your ears, my darling. The silky smoothness of them, the piquant taste of the furry tips, the sensual little shiver you do when I engulf them in my mouth . . . I yearn for you, my sweet love. Do you yearn for me, too?

Slurps and sniffs,
Jim

To: demonsdoitbetter@dragonsepts.com
From: AGrey@dragonsepts.com
Subject: Re: My love!

Jim:

For the fifth time in a week, will you *please* check your address book? I'm tired of getting these canine semi-pornographic e-mails because something is messed up in your address book and they're going to me instead of Amelie.

Aisling

PS—That's just sick that you make Amelie read those aloud to Cecile. Have you no shame?

To: Amelie@grimoirefrancais.com
From: demonsdoitbetter@dragonsepts.com
Subject: My love, part deux

Dearest Cecile:

How do I love thee? Shall I count the ways? I love the way your butt waddles when you walk. I love the grunts you make when you get to your feet after a long evening of cuddling with yours truly. I love it when we go for walkies and you let me have the good poop spot. In other words, I love thee to the depth and breadth of my heart. Or something poetic like that.

Longing to sniff your butt,
Jim

To: demonsdoitbetter@dragonsepts.com
From: AGrey@dragonsepts.com
Subject: Re: My love, part deux

Jim:

You don't have a heart. Fix the address book.
Now!

Aisling

To: Amelie@grimoirefrancais.com
From: demonsdoitbetter@dragonsepts.com
Subject: Adorable one!

My beloved scrumdillyicious Cecile:

I have written three haikus for you in celebration
of our eternal love.

You walk under me
With your tiny little legs.
I drool on your head.

A tailless butt wags.
It entices, arouses.
Come to Daddy now!

I love you so much.
There is nothing I love more.
Oh, look! Dinner time!

Ever thine,
Jim

To: demonsdoitbetter@dragonsepts.com
From: AGrey@dragonsepts.com
Subject: Knock it off!

Effrijim, I order you to examine your address
book and remove my name from it! Immediately!

A very annoyed demon lord

To: Amelie@grimoirefrancais.com
From: demonsdoitbetter@dragonsepts.com
Subject: Demon lords are *so* overrated.

Cecile o' the ears:

Aisling is off her rocker. Yeah, again. I know it just seems like it was yesterday that she was completely gaga—oh, wait, it *was* just yesterday—but at this point, she's several onions short of a tuna salad.

First, she got all bent out of shape over a couple of misdirected e-mails. Then, this morning, this little conversation took place:

[Scene—living room. I had the sunny spot on the couch and possession of the Sunday papers. Life was good.]

Aisling came into the room, followed by that butt-kissing demon Tracy.

"But my lord," Tracy said, trying to foist a clipboard on Aisling. "You said I only had to be Venediger for a day or two, until the citizens of Paris rose up and elected one themselves. It has been three weeks now. Three weeks! I cannot possibly do justice to your lordship's business and be Venediger as well. I beg you, please find someone else to do the job."

"I told you yesterday, and the day before that, and the day before the day before yesterday that I

was doing everything I could to de-Venediger
you, but until things settle down in Paris, you're
just going to have cope."

"But my lord—" Tracy said in one of those
annoying whiny voices that I knew grated on
Ash's nerves.

"Look!" she snapped, whirling around from
where she was gathering up her cell phone and
purse and keys and stuff from where she'd
strewn them around the room (and she has the
nerve to call *me* a slob!). "I am doing the best I
can, okay? But it's not a bowl of kumquats for
me, either!"

"Cherries," I corrected her, smirking to myself
at the frustrated look on Tracy's face. I just know
it wants my job. Ha! Fat chance it'll get it from
me! Aisling is devoted to me.

"You!" she snarled, spinning around to point a
finger at me. "How many times do I have to tell
you? That's Drake's antique couch, and your
shedding butt is not allowed on it. Get off it now,
or I'll send you to work in the software factory!
Pronto!"

"Crikey, keep your grimoire on. It's just a few
hairs," I said with much dignity as I withdrew
from the couch onto the dog bed she insists I use.
Like I'm an animal or something! Sheesh!

"I understand that your lordship is having a

difficult time adjusting to being a prince of
Abaddon, but I, too, am having problems. The
amount of stress I'm under having to do both
jobs with which you've saddled me—" Tracy
started to say.

"Stress!" Aisling shrieked. I mean, a real
shriek, the kind that is so high and screechy, it
makes you squint your eyes when it pierces your
eardrums. "*Stress!* You think *you've* got stress?"

Tracy started backing up when Aisling stalked
toward it. I have to say, I felt a bit sorry for the
demon—Ash's eyes are bad enough under normal
situations, but when she's all wigged out, they
are positively creepy.

"I . . . I . . . ." Tracy stammered.

"You only have two measly little jobs! Try
being a demon lord, a wvyern's mate, a Guardian,
and a prince of Abaddon all at the same time if
you want to know what *stress* is!" she snapped,
still walking forward toward the demon.

"I understand, but—"

"Try being proscribed, just a hairsbreadth
away from eternally damned for a little stress,"
she continued, backing Tracy into a corner.

The demon looked around nervously, licking
its lips. I snickered to myself, but quietly, 'cause
there was no way in Abaddon I wanted to draw
Aisling's attention to myself.

"You think *you're* stressed?" She snatched the clipboard from the demon, scrawled her name on the top piece of paper, and slapped it back across Tracy's chest. "I'm mated to the wrong friggin' dragon! Now *there's* some stress!"

"Yes, but—"

She took a deep breath. I slid off the dog bed and went to stand behind the couch. Not to hide, you understand. But dark power had started to glow in a corona around Aisling, and that's never a good sign.

"And on top of it all, as if all of that wasn't enough to give a girl an ulcer, I have a wedding to plan."

"A wedding?" Tracy squeaked, pressed so tightly against the wall that its body started to flatten. "Yours? Con-congratulations."

"Thank you!" Aisling leaned forward, her face in the demon's, her weird white eyes glowing with vivid intensity. "But even that I could cope with. No, it's the other part, the truly frightening event, the thing so horrific that I can't sleep at night, I can't eat, I can't enjoy Drake's fabulous body. It's so completely terrifying, I'm ready to throw out everything and run away to live in a cave in the deepest, darkest reaches of Tibet."

Tracy's mouth dropped open for a second. It swallowed hard a couple of times before it finally got out in a hoarse, frightened whisper, "Fires of Abaddon—what's happening?"

Aisling stood up straight, a look of martyred, hopeless doom etched deep upon her features as a little tremor shook her body. "My family is coming for the wedding."

Tracy fainted dead away. Aisling struck one final dramatic pose, then gathered up her things, told me I'd better not be peeing on the back of the couch (geesh, you have one little error in judgment, and they never let you forget it!), and stormed off to inflict herself on some poor innocent at Hannah's House of Bridal Joy.

And so you see, my beloved and adorable one, just how bad things are here. Ash is running around like a hellhound with its head lopped off trying to get ready for this wedding and her family's visit, Drake is being all manly and bossy like he normally is, and me . . . well, I'm a bit lonely. I miss Nora, but she can't come by anymore because of Aisling being proscribed and all. I miss taking walks with Aisling—István or Pál goes out with me now, ever since one of the red dragons tried to do me in with a hacksaw. I miss yacking with Rene—he's gone back home to take care of his own family. But most of all, I miss seeing you wiggle. I just hope this wedding business is over soon, so life can settle down to normal again. Or as normal as it gets around here, which, admittedly, doesn't really follow the definition of the word.

Mucho lickies, babycakes.

Your everlovin',
Jim

KATIE MACALISTER

EVEN VAMPIRES GET THE BLUES

Paen Scott is a Dark One: a vampire without a soul. And his mother is about to lose hers too if Paen can't repay a debt to a demon by finding a relic known as the Jilin God in five days.

Half-elf Samantha Cosse may have gotten kicked out of the Order of Diviners, but she's still good at finding things, which is why she just opened her own private investigation agency.

Paen is one of Sam's first clients and the only one to set her elf senses tingling, which makes it pretty much impossible to keep their relationship on a professional level. Sam is convinced that she is Paen's Beloved— the woman who can give him back his soul—whether he wants her or not.

0-451-21823-X

Available wherever books are sold or at
penguin.com